A SIGNAL VICTORY

A Signal Victory

DAVID STACTON

FABER & FABER

This edition first published in 2014
by Faber & Faber Ltd
Bloomsbury House, 74–77 Great Russell Street
London WC1B 3DA

Printed by Books on Demand GmbH, Norderstedt

All rights reserved
© The Estate of David Stacton, 1960

The right of David Stacton to be identified
as author of this work has been asserted in accordance
with Section 77 of the Copyright, Designs and Patents Act 1988

This book is sold subject to the condition that it shall not, by way of
trade or otherwise, be lent, resold, hired out or otherwise circulated
without the publisher's prior consent in any form of binding or cover other than
that in which it is published and without a similar condition including this
condition being imposed on the subsequent purchaser

A CIP record for this book is available from the British Library

ISBN 978–0–571–32012–7

For

JAMES WORKMAN

otherwise Jamie

A fellow Carthaginian historian

The future is unknowable, but the past should give us hope.

Churchill

Un acteur juge réellement ... avec sa sensibilité et sa personne physique—non avec son esprit.

Jouvet

INTRODUCTION
The Case of David Stacton

Might David Stacton (1923–68) be the most unjustly neglected American novelist of the post-World War II era? There is a case to be made – beginning, perhaps, with a simple inductive process.

In its issue dated 1 February 1963 *Time* magazine offered an article that placed Stacton amid ten writers whom the magazine rated as the best to have emerged in American fiction during the previous decade: the others being Richard Condon, Ralph Ellison, Joseph Heller, H. L. Humes, John Knowles, Bernard Malamud, Walker Percy, Philip Roth, and John Updike. It would be fair to say that, over the intervening fifty years, seven of those ten authors have remained solidly in print and in high-level critical regard. As for the other three: the case of H. L. Humes is complex, since after 1963 he never added to the pair of novels he had already published; while John Knowles, though he continued to publish steadily, was always best known for *A Separate Peace* (1959), which was twice adapted for the screen.

By this accounting, then, I believe we can survey the *Time* list today and conclude that the stand-out figure is David Stacton – a hugely productive, prodigiously gifted, still regrettably little-known talent and, yes, arguably more deserving of revived attention than any US novelist since 1945.

Across a published career of fifteen years or so Stacton put out fourteen novels (under his name, that is – plus a further raft of pseudonymous genre fiction); many short stories; several collections of poetry; and three compendious works of non-fiction. He was first 'discovered' in England, and had to wait several years before making it into print in his homeland. Assessing Stacton's career at the time of what proved to be his last published novel *People of the Book* (1965), Dennis Powers of the *Oakland Tribune* ruefully concluded that Stacton's was very much 'the old story of literary virtue unrewarded'. Three years later Stacton was dead.

The rest has been a prolonged silence punctuated by occasional tributes and testaments in learned journals, by fellow writers, and around the literary blogosphere. But in 2011 New York Review Books reissued Stacton's *The Judges of the Secret Court*, his eleventh novel and the second in what he saw as a trilogy on American themes. (History, and sequences of titles, were Stacton's abiding passions.) In 2012 Faber Finds began reissuing a selection of Stacton's novels.

Readers new to the Stacton *oeuvre* will encounter a novelist of quite phenomenal ambition. The landscapes and epochs into which he transplanted his creative imagination spanned vast distances, and yet the finely wrought Stacton prose style remained fairly distinctive throughout. His deft and delicate gifts of physical description were those of a rare aesthete, but the cumulative effect is both vivid and foursquare. He was, perhaps, less committed to strong narrative through-lines than to erecting a sense of a spiritual universe around his characters; yet he undoubtedly had the power to carry the reader with him from page to page. His protagonists are quite often haunted – if not fixated – figures, temperamentally estranged from their societies. But whether or not we may find elements of Stacton himself within said protagonists, for sure his own presence is in the books – not least by dint of his incorrigible fondness for apercus, epigrams, pontifications of all kinds.

He was born Lionel Kingsley Evans on 27 May 1923, in San Francisco. (His parents had met and married in Dublin then emigrated after the war.) Undoubtedly Northern California shaped his aesthetic sense, though in later years he would disdain the place as an 'overbuilt sump', lamenting what he felt had been lost in tones of wistful conservatism. ('We had founding families, and a few traditions and habits of our own . . . Above all we had our sensuous and then unspoilt landscape, whose loss has made my generation and sort of westerner a race of restless wanderers.') Stacton was certainly an exile, but arguably he made himself so, even before California, in his estimation, went to the dogs. In any case his fiction would range far away from his place of birth, for all that his early novels were much informed by it.

Precociously bright, the young Lionel Evans was composing poetry and short stories by his mid-teens, and entered Stanford University in 1941, his studies interrupted by the war (during which he was a conscientious objector). Tall and good-looking, elegant in person as in prose, Evans had by 1942 begun to call himself David Stacton. Stanford was also the place where, as far as we know, he acknowledged his homosexuality – to himself and, to the degree possible in that time, to his peers. He would complete his tertiary education at UC Berkeley, where he met and moved in with a man who became his long-time companion, John Mann Rucker. By 1950 his stories had begun to appear in print, and he toured Europe (what he called 'the standard year's travel after college').

London (which Stacton considered 'such a touching city') was one of the favoured stops on his itinerary and there he made the acquaintance of Basil 'Sholto' Mackenzie, the second Baron Amulree, a Liberal peer and distinguished physician. In 1953 Amulree introduced Stacton to Charles Monteith, the brilliant Northern Irish-born editor and director at Faber and Faber. The impression made was clearly favourable, for in 1954 Faber published *Dolores*, Stacton's first novel, which *Time and Tide* would describe as 'a charming idyll, set in Hollywood, Paris and Rome'.

A Fox Inside followed in 1955, *The Self-Enchanted* in 1956: *noir*-inflected Californian tales about money, power and influence; and neurotic men and women locked into marriages made for many complex reasons other than love. In retrospect either novel could conceivably have been a Hollywood film in its day, directed by Nicholas Ray, say, or Douglas Sirk. Though neither book sold spectacularly, together they proved Stacton had a voice worth hearing. In their correspondence Charles Monteith urged Stacton to consider himself 'a novelist of contemporary society', and suggested he turn his hand to outright 'thriller writing'. But Stacton had set upon a different course. 'These are the last contemporary books I intend to write for several years', he wrote to Monteith. 'After them I shall dive into the historical . . .'

In 1956 Stacton made good on his intimation by delivering to Monteith a long-promised novel about Ludwig II of Bavaria, entitled *Remember Me*. Monteith had been excited by the prospect of the work, and he admired the ambition of the first draft, but considered it unpublishable at its initial extent. With considerable application Stacton winnowed *Remember Me* down to a polished form that Faber could work with. Monteith duly renewed his campaign to persuade Stacton toward present-day subject matter. There would be much talk of re-jigging and substituting one proposed book for another already-delivered manuscript, of strategies for 'building a career'. Stacton was amenable (to a degree) at first, but in the end he made his position clear to Monteith:

> I just flatly don't intend to write any more contemporary books, for several reasons . . . [M]y talents are melodramatic and a mite grandiose, and this goes down better with historical sauce . . . I just can't write about the present any more, that's all. I haven't the heart . . . [F]or those of conservative stamp, this age is the end of everything we have loved . . . There is nothing to do but hang up more lights. And for me the lights are all in the past.

Monteith, for all his efforts to direct Stacton's *oeuvre*, could see he was dealing with an intractable talent; and in April 1957 he wrote to Stacton affirming Faber's 'deep and unshaken confidence in your own gift and in your future as a novelist'.

The two novels that followed hard upon *Remember Me* were highly impressive proofs of Stacton's intent and accomplishment, which enhanced his reputation both inside Faber and in wider literary-critical circles. *On a Balcony* told of Akhenaten and Nefertiti in the Egypt of the Eighteenth Dynasty, and *Segaki* concerned a monk in fourteenth-century Japan. Stacton took the view that these two and the Ludwig novel were in fact a trilogy ('concerned with various aspects of the religious experience') which by 1958 he was calling 'The Invincible Questions'.

And this was but the dawning of a theme: in the following years, as his body of work expanded, Stacton came to characterise it as 'a series of novels in which history is used to explain the way we live now' – a series with an 'order' and 'pattern', for all that each entry was 'designed to stand independent of the others if need be'. (In 1964 he went so far as to tell Charles Monteith that his entire *oeuvre* was 'really one book'.)

Readers discovering this work today might be less persuaded that the interrelation of the novels is as obviously coherent as Stacton contended. There's an argument that Stacton's claims say more for the way in which his brilliant mind was just temperamentally inclined toward bold patterns and designs. (A small but telling example of same: in 1954 at the very outset of his relationship with Faber Stacton sent the firm a logotype he had drawn, an artful entwining of his initials, and asked that it be included as standard in the prelims of his novels ('Can I be humoured about my colophon as a regular practice?'). Faber did indeed oblige him.)

But perhaps Stacton's most convincing explanation for a connective tissue in his work – given in respect of those first three historical novels but, I think, more broadly applicable – was his admission that the three lives fascinated him on account of his identification with 'their plight':

> Fellow-feeling would be the proper phrase. Such people are comforting, simply because they have gone before us down the same endless road . . . [T]hough these people have an answer for us, it is an answer we can discover only by leading parallel lives. Anyone with a taste for history has found himself doing this from time to time . . .

Perhaps we might say that – just as the celebrated and contemporaneous American acting teacher Lee Strasberg taught students a 'Method' to immerse themselves in the imagined emotional and physical lives of scripted characters – Stacton was engaged in a kind of 'Method writing' that immersed him by turn in the lives of some of recorded history's rarest figures.

Stacton was nurtured as a writer by Faber and Faber, and he was glad of the firm's and Charles Monteith's efforts on his behalf, though his concerns were many, perhaps even more so than the usual novelist. Stacton understood he was a special case: not the model of a 'smart popular writer' for as long as he lacked prominent critical support and/or decent sales. He posed Faber other challenges, too – being such a peripatetic but extraordinarily productive writer, the business of submission, acquisition and scheduling of his work was a complicated, near-perpetual issue for Monteith. Stacton had the very common writer's self-delusion that his next project would be relatively 'short' and delivered to schedule, but his ambitions simply didn't tend that way. In January 1956 Monteith mentioned to Stacton's agent Michael Horniman about his author's 'tendency to over-produce'. Faber did not declare an interest in the Western novels Stacton wrote as 'Carse Boyd' or in the somewhat lurid stories of aggressive youth (*The Power Gods, D For Delinquent, Muscle Boy*) for which his *nom de plume* was 'Bud Clifton'. But amazingly, even in the midst of these purely commercial undertakings, Stacton always kept one or more grand and enthralling projects on his horizon simultaneously. (In 1963 he mentioned almost off-handedly to Monteith, 'I thought recently it would be fun to take the Popes on whole, and do a big book about their personal eccentricities . . .')

In 1960 Stacton was awarded a Guggenheim fellowship, which he used to travel to Europe before resettling in the US. In 1963 the *Time* magazine article mentioned above much improved the attention paid to him in his homeland. The books kept coming, each dazzlingly different to what came before, whatever inter-connection Stacton claimed: *A Signal Victory, A Dancer in Darkness, The Judges of the Secret Court, Tom Fool, Old Acquaintance, The World on the Last Day, Kali-Yuga, People of the Book.*

By the mid-1960s Stacton had begun what he may well have considered his potential *magnum opus*: *Restless Sleep*, a manuscript that grew to a million words, concerned in part with Samuel Pepys but above all with the life of Charles II from restoration to death. On paper the 'Merrie Monarch' did seem an even better subject for Stacton than the celebrated diarist: as a shrewd and lonely man of complicated emotions holding a seat of contested authority. But this work was never to be truly completed.

In 1966 Stacton's life was beset by crisis. He was in Copenhagen, Denmark, when he discovered that he had colon cancer, and was hospitalised for several months, undergoing a number of gruelling procedures. (He wrote feelingly to Charles Monteith, '[A]fter 48 hours of it (and six weeks of it) I am tired of watching my own intestines on closed circuit TV.') Recuperating, he returned to the US and moved in once more with John Mann Rucker, their relations having broken down in previous years. But he and Rucker were to break again, and in 1968 Stacton returned to Denmark – to Fredensborg, a town beloved of the Danish royal family – there renting a cottage from Helle Bruhn, a magistrate's wife whom he had befriended in 1966. It was Mrs Bruhn who, on January 20 1968, called at Stacton's cottage after she could get no answer from him by telephone, and there found him dead in his bed. The local medical examiner signed off the opinion that Stacton died of a heart attack – unquestionably young, at forty-four, though he had been a heavy smoker, was on medication to assist sleeping, and had been much debilitated by the treatment for his cancer. His body was cremated in Denmark, and the ashes sent to his mother in California, who had them interred in Woodlawn Cemetery, Colma.

From our vantage today, just as many years have passed since Stacton's untimely death as he enjoyed of life. It is a moment, surely, for a reappraisal that is worthy of the size, scope and attainment of his work. I asked the American novelist, poet and translator David Slavitt – an avowed admirer of Stacton's – how he would evaluate the legacy, and he wrote to me with the following:

> David Stacton is a prime candidate for prominent space in the Tomb of the Unknown Writers. His witty and

accomplished novels failed to find an audience even in England, where readers are not put off by dazzle. Had he been British and had he been part of the London literary scene, he might have won some attention for himself and his work in an environment that is more centralised and more coherent than that of the US where it is even easier to fall through the cracks and where success is much more haphazard. I am delighted by these flickers of attention to the wonderful flora of his hothouse talents.

At the end of 1957, having settled the sequencing of the 'Invincible Questions' trilogy, Stacton advised Charles Monteith by letter that his next novel would concern 'Guerrero's adventures in Yucatan: joining the Mayas and helping defeat the Spanish for a while, *and all that* . . .' The italics are mine. Note, too, the presumption (or affectation?) that Monteith would know precisely whom Stacton was talking about. And yet Gonzalo Guerrero was an obscure historical figure, the evidence of his existence based on patchy sources. The legend as Stacton must have known it described a shipwreck that brought the Spaniard Guerrero to the Yucatán in the early 1500s: there he would renounce his Spanish identity, marry a princess, father the first *mestizo* children and, finally, take arms in resistance against the advances of conquistadors from his native land. Whomever Guerrero might have been, though, the lineaments of this account were undeniably useful to an imaginative historical novelist, offering the example of a doomed but noble hero interposed between the steel-helmeted colonisers from Europe and the indigenous peoples of the Americas.

Stacton promised Monteith that *A Signal Victory* would be 'fairly short . . . concise, anyway, and rather explicit'. Though he could at times be disingenuous in issuing such assurances, he was, on this occasion, as good as his word. The novel flows fast, Stacton as assured as ever of the epoch and terrain and human character that he is re-imagining into life on the page. You sense, as usual, his conservative-minded confidence that all lives have been lived before, all achievable truths established, and available as such to the questing author of fiction. And Guerrero's story is no way impeded by Stacton's penchant for ruminating upon history even as he restages it.

With the work done and dusted in May of 1960 Stacton would confess to Monteith that *A Signal Victory* was 'a book I feel squeamish about . . . it's a book *about*, whereas a book should *be* its subject'. But here Stacton was only belatedly setting himself a bar that he never truly tried to clear: he is always a presence in his work, his choice of subject just as revealing of him as his work is in revealing that subject. He need not have offered the self-criticism: *A Signal Victory* is among Stacton's most compelling productions, and draws the reader into his vision of history as engrossingly as any.

Richard T. Kelly
Editor, Faber Finds
April 2014

Sources and Acknowledgements
This introduction was prepared with kind assistance from Robert Brown, archivist at Faber and Faber, from Robert Nedelkoff, who has done more than anyone to encourage a renewed appreciation of Stacton, and from David R. Slavitt. It was much aided by reference to a biographical article written about Stacton by Joy Martin, his first cousin.

ONE

I

If you live close to the end, as today we all do, you want to see the course by which the eagle makes his swift descent. Unlike the dove, he leaves a trail of smoke, somehow, in the air. Not that there will not be a new world, but this is the end of ours. And being selfish, we are concerned with that.

Against the air of Yucatan one sees that trail very well, even after 400 years, for the sky down there is indelible. Nothing that has ever happened under it has ever been erased.

Wandering round those serene ruins, from which the jungle has by science been temporarily protracted, climbing those fatiguing stairs, looking at those toothy and imperturbable processions carved on stone, one finds oneself baffled and anxious, as usual, in civilization's historic consulting room. Diagnostics, as we know, proceed by parallels. What, then, will the judges of the secret court make of our case?

The ruins of Yucatan impose sobriety. They were a world. They are a world. Like the ruins of Angkor, they have something to teach which no one would ever be fool enough to learn. And there, often, one cannot help thinking, as the Mexicans sometimes think, of one who went down with them. In our time, for us, that is the only hero we can have: the one who tells us how to go.

No man would ever be defeated by himself. It is better, in that case, to go.

Yet though a taste for elegies is pleasing to the elegiac, it does not represent our true feeling, nor, 400 years ago, was Yucatan a ruin.

Instead, it was not a wilderness, but an Empire, a little broken, overwhelmed by flood and invasion, yet populous, orderly, and coherent with more than a thousand years of prosperous tradition. They knew how to live there, even if they had forgotten why.

Nor, in those days, was a young man so old as he is today. In those days he still had a choice.

White causeways ran through the forests and the fields, to connect the cities of that endless plain. At night the temple beacons lit up the lower sky, or shone above the flaccid sea.

There was nothing like it in Spain. There was nothing like it anywhere, divided though it was into a series of small warring states which only had the appearance of cohesion.

Among these states Chetumal was one of the most secure, and he had done his best to make it so. Loyalty and gratitude had seen to that. And perhaps love.

His name was Gonzalo Guerrero, a Spanish name, though he was not Spanish any more. Perhaps he never had been, though he had often wondered what he would do when at last the Spaniards came.

He was a gipsy. Under that definition he belonged anywhere, but now he belonged here.

Chetumal was half way down Yucatan, on the eastern coast, but news in that flat country could travel rapidly, and the ruler of Ecab had sent news. A great sea bird had appeared far to the north, at Cape Catoche. It contained white men in black clothes, perhaps those gods whom prophecy had it would one day walk back out of the sea. Some men believe in some gods and some men in others, but a realist believes in the present. In the present events do not have divine causes. Therefore the ruler of Ecab had driven them back into the sea, and waited for advice. A picture of both bird and men would follow.

Guerrero did not need a picture, nor had the men been driven away. Nor were they gods. The Spanish had come at last, as he had always feared they would. Greed, and its great goad, inefficiency, had seen to that.

Five years ago he might have hesitated, but not four, not three, and certainly not now. He would fight them, and there were reasons for that. He had always fought them, but now there was much to save, and he expected to win.

Why should he not?

He followed the messenger back to Nachancan, the ruler of Chetumal and his own father-in-law. There was nothing to say. They had talked of this for years. But there would be much to do.

He found Nachancan waiting in the cool inner rooms of the upper platform of his house, alone, and entered without ceremony, for there had never been any pomp between them. Nachancan was formal enough, he respected pomp, but he knew where it belonged, and equals provide their own ceremony.

If he had doubts, at this dangerous moment, he did not show them. Guerrero did not blame him for the doubts, but it was for the not showing of them that he loved him.

And looking at him now he saw, that yes, he did love him. That made things easier.

"So they have come," he said. He did not really expect an answer. He watched. He was content to watch. He was content to be a pet dog, given such a master.

But there was nothing to watch. These people of oriental blood, they know better than we do how to control their features. Guerrero could see nothing but an alert calm. It was not stoicism exactly, for stoicism pretends to care nothing for events, and is passive. It was merely the best way of dealing with things.

There is a moment between the expected and its occurrence, when most of us would hesitate and find a way out through the slight dissimilarity between the prediction and the event. But Guerrero did not think like that. He had made his decision years ago. He was not a scholar. He knew what he liked and what he did not like. He had not that fear of being committed which tries to conceal its moral nakedness behind second thoughts.

"They will sail down the west coast," he said. "We must warn Campeche and Champoton."

Nachancan let out a little sigh. It was almost inaudible. But it showed what he had been wondering.

"We can expect nothing of Campeche," he said, but he was a little less formal now.

It was the way they had always been together. Guerrero saw that his father-in-law was pleased behind that mask. If one man believed in another, that is enough. It had been for years. They understood each other.

Unfortunately Nachancan was old, and there was no one else to hold even Chetumal together, should he die.

That was in the future, and made no difference. At least Guerrero did not think it did. He would do his duty. It would be a pleasure to do so. Experience had etched the lines of his conduct upon his face. To do one's real duty is always a pleasure.

All the same he was thoughtful. How could he help but be? Though he was not a literate, he was a thoughtful man. Those thoughts had no names, but they did have a nature, and they told him what to do. For seven years they had told him what to do, even though the man Aguilar had told him something else. He had not listened, knowing the man was a bigot. But a bigot must destroy everything he does not understand, out of inner uncertainty about the security of his own beliefs, and that must not be allowed to happen here, for about the goodness of this world Guerrero had no doubts.

He went back to his own house. Yes, the man Aguilar had much to do with it.

But for that, too, one must go back seven years. One must go back to the year 1511.

II

Like many such stories, his began with the weather; and it is as aspects of the weather, says Spinoza, that we must regard the emotions of men, if we are to understand their politics, without his adding, as men once believed, that weather is the emotion of the world.

We are apt to forget that geography defines not the nature of the world, but only the extent of our knowledge of it. And in 1511 men knew very little of it, and of the Caribbean, not much more. So they were not prepared for the hurricane of that year, the worst since the national disaster of 1464, for to them the Caribbean was a dangerous darkness with an island coast, of which were inhabited only San Fernandina, which we call Cuba, Santo Domingo, which we call Haiti, and in Panama, the colony of Darien. To the west they expected the Indies, but no longer with much hope. Their greed had been frustrated there. In particular they knew nothing of that whorl of the Gulf Stream which, sweeping through the Straits of Trinidad, carries danger with it up past Yucatan.

Of Yucatan, of the ancient glories of Yucatan, no man had ever heard. Ancient glory, to them, if they thought of it at all, meant Rome, or something Ferdinand had captured from the Moors.

When the storm struck there was only one Spanish vessel on that sea, a caraval bound back from Darien, for the Spanish had not the art of navigation, and put to sea only of necessity. There had been a squabble in the colony, and the official Valdivia was going back to Santo Domingo to plead his case. He was a practical man, so that in addition to being by its nature unsuited to that sea, the caraval was doubly burdened with twenty thousand ducats of gold in the cargo, which were what he planned to plead his case with. And though gold is the best of bribes, it makes a poor ballast for eternity.

The boat was overpacked with the military guard from Darien, a posse of priests headed by a white-skinned, wincing Franciscan of the worst sort, named Jeronimo de Aguilar; with two women, who always bring sailors bad luck; and with cattle and goats for the voyage, as well as crates of chickens, pigeons, and fruit.

A storm in the Caribbean cannot be predicted unless you have lived long enough on those shores to recognize the approaching signs, the heat which makes men boil in their armour, the viscous calm, and the purple shimmer of something about to happen.

The pigeons recognized the danger first. They broke loose, rose like torn paper in a go-devil, and took off for the nearest land, though there was no landfall to be seen.

Then, with a sudden heave, the storm, twirling inconsequentially out of the horizon like a toy, grew bigger than a toy, and struck.

It was more than any of them knew how to handle. The ship could not be controlled. It pitched in the sudden darkness, was swept off balance, careened up and down gigantic hills of water, hit Los Viboras, smashed, split, and with a gurgle in the holds, began to sink.

The Spaniards did not know where they were. They had never heard of Los Viboras, or, for that matter, of Jamaica, off whose shore those razor shoals still lie. The two women and fifteen of the men managed to get away in the only boat. The fifteen men included Valdivia, who was a person of importance, and so went first; Aguilar, because a priest to save others must first save himself, which in those days was his perquisite; and a sailor from Nieto, Gonzalo de Guerrero, taken at the last moment, because priest to overweigh the boat or not, Valdivia wished one man with him competent, and Guerrero was competent. So competent, indeed, that Valdivia had mistrusted him until now. He did not know his station. But in a time of danger, fear means nothing, and neither does station. He was the best man, and Valdivia meant to reach land.

The question was, what land?

For fourteen days they drifted, they scarcely knew where, across the surface of that once more deceptive sea. The arm of the Gulf Stream carried them north, but they knew no more than that. Nor is their suffering a part of this story. Sufficient to say it was the women who died first.

They had given up all hope of land. Yet by a swerve in that cold river of whose existence they knew nothing, when they were ready for death, they began to approach a shore.

III

Nowadays a man shipwrecked and cast adrift is not so hopelessly at sea. He knows which waters these are, and where the shores are, that monsters are rare, currents certain, sharks timid without the lure of blood, so they say, and that to drink salt water will not kill him. There are other ships, he had time to send out an S O S, and he really does believe that he lives in a known world. He may suffer, but he is not doomed.

Of the men in that boat of 1511, some could retreat into delirium, some into faith, but the others had no comfortable knowledge to pull them through. It was only the will to survive itself that survived there, for the calm would not end and the sun was not the glorious light of heaven, but the Devil's eye. The eye came closer and closer. It swooped crackling down, it became a coal, they felt the heat against their eyelids, were conscious of the hiss of steam, and went black blind.

Was the will to live then, only an impiety, that we are justly punished for?

Aguilar would have said so. He belonged to the heresy we take with us. He was a Manichee. That was the thing that made bigots out of Christians, nothing else, but then that was also the thing that made Christianity a slave religion and was essential to it.

Guerrero watched him. He was not a Christian, but a gipsy. He belonged to the older dispensation. He knew how dangerous to others your man of faith could be.

He was also an ordinary man, and an ordinary man learns a certain rule of thumb, which serves him well enough. He measures the world up into women, men, and real men, and that simplifies things. The women were gone. You couldn't keep a corpse in that sun. So they went back into the sea they came from, while Aguilar mumbled the office for the dead. Valdivia was a real man. He could depend on Valdivia. But Valdivia had a wound in his leg, it festered fast, and he wasn't competent just now, only quarrelsome and almost motionless.

On the late morning of the fourteenth day they left that almost invisible current and were caught up by a little ripple thirty miles off the coast of Yucatan. But Yucatan is low and invisible from that far at sea, and though they heard the sound of surf, they had heard the sound of surf before. It only meant another reef.

And besides, the movement of this ripple was so slow.

There were only two erect in the boat now, one at the stern, the other at the prow. The one at the stern was the Franciscan, Aguilar, white, scrawny, and sacred. He had dealt so long with death, which was all of the world he understood, that he recognized the symptoms. His face glistened with stale sweat. He had assumed that mummified look the Spaniards like to see on their saints. He was prepared.

But Guerrero knew Aguilar was no saint. There were no saints. There were only brave men, the rest of us, and fools, and a brave man does not die that way, You may kill him, but he does not submit, to earth or heaven, in quite that self-deluded way.

In his lap the Franciscan held his breviary. He had not read it for days, but he kept turning the pages, as though looking for something that wasn't in this volume at all, but in some other one, the same size and shape, that he had left behind by mistake.

Guerrero found it an interesting problem: how long could a Franciscan live without water? There was something in the man's eyes Guerrero did not wish to see, something thirsty, greedy, and obscurely shy. The man hated everything, and yet he wanted to live. It seemed incredible.

Between them the others lay piled over each other, faintly awash at the bottom of the boat.

He knew he had to stay awake, but he couldn't. He looked at the sun, all the spots before his eyes merged into each other, and he became unconscious.

Aguilar pursed his lips. He wasn't really staring. He wasn't really thirsty. He could see things only as a blur, and he had forgotten the taste of water. But he saw Guerrero's thick bronze neck twitch and topple, and that pleased him in an idle, drifting kind of way. If they all had to die, he at least wanted to be last, and now he was. Nor did he care for strong animal men, or anyone not like himself. He suspected sometimes that perhaps they were not devout.

He went on staring, and seeing less and less.

It must have been the fog that revived him.

It was a thin, eddying, almost invisible fog, and condensed in long seminal streamers, here and there, clotting in the air, recruited with a sudden spurt into visibility, until the boat was drifting through a corridor of cobwebs. The air was suddenly cold.

The sound of the surf was louder.

According to Ptolemy, the world is surrounded by a river, which, since its symbol is a snake with its tail in its mouth, must always be cold. According to Strabo, there is nothing at the end of the world but England, and beyond England, ice, a solid wall of ice. Someone must have seen it once. It stretched from Norway to Greenland, and sometimes came as far south as Reykjavik.

Is there really such a place as Reykjavik? Do the people there have one foot and one eye?

According to Dante, the lowest circle of hell is merely ice, solid ice, and you sit there up to your neck, suffering for your sins.

Aguilar stirred and opened his eyes. He was too weak to believe what he saw, but he felt much better. He was not damned. He had always thought it impossible that he could be. Only other people were damned, for he had been careful always to avoid sin, and since, like all fanatics, he thought in negatives, therefore he was one of the saved.

For Bishop Brendon, that obscure Irish cleric, has his own vision of Ultima Thule. Sailing due west he beached on Hy Brasil. And Hy Brasil, as we know, was paradise, an island with steep cliffs, heavily forested, ecclesiastically scented, with great white cliffs, and nothing but innocence everywhere.

The surf was now louder. It was a low surf, imminently booming. Aguilar stared with a certain horror. The fog had gone. It was evening, the soft, purple evening of the tropics. The cliff was shaggy, and abrupt. It was draped with foliage. And shimmering there, against a hovering sky, already faint with stars, were the towers and battlements of a white and quiet city.

He heard drums. He heard wisps of chanting, lonely, empty, and far away. He heard the great entry of a conch, but he had never heard a conch before, and thought it a trumpet. Was that the way a trumpet sounded in heaven?

He glanced down the boat. No, it was not there after all. It was a mirage. For if it was heaven, then how could a common sinner be here in the boat with him, and Guerrero was still there.

The surf was threatening now. There must be a barrier reef. Saved or damned, Aguilar did not want to drown. He found that he could move. The trouble was that he could not move enough. He could just raise his arm, and no more. The Japanese at that period, when their voyages failed, or so they claimed as a joke, kept themselves alive by eating their own lice. But Aguilar had no sense of humour, and his lice merely clotted his sleeve. He had had nothing to eat for days.

Starvation was to save his life, but now he only thought it meant he was going to die anyway. Whatever else he might be about to become, he did not want to die, for no matter how reduced he might be, Aguilar would always have the strength to feel afraid.

Painfully he tried to move his cracked tongue, and some sound must have come out. Guerrero stirred.

Or perhaps the conch wakened him. It did not seem to him a strange sound. It seemed to him a sound he had always expected to hear.

He saw Aguilar's quivering hand. He heard the surf, felt the water choppy under the keel, and grabbed the tiller with a chapped and blood-clotted hand.

The next minutes were quick, sure work. Even so it was not his skill that brought them through. In those sudden waters he had no skill. It was his luck.

Being a realist, and so able always to make the better of any choices, Guerrero always had luck.

When he straightened up, the reef was behind them, and they were in quiet water, though water with a slight surge, enough, at any rate, to bring the boat to the shallows.

It's amazing how much strength you have at the last moment. Guerrero jumped out and tried to beach the boat. He couldn't stifle a slight scream, for since the skin of his legs was sun-dried and salt-caked, the warm water split it up the bone, as though slitting the belly of a fish.

He paid no attention. He knew they should get under cover. There was no way to tell where they were, or who lived here, and he had had enough of natives in Panama. Unfortunately he was too weak to do more than count the living, and see if Valdivia was among them. Valdivia was his captain, and though he did not need orders, if there was anybody to give them, it was his place to take them.

He squinted up at the cliffs and caught a glimpse of the white buildings. As far as he was concerned, they were just buildings, but he didn't like the abrupt silence up there, and the night was full of watching.

A narrow, snake-like line of light caught his eye, undulating against the cliff face. He knew what it was. Fresh water.

Behind him he heard the most peculiar sound, a muffled, high-pitched giggle. He turned around. It was Aguilar, crying with joy, because he wasn't in paradise after all, this wasn't Bishop Brendon's island, and he was still alive.

There was no gratitude in that sound, for such salvation,

but only triumphant hatred of a world that had once more not quite put him down.

With a shrug of disgust, Guerrero dragged himself up the beach towards the ribbon of water.

IV

They had beached at Tulum. It was a pitiable little city, jerrybuilt and holy, eight hundred years old, and half deserted now, for no noble could be bothered to live there. Yet it was the end of that long pilgrim road from Chichen Itza and the interior which led to the embarkation point for the sacred island of Cozumel, so perhaps it was not so pitiable after all. It still had its priests, and the temple of the Diving God was whitewashed every year. It was powerful enough to overwhelm fourteen men weak from exposure on the beach below.

Of all this Aguilar was unaware.

He was one of those men who, having no character of their own, but only a vast desire to be safe, derive one from precedent, and take on the character of whatever shell they find that fits them. Like the hermit crab, they scuttle along from birth towards the nearest conformable security, isolate and terrified, In his case that shell was the Church, which gave him a precedent for everything, and a weapon against everything he was afraid of. That was what made him so useful to anyone conservative enough to hire him. He had an absolute terror of anything he had never seen before which, when he felt secure, turned into hate. He was a groveller by nature. He would have grovelled to God, until the proper time came, and he was secure enough to put Him in His place.

Meanwhile, he had that shell, the Church. So he knew exactly what to do in an emergency. In an emergency one had merely to follow the proper forms. He decided to say mass.

It was almost dawn, which in the tropics brings the colour up as suavely as does a flood of varnish. The sea glistened and the land crabs swept away. One hungry sailor might reach to crack a scuttling shell and suck the claws, but not Aguilar. Aguilar was looking for a flattened stone.

Valdivia, who was hungry enough to suck a crab himself but too weak to get one, propped himself up to watch, sweltering in what was left of his armour, in that sudden lobster heat, and waiting for Guerrero to bring him water. Behind them the cascade dribbled down the cliff.

"What is he doing?"

Guerrero shrugged, grunted, and looked at the men, some of whom were still too weak to leave the boat.

"He wants to say mass."

Valdivia did not object. Not only was the saying of mass appropriate, but it would give him time to think, and Christ might serve to pull the men into order, for certainly at the moment he could not.

Wearily the men lined up, facing that flat stone which Aguilar had chosen as an altar, so that it was he who first saw what was behind them.

He faced problems in his own way, by putting in front of them little contrived problems small enough for him to handle, out of which he could make enormous tasks. It was true that under such conditions anything capable of being swallowed and digested could serve as a Host, but what in this alien bright green world was edible? Even though starving, he had saved a piece of hardtack. Now he offered it up and smashed it to bits with a stone. Then he was ready.

He looked around him with satisfaction. Life was settling into its accustomed place, and later, no doubt, when the men found food, they would feed him.

Guerrero was standing beside Valdivia, who closed his eyes. Aguilar had seen that courteous gesture of impatience before. It is all very well for a prelate, but a common priest cannot feel at ease with gentlemen, for it is too hard to hold their attention. Nor was the look in Guerrero's eyes any more reassuring. Aguilar turned his back on his congregation and stared blankly at his stone.

When he turned round to administer the Host, they were there, just behind the men. They were not devils. He could see that at once. They had too much dignity.

Though he had no courage, he was stubborn and narrow-minded, which sometimes does just as well. He affected not to notice and chanted on, even while he watched.

Behind the kneeling men the wall of the jungle was every shifting shade of green. It rustled in the morning breeze. But some of those leaves detached themselves, they flowed differently, with a high and undulating motion, out of the wood, and became the feathered head-dresses of a small party of coffee-coloured men. These drew aside, and there was carried from the wood a kind of papal palanquin, of that sort derived from ancient Rome. Indeed the party was senatorial in its gravity, as though made up of the judges of some secret court.

Having administered his last crumb of wafer, Aguilar straightened up, made the sign of the cross, and delivered himself of a palindrome against dragons, in his best Latin. He was perhaps feverish, but even so a little magic did no harm.

The men turned round to look, but the party did not vanish. Instead it rustled uneasily and then stood still. An old man looked out of the palanquin.

In his nose he wore a long carved rod, a dragon with a waving tongue hung out of his lower lip, his ears were distended with wide jade plugs, and his head-dress was taller and more elaborate than that of his escort. He looked venerable and extremely jolly. Unlike the rest of his party, he was not armed.

He said something and then jerked back out of sight, without waiting for an answer. Clearly he was accustomed to obedience. His bearers manœuvred the palanquin back into the jungle, while his escort moved forward.

So did Aguilar. He had much to say, all of it in Latin.

It was the month of Zul, sacred to Kukulcan, celebrated according to the Mexican usage, which made their arrival convenient, but he had no way of knowing that.

Guerrero moved to stop him. It was useless to antagonize people who might be friendly but could certainly overwhelm them. It was better to follow, as they were beckoned to do, than to treat them to a harangue. Valdivia agreed.

Indeed, they soon saw, so long as they followed peaceably, no harm did seem to be meant. On the contrary, these feathered men were considerate and seemed extremely pleased. Their language was unintelligible, flexible and high-pitched, like the language of birds. St. Francis might have been able to speak to them, but Aguilar could not.

The jewelled warriors closed behind the Spaniards, the jungle closed behind them, and the palanquin was far ahead. They began to climb.

The jungle was not so venomous as that at Panama. It looked domestic and weeded out. As they ascended the cliff path, the leaves of the trees became a healthier and larger green. The air was less damp.

In about half an hour they left the jungle and found themselves on the edge of a large field crowded with corn tassels. The corn was high. They could see nothing over it. Led by the palanquin, the party advanced to a ramp, mounted it, and turned to the right.

The Spanish now stood on a broad causeway, not in very good repair, slightly topped by corn tassels on either side. Before them, at no great distance, rose the glittering gypsum walls of a sizeable city, with beyond those, several tall towers on which people were standing. One could pick out only the quivering masses of those enormous head-dresses, as though the sky were a sea, and these natives anemones at the bottom of it.

The world seemed curiously hushed.

The only clean cities Aguilar had ever seen were Moorish, and so infidel. He crossed himself.

In those days the Spanish had not yet invented Spain, or even, for that matter, the habit of being Spanish. They had lived by sacking each other and the Moors for so long, that carpet bagging and flight were the only ways they had yet found to display their dignity. The exigencies of such a life meant that they took with them no private possessions but their God, and so they were always confronted by devils. Aguilar felt weak. Converting the infidel with a group of Spanish gentlemen no better than *condottieri* at one's back was one thing, being on the wrong end of a crusade was quite another.

Guerrero, on the other hand, felt no such doubts. What he felt was a thrilled and yet familiar wonder. The sun was hot and he liked what he saw. He was one of those men born into the wrong world, who spend their lives searching for the right one. They may not even be aware of their own discontent, but if by chance they encounter the right one, they recognize it at once, because for the first time in their lives they feel at ease. He felt at ease.

Thus they entered Tulum.

On the other side of the wall was a broad street, half a mile long, and lined with loosely built stone palaces. It, too, was deserted, but they heard far off a murmur, like the swarming of voices at dusk in the *paseo* of any Spanish city. The street they found eerie. Everything was neat and clean, yet weeds sprouted out of the walls. Above them the sky had the blue shimmer of steel.

They did not go so far as the square, but were taken into one of the buildings on their right, guarded, and left there.

By now they were frightened. They were also tired, weak, and comfortable for the first time in weeks, and that made them apathetic. In the centre of the building was a patio. There they were brought food, and from there beckoned into the sweat bath. A sweat bath was a new experience for them, it frightened them, but it did make them feel better.

They would have relaxed, had it not been for glimpses of that barbaric guard at the outlets of the building. Aguilar did not speak. He was preoccupied by the imminence of devils. He sat in the midst of all that unexpected splendour and read his breviary. A priest was sacred. He had no fears. Later he would be taken to someone in authority, explain himself, and convert the heathen. He would have read his breviary in Hell with the same composure, and indeed did daily, for Hell was what the world was to him.

Guerrero and Valdivia were more practical. Hospitality from the enemy, and the world, though a good place, was full of enemies, never meant anything good. They had defeated Caribs, who were ferocious but debased, and the shivering Indians of Panama, but here, they knew, they were up against something else. Here they were up against not a tribe, but a world.

They could not even ask questions. And without weapons, their men were demoralized and grateful to be fed. For they were fed, at about noon, fruit in strange shapes and sizes, a heavy, frothy drink, served in glazed bowls, which they did not yet know was cocoa, and a rich red dish of some kind of porridge, hot with spices, served with a crisp rolled bread stuffed with chopped meat.

They were given the best care, and that was what made them nervous, for in their experience prisoners did not receive the best care, but, at most, a grudging second best. There was something, too, disturbing about the manner of their attendants, something mocking, considerate, and perhaps a little sad. Valdivia did not know what to make of it.

Neither did Guerrero, but he set himself to learning how to ask questions. He pointed to things until the attendants told him the name. By late afternoon he knew the names of twenty things in the house, but how can you ask what is being done to you, if you have no verbs? The words came easily to his tongue, but not to Valdivia's, and Aguilar would not even try. If God speaks Latin and Spanish, why should one bother to learn anything else?

At evening two men came to see them, a religious-looking one, some kind of overseer, surrounded by apprentices, who looked them over carefully but said nothing, and another who insisted upon examining the men with care, probing here and pinching there. Both were ritually dressed, and neither seemed to care for what he saw. Valdivia they singled out at once, as the obvious leader of the party. He seemed to displease them least. They also paid particular attention to one of the soldiers, a man from Estramadura named Léal, no more than a boy really. Then they left.

Guerrero and Valdivia were alarmed, but nothing more happened. They were allowed to remain by themselves all next day. They were fed, as usual. They were bathed. But something made them uneasy.

A little before dawn, on the second day, while Aguilar was setting up his equipment (he had already smashed several small idols, in order to reconsecrate what was clearly an altar), about twenty soldiers, a party of priests, and the same sacerdotal personage they had seen before, who was this time elaborately dressed and painted a curiously vibrant shade of blue, came into the house. Chocolate was served to all the Spaniards.

Aguilar signalled that they should not drink before mass. Since the visitors paid no attention to this, Valdivia thought it better that they drink. Their rooms were still cool and shadowy. The sun had not yet warmed them.

When the chocolate was finished, the guard beckoned to Valdivia and Léal, smiling amiably, and the priest and the man who seemed to be a doctor or shaman, led them into a side corridor.

Without their leader, the Spaniards felt uneasy. There was no sound but that of Aguilar droning through his interrupted service.

The mass ended, and still Valdivia did not return. Aguilar blinked and clutched his breviary tighter. Far off, somewhere, over the roof-tops, they heard the rumble of drums, and then, one by one, the entry of whistles and flutes. They had no way of knowing what was out there.

At last they heard footsteps, turned towards the corridor, but did not at first recognize what they saw.

Valdivia and Léal had been drugged, that was clear. They moved heavily and almost complacently. Both men had been stripped naked and painted that same shade of ominous blue. Even Valdivia's beard was painted blue. He was still a muscular man. Under the paint his body glistened. He wore an elaborate feathered breechclout, such as the natives wore, high masked sandals, and a peaked feather head-dress. Léal was dressed the same way. Each man was flanked by priests to hold him.

What did that drug do, that it could make you so docile? Guerrero was excited. He wanted to know what it felt like to be tricked out so. Yet even painted up that way, Valdivia was a gentleman and Léal was not, so the priests were the more considerate of him.

Guerrero caught the eye of the high priest, who was watching him with some sudden interest, and looked away.

Valdivia and Léal left the building, surrounded by the priests. Guerrero, Aguilar and the others were herded out behind them.

Guerrero was not worried. He knew that for the moment he was safe. Aguilar ran forward. He had taken up the scent at once, and had officiated at executions before. It was his duty to offer the consolations of a pious Latinity. Guerrero hauled him back.

"Do you want them to kill all of us?" he snapped.

Aguilar glared at him, but no, he did not. He fell back.

They went out not the way they had first entered the building, but through a corridor. The sound of drums and flutes was now louder, and to it was added the great peremptory braying of a conch.

They came out into abrupt sunlight and found themselves in a square, like the choir of a church without walls, but a choir somehow magnified. At one end rose the altar, but high, in two stages, like a pyramid, with some structure on top that might have been a monstrance. On either side of the square solemnly danced and chanted those dignitaries the worshippers are usually prevented by the rood screen from seeing.

At the top of the pyramid two columns of incense rose

like scented candles. The music now was faster, and even so, beginning to quicken. It had a rapid and yet stately rhythm, impetuous but grave, as though the jungle had learned order and polyphony. It was full of birds and omens.

It was hypnotic, and over it all came that deliberate, hopeful, and hungry chant, from everywhere around the square, spaced by the double drums.

Valdivia and Léal were led towards the altar.

The drums beat faster.

It was all too bright and cruel out there. Yet Guerrero understood it very well, better than Aguilar, whose sort of business it was. When the body runs wild, or when it is driven so, we cross a border. Then we either scream our heads off when they beat us, or laugh with delight, according to our nature, according to the nature of the God we worship. And that is what these people were doing. As at all religious rites, they were crossing a border. They drove the body wild. They whipped the hell out of it, slowly, and with compassion. A little under-sexed, they had to find release in other, indirect, and sadistic ways. Well, a Spaniard could understand that. That was how a Spaniard worshipped his own phallic ethnic gods, and only called it Christianity.

Guerrero was excited, and therefore impatient with Aguilar. For Aguilar was cringing. To him it was as though someone had suddenly slit a bull's throat in the middle of a mass. It was a little more of religion than he wished to know about.

Guerrero, Aguilar, and the others were driven into the middle of the square and up some steps to a platform. In the middle of the platform was a large wooden cage, ten feet on a side, seven feet high, and barred at the top. They were shoved into this and the gate fastened behind them.

Guerrero looked around him. The Spanish were in love with death. But these people must be terrified of it, to have to make so much of it.

From the elevated cage he could see the pyramid, which was low and crudely made. He could even see the stone at the top of it, where four blue priests were waiting, for the stone was placed to be seen from below.

Valdivia and Léal had reached the foot of the stairs.

The drumming stopped. There was not even an overtone to ripple out into that sudden hush.

The party went up the steep stairs towards that stone. The sun was risen now. The priests helped the men up.

Léal was sacrificed first, being the lesser man, and then Valdivia. That procedure was a customary honour. But Valdivia was a gentleman, one who made an idol of self-control, he had therefore made an effort to throw off the effects of the drug, had succeeded, and therefore saw what was to be done to him.

The crowd was motionless. Then, it was to be expected, not a mass bell sounded, but a single note on a double drum.

Guerrero looked up.

The priests had laid Valdivia on the stone, holding him down by his wrists and ankles. The stone was convex, so that his head and feet hung down, and his chest thrust up as though straining towards heaven. He did not flinch.

The high priest stepped forward and made an expert upward incision with an obsidian knife. Valdivia screamed. His body twitched. But he was not yet dead. The priest groped his right hand into the incision and tore out the heart. Valdivia's soul flew out of the top of the life tree, like a bird, as may be seen in the *códices*. The priest held the heart up and then passed it to an attendant.

It is unforgettable to hear a self-controlled man scream.

Aguilar began to mumble the office for the dead, turning his back on everyone.

The four assistant priests flung the empty body down to the courtyard.

There other priests took the body and flayed it, peeling it from the back. The drumming and chanting began again. The corpse was carted off, red and fatty, except for its feet and hands, which had not been skinned.

The Spaniards sat down in their cage. Now they knew

what was in store for them, and it left them without the desire to go on watching. One of them was sick.

Only Guerrero remained standing.

Except that he did not want to die, and did not intend to, which gave him confidence, what he had seen did not distress him. It was easier to take than the Inquisition. The Inquisition was a system of oppressive punishment. Being self-righteous, the Church offered you dirt, filth, squalor, torture, and damnation. This hazard was different. It was a risk you took, everybody believed in it, and at least you were fed properly until it was over. The victim was drugged. It took only a moment. And besides, he understood: to watch someone else die violently was a way of being reborn yourself. It wasn't a punishment, but a communion. It did not, like the Inquisition, cast you out, but took you in.

He knew now why they were in the cage. They were in the cage to be fattened up. He went on watching.

The priest came down the steps of the pyramid, surrounded by his acolytes, who at the bottom closed in around him.

Again there was silence, and again, the sudden shrilling of pentatonic flutes, the snake-like slither of rattles. The acolytes moved away into their ritual positions.

Then the high priest began to dance, slowly, solemnly, and wet with blood.

He was wearing Valdivia's flayed skin, fastened over him at the back, with the face drawn over his own face. Slowly he forced Valdivia's appearance into the movements of another world, the beard waggling up and down, quite dead, a rod through his nose, but the body alive, and his thighs quivering with the hieratic movements of a sad, gentle, and yet wryly hopeful ritual. Please, death, the flutes seemed to say, let us live, now that you have this offering, for life is so beautiful. It was something Valdivia alive would never have thought to say, something no Christian would ever have said, for to Christians Man was the earth's Manichee, to whom loveliness was only a heap of cinders, and the moon an ash dump for souls.

Aguilar had turned around, white faced and round eyed. He had seen the Devil at last, and it had almost destroyed his faith in God. He had always suspected the two were identical twins.

But it is something after all to see the devil dancing in a dead man, particularly when that man was an hidalgo and in some wise your friend. The little beard wagged up and down, and Guerrero almost envied Aguilar. He was almost sick himself.

For everything is so easy for people who believe in the Devil. For them the problem of good and evil is solved, because for them it exists. And then, it is so much easier to believe in evil than in good. But if one is a realist, and therefore believes in neither, and yet in both, then one has to face events for one's self. That is harder.

Not that Guerrero thought of it that way, but there was something here he understood. He heard it in the sound of the flutes and trusted it. And as for the horrors, he had seen worse horrors, and these people were like flowers. There was something absurd and touching about the way they opened so uxoriously to the sun.

He meant to live.

It was to be many years before he realized why.

v

They spent a month in that cage.

It was better, at any rate, than a Spanish dungeon, or being kept below decks, in the bilge, as discipline. They had the sun and the nights were warm. Guerrero became brown as an Indian, which was what he wanted.

They were fed and watered like animals, but like animals in captivity, began to bore their captors. After a week the life of the town went on around them as though they were not there. Guerrero set himself to learning what he could of the language, and made rapid progress. Aguilar would only learn the names of things he wanted. The rest of the men made no effort at all. They had no ingenuity, and felt hopeless without weapons. They did not have any idea where they were, and only by the sun and at night the stars, whether they were north, south, or east. At night sometimes they could hear the susurration of the gentle surf, below the cliffs.

By asking questions, Guerrero managed to make friends of the townspeople who used the square as a market. Except for their religion, they seemed a gentle, humorous, and interested people. They moved with an indolent but wiry grace, perhaps because they were so short, as Guerrero was himself.

Aguilar was tall and lean. Naturally, because it was foreign to him, he complained of the food, but that did not prevent him from stuffing himself with it. But it did not make his body any pleasanter, and his cassock was in shreds.

The men did not entirely realize, because they did not want to know, why they were there. Aguilar, in particular, acted as though he expected to be ransomed, and therefore had nothing to fear. They were now a party of eight.

The others had become so apathetic, that Guerrero feared drugged food. Yet he ate the same food, and his mind was watchful and sharp.

Once every five days the priest and the doctor came to inspect them. The men were fleshing up, and he himself seemed an object of close attention. Somehow he knew they would save him until last. He did not know why.

It was because they thought him a leader, and so particularly attractive to the gods.

As the days went by and nothing happened to them, the men began to grow restless. Their cage was small, and they had nothing to do but listen to Aguilar talk to them about God and how He would save them. Guerrero said nothing to that but he did not agree. This country, he suspected, could be reached only by accident or storm, and a force washed ashore would be in no position to rescue anyone.

On the nineteenth day, at sunset, they were taken back to the house from which they had come, stripped, bathed and fed. Their clothes were taken away from them, and they were given the sandals and breechclout of the country. Guerrero tied his without any trouble. He was observant and had no *pudeur*. He also had a narrow waist, which made the fold easier to hold up. The ends of his cloth were more elaborately fringed than those of the others. Aguilar refused to part with his tattered robe, which was his sole distinction, but which now made the other men seem more naked and self-conscious.

They were inspected and then taken back to the cage, though two were left behind.

The others did not spend an easy night. The weather was hotter than usual, and the mosquitoes a worse plague. The only light was the signal beacon on top of the temple, for the moon was merely a nail paring above them. At night they could hear jungle noises not audible by day, strange unexpected wooden sighs, frogs, and distant prowling screams.

Aguilar lay on the paving, curled into a ball, but he was not asleep. He was staring sightlessly in front of him. Guerrero watched him suspiciously, and then, with his hands gripped round the bars, stared at the temple stairs across the square. A few priests flitted up and down them, even during the shallow watches of the night. They came and went like the shadows of prowling animals, and sometimes the beacon fire would crackle up, or hiss with incense, as a breeze blew the resinous smell across the square to the cage.

No one else slept much either.

At dawn the square began to fill up with people. Aguilar cleared his throat and said his office. The morning grew longer, but still nothing happened.

At eleven the music began, and the crowds lined up. The two sailors were led up the stairs and sacrificed, though not flayed. Nor did the priest dance afterwards. Guerrero knew in whose skin the priest meant to dance, and the knowledge gave him an odd feeling of being possessed, as though the priest were inside him already. He looked down at his hands and feet. They were strong hands, but they trembled.

Aguilar did not tremble at all. Guerrero knew that kind of hysteria, and now that they were reminded of what they might expect, and of why they were being fed so well, few of them could eat their dinner when it was served.

The priests had long since gone, but most of them had been in prison or the stocks at one time or another. They knew there was no way out of a prison. They began to feel like the animals one or two of them, as farm boys, had tended. That made them eager to confess their sins, while Aguilar absolved them in a corner.

Guerrero did not join them. He had no objection to what God might know, but no desire that Aguilar should know it too. Aguilar was the wrong kind of priest.

At last, when the darkness was thick enough, they slept.

Guerrero did not know what woke him, but he did know what he heard, the sound of a low, continual, and insane sobbing. He sat up. The others still snored, but over against one end of the cage someone was huddled against the wall, and from the blackness of the shadow, he knew it must be Aguilar. He got softly to his feet and went over there.

The temple beacon was burning low. What light it gave was directed towards the sea. There was no moon, and though the stars were bright, the buildings were a series of architectural ghosts which cast the cage into deep shadow.

Aguilar was very close to the bars. His shoulders heaved, tears streamed down his face, and he gave little gasping noises. His bony hands were clenched round the bars, and he was chewing at the knotted binding of the uprights.

Guerrero pulled him back and looked for himself. The cage was made of upright lengths of cane, socketed in the platform, braced at the corners, and held in place by lengths of interwoven sisal worked in a warp and woof pattern. The roof was made of the same bars, with the join bound with the same hemp.

The cage had been built to receive them. That was why they had been kept at the house overnight. But in twenty days the green cane had turned dark brown, and the sun had made the hemp almost frayed. Aguilar had been trying to gnaw through the hemp, which was slimy with spittle.

There are advantages to being born outside of a culture in which you find yourself. No native would have thought of doing such a thing. But Aguilar had thought of it.

There was nothing to be done with him. He was more than a little crazy. Guerrero leaned his own face to the bars and began to chew. Aguilar gave him an odd look. Plainly he did not want to share his secret way out, but unless he did, none of them would escape. Quietly Guerrero went to wake the men and to explain.

He knew now at what intervals the priests came to tend the fire. He set the men to work, grateful that there was no moon.

The hardest task was to release the ceiling bars in order to work the uprights loose. Guerrero had to hold a man on his shoulders, and the work was slow.

From the fading of the stars, they saw it must be only a short time before dawn, which did not give them much chance to go unnoticed for long. They worked faster.

The roof bars gave. Gently they eased out two uprights, which gave them enough room to slip out and drop the three or four feet to the courtyard. One of the men broke his ankle in jumping. He was a good man. He made no complaint when they left him there. But now there were only five of them, against a whole society.

Flitting from building to building, they reached the sacbe, the raised causeway through the cornfields. It was the only way out, but Guerrero did not care to use it. There would be merchants about soon, with their guards, and the agricultural slaves would be going out to the fields. But Aguilar was out ahead and there was no way to stop him.

He seemed to be looking for something, found it, and darted to the left, down a ramp to the ground. He was heading back to the beach.

On the other side of the fields loomed the forest.

"Not there, you fool," said Guerrero. "They'll find you at once."

"The boat," shrilled Aguilar. To him the beach meant the sea, with Spaniards on the other side of it. Guerrero knew they could never escape that way, even if the boat was still there. These were busy trading waters, and they had no sail.

The men sided with Guerrero. It was the jungle or nothing. Aguilar would not agree.

"Then go by yourself. At least this way we have some chance," said Guerrero. He jumped off the sacbe, on the maize-field side. Some men are born leaders, but others have to do their best, when there is nobody else to command. That was his role now and the others followed him. They wanted to live.

Aguilar plopped down in his turn and hurried to catch up, but said nothing.

Neither did Guerrero.

The maize was tall enough to close over their heads. It was also ripe. He told the men to snap off a few ears and stuff them into their breechclouts. There was no telling what or when they would eat again.

For half an hour they worked their way through that field. Aguilar's cassock caught on everything. He stumbled and tucked it up round his girdle, but even so, it was too bulky. It caught on the corn plants, so that anyone on the sacbe could have told where they were going by the movement of the tassels above them; whereas half-naked, the men made less commotion in the stalks.

Guerrero halted and told him to strip. He would not and the men refused to strip him. Angry, Guerrero did it himself, while Aguilar rolled his eyes up to heaven. The men did not interfere. He might be a priest, but they were tired of him.

Still, he had saved their lives. Guerrero ripped out a length of the cassock and gave him that to wrap around him, since modesty seemed more important to him than survival. Clutching his breviary and his beads, Aguilar plodded on. From the look he gave Guerrero, he would cause trouble as soon as it was safe for him to do so, but then he would have done that in any case.

They came to a small clearing. At the other end of it was a thatched hut on the raised stone platform of the country. A man appeared in its doorway, carrying a jar. When he saw them, he called out for help.

Guerrero had to strangle him. In the hut they found another man, trying to break out through the thatch, whom they also killed. Then they searched for food.

Guerrero preferred to search for a weapon, but could find only a flint knife, badly chipped and dull, but better than nothing. He stuck it through his breechclout, and then gave the first peasant's loincloth to Aguilar.

What food they had been able to find Guerrero shoved into a woven sack, which he slung over his shoulder. They would be missed by now. There was no time to form any plan. The essential thing was to pretend that he had one, so as to keep the men in order. What they must do now was to sleep by day, travel by night, and hide until they knew their way about. He led the party into the jungle.

Aguilar might trust in God, but Guerrero put his faith in providence. With providence one could improvise, with God never. He had learned enough of the language to know that the country was divided into a series of squabbling provinces whose hobby was war. He had the advantage that to him war was not a hobby, but a profession. If he could find the enemy, any enemy, perhaps he could barter their services for their lives. The trouble was to find the enemy, and in any such plan Aguilar was a dead weight.

He went right on being a dead weight.

VI

That part of Yucatan, on the north-west, near the coast, but more deeply inland than Tulum, was a rain forest. It was something outside their experience, a rain forest, except in Panama, beyond the boundaries of their wretched town there. It dripped day and night and was crowded with foliage. On that first march they did not get much farther than a mile or two.

Fortunately for them, the natives avoided the forest, and feared it. To the natives it was the garden of the house of death. They were among the enormous trunks of the palm, the cacao, and the mahogany. Lianas coiled down like snakes, and if a tree did not burst into gangrenous orchids, then it was a flight of parrots that whirled away screaming to blossom on some other tree. A peccary charged them, which they could at least see was some sort of pig, and a tapir ran away from them, a thing they could not identify at all.

At night the howler monkeys made their uproar, as did, from various directions, keening bats, all chattering from the same leathery tree, and the jaguar, hunting. Underfoot and overhead the liana slithered to life as the python, the fer-de-lance, the moccasin, and the pit viper.

On the second day Aguilar's jaw began to swell. He had broken a tooth chewing the sisal of the cage. He could not stand the pain. In that damp the pain was incessant.

Sandals were no protection against the fer-de-lance, so they had to watch one of their party go into convulsions. There was not enough soil in which to bury the body, though Aguilar said the office for the dead.

At night they were plagued by ticks, chiggers, mosquitoes, termites, and ants. Between the trunks of the trees they could see the lights of enormous fireflies, like those of some spectral search party.

Once they felt safe from their captors, it exacerbated their nerves that they came across no one. The jungle was empty, inimical, and lonely. They caught ague from the hot, sticky, and metallic rain. Nor did they have any glimpse of the sky, from which to judge their direction. All they could do was to plod along until they had gone far enough to reach the boundary of some hostile state or, they were by now in such bad condition, of any settlement at all.

Water would have been a problem, had the rains not been

so frequent. But there was no lack of small game. Having no weapons but the knife, they fed largely on the very young, who could not flee, but even so, gorged on fowl and meat until both made them belch.

Underfoot the ground began gently to roll.

At night the jaguars roared to each other, from all around them, as though the whole forest were one ambush. They were now four, getting on each other's nerves in all that green steaming wilderness. Aguilar was making a pious nuisance of himself. What was the point of grovelling piously to someone who is not even there? It was a waste of time, for this country had its own gods. They heard them every night.

They began now to travel by day; and on the afternoon of their eighth, came out, without any warning, on the shores of a small lake. It was the first glimpse of the sky they had had in a week, but they drew back at once, for on the far shore of the lake rose the towers and platforms of an enormous city.

The unexpected is always frightening. They decided to rest until night and then reconnoitre. There was nothing else they could do. They slept where they were, too tired to post a guard.

When they woke the world was damp and dark. What most oppressed them was the stillness. The insects made their customary noises, but nothing else did. They worked their way along the shore, sensing that something was wrong, huddling close together, and moving as quietly as they could.

The lake was a mile long and half a mile wide. The water glittered in full moonlight, each choppy little wave a row of metal teeth. More things stirred in that dark than they knew the shapes of, and though the supernatural exists, we can never be sure that our own system of belief is the right way to deal with it.

It was curious to walk behind Aguilar. Some priests might be theologians stark naked, but not he. His shoulders showed his fear. It made even him believe in the powers of darkness, to be thrust among them in that way.

The city, which cast no beacons towards the sky, but which loomed against it, as they came closer, began to sink beneath the trees.

Guerrero looked around him. In this world we have the ability to watch. It is the ultimate luxury. A peasant can understand that attitude, because he has spent his life watching. It is only an intellectual who becomes bitter and confused when confronted by something to see. An intellectual wants the right to rule and can't have it. But even after the young light in his eyes goes out, a peasant likes to watch. That's why he wants to survive.

Aguilar began to balk. It wasn't that he was scared. They were all in too much danger to be scared. It was just that he resented being led by an inferior, or, for that matter, being one. Now they were approaching someone to observe them, he wanted to tell Guerrero what to do.

Guerrero paid no attention to him.

The borders of the lake were squishy and uncertain. Some distance to the left he caught sight of a dull glitter of stone, and lead his party that way.

It was another sacbe, here perhaps eight feet high. Guerrero was for scrambling up to it. Aguilar was not. Aguilar wanted to dawdle. The thought of a second captivity had made him suddenly rebellious.

They scrambled on to it, with Aguilar well behind. The surface of the road was cracked, broken, and choked with weeds, some of them two-foot shrubs, which in the distance looked like crouching men, but even so it glittered in the moonlight. Five hundred yards ahead of them it made a curve. They had no way of knowing what was beyond that curve.

Guerrero was puzzled, but pretended not to show it.

He was beginning to wonder if everything in this ponderous country was in disrepair. He led them through the shrubs.

At the bend of the road they saw through the vines a ruined

village. Its empty doorways stared at them, and a spider monkey darted forward and up the nearest tree, chattering.

That set the invisible parrots screeching, as though to raise an alarm. Aguilar stumbled and fell. He did not get up at once. The thing that had tripped him was a stone road roller, cracked and left there who knew when.

Beyond the bend they saw a well of light, glittering against the black jungle. It startled them. But it was not human light, it was only the moonlight on another lake. They reached an intersection and turned left, though there was nothing to see at the end of the new sacbe. The air seemed heavy, the jungle ominously hushed. They had walked into the middle of a lull. Aguilar began to pray.

They were waiting now to be captured. The air felt warm, and they began to perspire. They were so dirty and so tired.

Far off, somewhere, there was a crack of lightning, and the sky jumped into high relief. The thunder growled like a jaguar. The moon had gone. The sky was rolling with pendulous clouds.

The sacbe did not so much end as seem to flow out among the trees. They found themselves in an extensive overgrown court with to their right, in a second sheet of lightning, the wide stairs of a large pyramid clogged with trees and shrubs, and shrouded in darkness, until another flash showed them the polychromed gods in their niches, high above them, gesticulating wildly in the electric chiaroscuro.

It was Coba, founded nine hundred years ago, during the Little Descent, but abandoned for six generations now, a sacred city, inhabited only by bees.

The storm opened like a weir and the rain poured down.

Before the temple was a row of carved monoliths. Before two of these incense smouldered in cracked pots. Hunters had left offerings before the sacred stelae. Guerrero made a dash for one of the pots and covered it with his body. It could be fanned alive, and they would need fire, if they could find anything dry enough to burn.

The downpour was too strong. Bending double, he dashed

forward, the warm bowl to his belly, veered at the foot of the temple stairs, and then rushed straight up. The steps had very high risers. He crossed a wide landing, and then went up again, without looking behind him. The others could follow as they would. The stairs were broken and slippery, but the overgrowth of weeds and shrubs helped him. He tore off a large leaf and protected the pot with that.

At the top, breathless, he stopped and then plunged into the temple, a roofed building open at the front. There he set down the bowl and began to blow on it. There were dry leaves on the floor, and other dead matter with which to get the fire going.

As the coals began to glow, the flames to lengthen, the painted idols began to dance in the shadows, and with a high-pitched scream, bats detached themselves from the corbel vaulting and looped eccentrically out the doorway. He paid no attention.

They spent eighteen hours there, huddled around the fire, while the rain came down, and they half choked from the wet wood smoke. The wait did not improve their tempers. Though some people think bats a delicacy, like most delicacies, they were not nourishing. Nor was it pleasant to be watched by those strange gods. There were stealthy movements, too, on the temple stairs beneath them.

And then, with less ceremony than it had begun, the rain stopped. The sky cleared. There was sun, the shadowless sun of noon.

Stiff, they crawled out into the healing light. From the front of the temple platform they could glimpse only the plaza and the lake. But from the rear, they could see that the temple was the prow of an extensive city. Steam rose up everywhere, as the sun dried out the stairs, the temples, the courtyards, and the symmetrical stone palaces. Beyond lay the waters of another lake, above the trees rose the tops of suburban temples the jungle had not yet climbed, but for the rest, the nap of the forest was healing back over the masonry scars in its endless furry skin, now heaving taut, now lax.

There was no sign of life anywhere. And then Guerrero saw the bees.

If bats inhabited the city by night, little gods who hung upside down in the underworld, that wooden hell, by day it belonged to the bees. In the past this had been the great honey producing centre of Yucatan. Now the bees made it for themselves, but with the same industry. Now they could put their hives anywhere they chose, in their own temple, or any other likely place.

Guerrero started down the stairs.

Aguilar wanted to know where he was going. He did not wish to be left behind. He was worried about whoever it was had left those pots of incense burning. In his hand he had a notched stick. He never let go of it. It was his last way of keeping European time, in a world that kept time some other way, but that did not matter to him, what was important was to know which saint's day it was, since one of them might save him.

Somehow Guerrero did not think so. Besides, he wanted to be alone. He wanted to go down there. When he left, Aguilar had turned his back on all that magnificence, and was thumbing his breviary, as though testing the edge on a saw.

There are advantages to being illiterate. Guerrero walked right down into the city.

The sun was hot and he began to feel himself again. He spent all day wandering across those platforms and courts. They made him thoughtful. He could see what he was up against. If a people could afford to throw away such opulence, what on earth had they kept in its stead?

And yet it was an austere opulence. Wildly carved though it might be, there was something aloof and restrained about it. In particular he looked at the carvings. Mostly they were of a short, plump, well cared-for people, severe, oblique, and gentle. It was as though they were all acting out a charade, conscientiously and with great amiable care. You felt somehow that the charade was something that suited them, but also that they were eager to get through it, in order to relax and giggle later. Even the cruelty seemed a little disdainful.

Perhaps Coba misled him. It had been abandoned before the Mexicans came, with their cult of human hearts.

Yet in some sense he was right. They were a very old people. They had been doing the same things for two thousand years. Perhaps they were too old. They were a little hampered by themselves, by all that invariable time. What had once had meaning for them, was now only the traditional sensuous pleasure of the day. The things they had once rightly enjoyed doing, were now only the right things to do. That made them grateful for almost any harmless novelty that conformed to the ritual of their days, and that admired them.

Well, he admired them.

An individualist, born into a society, or a social class, to whose ideals and nature he does not conform, spends his life in solitary confinement. The world must be full of such individual padded cells, each containing nothing but a desperate man who could not, if he would, agree to the conditions of his release. He cannot demean himself even for freedom. But though he knows he is an anomaly, something tells him he is not, as others would tell him, an abnormality. There must be somewhere a society in which he would be normal, his critics or oppressors then beyond the pale.

Looking at this sculpture, Guerrero realized that he had at last found it.

It was Aguilar, here, who became the solitaire.

All day he wandered. It was to be in a museum, a thing which in those days did not exist. Menageries they had, but not museums, unless any world be the museum of the future, in which there is no way of telling whether we will be something of value or something to fling away.

For whatever reason the city had been abandoned, it had been abandoned complete. Foraging around, he found not only wild honey, but new sandals, weapons, and in a chest in a back room, a feathered cloak. These he put on. He liked the dusty rustle of the feathers, which gave him rank, though he did not know that.

Next he explored the sacbes, searching for traces of whoever had left the incense lamps, and at last thought he had found them on a causeway which seemed to lead back to the coast, to judge by the position of the sun.

He also found a better place for them to camp, so that night they feasted on fresh fruit and honey, and had a good fire. The fire helped to keep at a distance the reddish jaguar of which he had caught a glimpse, as it paced him all day.

A weapon, it was the studded club of a warrior, made him feel much better. Seeing his costume, Aguilar had started and then glowered at him, suspecting him of having gone over to the enemy.

Perhaps he had, but Aguilar had had all day to talk to the other two, who were now rested enough to be rebellious.

Guerrero was for going on.

The others were not. Aguilar cleared his throat and said they would stay where they were.

"And do what? And why?"

"We can pray for deliverance," said Aguilar, and rolled his eyes upward.

"To whose god?" Guerrero demanded scornfully.

It was what Aguilar had wanted to hear. He was always looking for heresy. A heresy proved to him how snug and warm it was to be orthodox. He wanted so much to see the whole world burn.

"You'd go over to them," he screamed. "You're a traitor."

It was absurd. It was also true, though he could not see how one could be a traitor to something one had never espoused. He shrugged. "They're here," he said.

"You should pray."

"I'd rather eat," said Guerrero. He walked out of there and left them. He wasn't worried. He wandered through the moonlit ruins. There was no real fight in Aguilar, just a fear of being flayed. There was, of course, that danger, and

Guerrero for a moment wondered how a priest would look dancing inside a priest. But he was not afraid for himself. He never had been, and he was not now.

It was something these people admired, courage.

Just the same he slept by himself that night. Courage is no defence against hysteria, and Aguilar was badly scared.

The jaguar, wherever it was, was explicitly vocal. By morning Aguilar had talked himself into the glories of incipient martyrdom. He had a thin and holy look. He agreed to follow Guerrero, but insisted upon saying mass first. Guerrero did not object. Such a thing seemed to help the other two.

Then he led them down the causeway.

In five days they reached a city on the coast, and were taken before its chief, a young man named Taxmar. Guerrero managed to make himself understood. The town was Ecab and no friend to Tulum, so they were not martyred after all. Taxmar was bored and they were a novelty. He enslaved them instead.

VII

They stayed two and a half years at Ecab. First they were forced to shave their beards and trim their hair, for they were slaves, and beards distinguish only rulers and old men of a certain wisdom. They also had to do without cloak and sandals, for those conferred rank. These, until Guerrero could prove his ability to fight, were taken away from him. But it did not take him long to prove that he could fight. He was enjoying himself. He enjoyed everything.

As a result Taxmar made a pet of him, and then a friend. He was curious about legendary worlds. Guerrero was curious about the one he was in. So Guerrero fared well and Aguilar badly. In the second year the other two died. They could survive neither the climate nor enforced labour in the fields. Few Spaniards could. It was what made them hidalgos.

Ecab was a handsome, prosperous place. Like all the Maya, the people were terrified of death, but also like all the Maya, this made them convivial and jolly. Except at night, when the gods of death were about, and Ah Puch watched everyone, they were a happy people, totally enthralled by small children and by flowers.

Guerrero underestimated neither them nor himself, but having at last found a place where he felt at ease, he meant to rise. He became a warrior. It was not difficult. Their wars were simple things, because they had a simple purpose. In a society like that, Guerrero towered up as a genius at strategy. His advancement was certain.

The purpose of war was offerings. It was the Mexicans who conquered them who had taught them what to do about death. They had always been a little puzzled about the matter before. The Mexicans were not. One offered death human hearts. Ah Puch ate them, and left you alone. And that was what the wars were for, to take captives for the altars. One only needed four or five at a time, for the monthly festivals. And since, after having thrown off the Mexican yoke fifty odd years before, the Maya had fallen into a series of mutually contentious states, all struggling for pre-eminence, but none strong enough to re-establish the Empire, there were many little skirmishes available.

So Guerrero prospered. There are advantages to being outside a culture, particularly if one is a soldier. One has only to see through the ethics of the opposite side, do something unheard of, and not only does one win, but one is quite safe. He soon got his cloak and club back again. He also enjoyed himself. He was becoming one of them. He was better fed and housed than he had ever been. He flourished. He was made much of. But he remained a slave. Taxmar refused to let him leave.

So long as Taxmar remained alive, to be a slave did not disturb him. In Spain he had been worse than a slave, and worse treated, for poverty makes slaves of us all. Here he had everything. There were even compensations. There were, for instance, women. Adultery was punishable by death, but Taxmar had concubines, and Guerrero was very fond of women. They were little women, plump but delicate, whose life consisted in pleasing. As a race, the Maya were sensuous, but not sensual, so Guerrero, who was both, given the opportunity, was a novelty again. He pleased.

That made Aguilar furious. Aguilar was by nature chaste, but only from a lack of desire. Yet the suspicion that the carnal may know something that the chaste do not drove him, as it always does the ascetic, but never the austere, to a frenzy. Never mind. It would be something to denounce later.

It was to please the women, really, or at any rate one of them, that Guerrero had his ears pierced and distended. It was not something he thought about. The world in those days was a bigger place, and having left one world, he naturally wanted to conform to the practices of another. Only low slaves were so plain as he, and even a slave, if a captive of war, which in a way he was, may have rank. The Spanish, he foresaw, would not come back for years, and might never come. Besides, he had one ear pierced already. Sailors did, by custom, and because it was supposed to improve their sight. For a year the distenders annoyed him. After that he wore jade tubes with flaring lips, and thought no more of the matter. They felt heavy and joggled when he walked, but that was not unpleasant, he grew used to them, and the women were delighted.

Tattooing came next. He did not mind that either.

He was beginning to move as they did, gravely, and with some pomp. An aristocracy is so. One way or another, it weighs itself down to the proper pace. Slave or not, he was one of them. It was something, after all, to become a gentleman, or at least, for he had always been such if in the wrong world, to be recognized as one. He found that condition suited him very well.

Aguilar was not one of them. He was put out to work in the fields. This he regarded as a martyrdom, and perhaps he was right. He had become a priest to escape such things. Now he was back at them again, and they did not please him. Still, even he had a certain novelty value. It was because he was celibate.

Taxmar could not understand that. He persisted, out of curiosity and a sense of fun, in attempting to find out whether the man was a eunuch or merely impotent. He must be one or the other, for a spiritual eunuch was something the Maya had never heard of. One might lacerate the flesh to please the gods, but certainly one did not deny it. To do so was unnatural, and therefore unthinkable.

Yet physically Aguilar seemed complete, and Taxmar was not without his informants. The man had wet dreams, so he could not be impotent. There must be some other explanation.

Guerrero, though amused, thought that investigations of that sort went too far.

Taxmar did not think they went far enough. He wished to try an experiment.

Aguilar tried to explain, but since he had refused to learn the language of a people he still called idolators and devils, could not explain very well. He looked ill. Forced labour had made him thin, and he had, even more than before, a tendency to cringe. Guerrero avoided him. He did not like to see people degrade themselves.

Aguilar grovelled.

To Taxmar, this was not priestly conduct. Priests did not grovel, except, of course, to each other. There must be some other explanation. He sent Aguilar out late at evening, to catch fish, and made sure that he would have to camp out overnight. He also sent along a concubine, with orders to tempt the man.

Aguilar was away for five days.

Taxmar awaited the result with the liveliest interest. But the concubine reported that he had merely gnashed his teeth and said something about St. Anthony, so they decided he was an idiot, and put him in charge of the harem.

Perhaps by this time he was one. A lust for revenge that goes unsatisfied for years can make a man so. At least the work was easy, and when they laughed at him, he could think of them as devils, which was some help. The Church was full of precedents for that sort of thing. But to be an anonymous martyr is full of futility. One wants at least to be on the official rolls. Would the Spanish never come?

Guerrero hoped not.

Then, unexpectedly, Taxmar died.

Guerrero put out to sea the same night. He had become a valuable person. He could win wars. Taxmar's successors were not likely to let him go, and he wanted to be free. He wanted to go on in this world, and knew not only what he was worth, but what he would be worth, when at last the Spanish came, when and if they did.

They would certainly try to, for though Yucatan had no gold, they did not know that, and though they had found a little among the Caribs whom they had slaughtered in the Indies, that had only made them reach out for more.

Guerrero did not know what he would do then, but he did know what he meant to do now. He meant to rise. Nor was he improvising any more, as he had at Coba. He had learned much of this country in the last two years, and he had decided where to go.

Taking five slaves with him, and such wealth as he could lay his hands on, cocoa beans mostly, but some trinkets and jewels, he got into a sea canoe and started south. He was ceremonially dressed in the full costume of a warrior, with rich cloak, shield, head-dress, and ornamented loincloth and sandals. His weapons were beside him. He lacked only the nose rod and tattooing of a noble of the first class, and those, as a slave, he was not allowed to have. He did not mean to be a slave again.

The north-east coast had estuaries, savannahs, sandbars, and dangerous shoals. They passed Tulum by night, and saw the temple beacons from the sea. But even had he been captured, he would not have been sacrificed now. He was too useful.

On impulse he had the paddlers turn towards the sacred

island of Cozumel, to which pilgrims went from Tulum. Reaching it, he rested for the night, and then went to one of the temples to offer sacrifice. He now looked like an Indian and was taken for one. Even the priests, who two years ago would have torn his heart out, took him for one.

Before leaving he took a long look at those templed gods. They were his now, and they were the ones he had always preferred. It was just that previously he had not known their names. And looking at them, he discovered his capacity for gratitude. Nothing had evoked it before, in his short life, but now that the emotion had sprung into being, he did not think that it would die.

Meanwhile there were adventures to be had. Of Aguilar he thought not at all.

Nor did he think of his European past. It never had been *his* past, and it was certainly not his now. This world was his now, and he was delighted with it.

He set out again. Beyond Cozumel a current caught his canoe and swept it far out to sea. He was often out of sight of land on that two-week journey, but that did not bother him. The water was calm, the sky marvellously young at night, the air cool, and he had brought much food. His slaves would get him back to shore.

To the south lay Chetumal, on a large bay, and he had heard much of Chetumal. It was the largest and the most secure of all these states along the eastern shore. He did not think they would make him a slave there. Its ruler did not sound that sort of man.

He had an Empire around him, and that being so, he found the world good. Why should he not? He was healthy, he was young, and he was loyal. To show that loyalty, he needed now only to be loved and love.

But loyal to what?

He was about to find out.

VIII

The state of Chetumal lived by trade, but had the advantage of being beyond the main periphery of Maya affairs, at the mouths of several navigable rivers, down which the merchants came from Guatemala, or overland from Mexico and the western coast. It was protected from the avarice of adjacent rulers by a series of savannahs and almost impassable swamps, and had been founded during the Lesser Descent of the Old Empire, in the sixth century.

Of its ambitious neighbours there were five, the Xiu, who had cast the Mexicans out and now wished to rule the peninsula in their stead; the Cocom of Sotuta; the Canek of Tayasal, who lived at Lake Peten Itza, in Guatemala; the Chel; and the Pech. Chetumal traded with all of them, and had been defeated by none. Its own borders and subsidiary fiefs stretched west of Lake Bacalar, and for some distance north and south of it.

Of all these dynasties, Chetumal felt close only to the Canek Itza, who had retreated to Guatemala from the holy but now long-deserted city of Chichen Itza, and who were the original colonists of the peninsula, both in the Lesser and the Greater Descent.

The name and title of the ruler of this land was Nachancan. There are different grades of nobility, from the ostentatious and therefore nervous, through the correct, to the true. From what Guerrero had heard, Nachancan belonged to the small company of the exact, who are so congruent with themselves, that we may always trust them not to budge from what they are.

He was excited.

Until a certain age, anyone of any sensibility is aware of his own life as a rehearsal. One plays the same scenes over and over again, but it does not matter what one does, for one will do it differently when the curtain goes up. But then comes a moment when one realizes that the play is on, and that the curtain, unnoticed, rose some time ago. By then one notices with a certain detachment both what will be done to one, and what one is doing. One scarcely knows then whether one is the puppet master of one's self, or the only possible person for the role, but one enjoys it so much, that all thought of audience or applause is forgotten. One's only left desire is to meet the other members of the cast on cue, and so take up one's lines. One knows where it will end, of course, but meanwhile one inhabits a world.

It is a mystery play but it includes, as do all things devout, much loving comedy.

All unknown to himself, Guerrero had reached both Chetumal and that point.

The city was a good fifty miles from the open sea, through a narrow passage and across a salty bay. When he had reached the sandbar which separated the bay from the sea, Guerrero beached his canoe and sent one of his slaves ahead with gifts, to announce his arrival.

As the efficient ruler of a trading state, Nachancan had as many sources of information as there were traders in the peninsula. He had long known who Guerrero was and was ready to receive him. Guerrero, who had rather expected that he would be, paddled up the bay.

He saw order, well cultivated fields, and prosperous villages. Chetumal itself, when he came to it, though large and populous, was not one of the great sacred centres of Yucatan, but a commercial town, often rebuilt, but stubbornly secular. Its temples were of a medium size. It did not go in fear of the gods, but preferred to bargain with them.

That too was good.

On landing he was surrounded by a small crowd which had come to see him and then taken to the palace. The crowd had come to see him as they would have flocked to any zoological curiosity. Legend had it that though their world would not end until 1697, which was comfortably far away, their new rulers would come out of the ocean and would be, as he had been, white skinned. But all the crowd saw was an Indian much like themselves. They went away disappointed.

Nachancan saw something more.

He had expected an oddity. Instead he found a healthy

young man with good legs, strong arms, and a determined but innate sense of dignity, a little too young perhaps, a little gauche, but then the person one becomes is not the person one was, and neither has anything to do with the person one is. Nor was dignity to be overlooked, for it was not in itself a quality, but a shape the mind has which even the self cannot hide. Nachancan liked the man and saw that the man, on sight, liked him. It gave their meeting a quality of predestination, for it is something in this lonely business, life, that spark of recognition. No wise man would stamp it out, for it can rekindle those fires in us which from neglect have almost burned out. To meet a lover is to have the illusion of youth back again, but to meet someone of one's own sort makes maturity endurable.

Besides, Nachancan was a practical person, and if his spies were accurate, Guerrero would be useful.

Affection and pragmaticism are not mutually exclusive. In fact they shore each other up. Guerrero saw a slightly wrinkled, but tight-skinned and amiable man of forty-five, sitting cross-legged on his bench of office, surrounded by his nobles, polite and smiling. He had come here to advance, and saw all would be well, but he also found something he had never had, and had never felt the want of, until now when it sat before him. He felt suddenly warmed inside. He had found a father.

Instantly he was at his ease. There was so much to say, that would not have to be said.

It was not something either of them ever bothered to consider, that recognition. It was not necessary. But there was, after that, no question of his being made a slave. Of course there were court jealousies to be dealt with, but they were dealt with, and besides, Guerrero was not ambitious in that way. Once the courtiers discovered that, even Nachancan's fifteen-year-old son relaxed. They, too, though warily, became friends.

For the next four years Guerrero became himself. It is something, after all, to find out where one belongs at the age of twenty-six, and he made the most of it. In doing so he became a grandee of that place, and a man of thirty.

He directed their battles and defences, and directed them well, for now he had so much to lose, he wished to make sure that he would not lose it.

Only sometimes, now that he had the ease, he would remember Spain, not his life there, which was not worth the remembering, but the country itself. As time went by he remembered it less and less. Born into the wrong environment, he had had the good luck to fall into the right one. He never tired of discovering how right it was.

He had first to prove his worth, and did, not once, but many times. He became adept at war. The object of native war was to capture the leader of the opposite side, for only warriors and great men made suitable sacrifices, the commonalty being good only for slaves. If the leader was captured, the others, not wanting to be slaves, deserted.

Most such expeditions were small, no more than foraging parties out to stock the gods' larder. In Mexico those sacrificed to the gods were sometimes used afterwards to feed the zoo. And for that matter, was not any pantheon, Christian or otherwise, good or evil, merely a theological zoo, which men stocked with one epitome each of the rarer of their own desires, either for amusement, or to assist by example the hunt?

Guerrero tried another method, capturing the rival party by ambush, which left the leader isolated and easy to pick off. In a war for such a purpose, men used their weapons defensively. They were easily bested by an aggressive European technique, which did not promise well for the future, when it should come. But it had not come yet.

Occasionally there was a real war, though Chetumal was so geographically secure, that such skirmishes were usually punitive. He had to put down the rebellious sub-chiefs of Lake Bacalar, which meant hand-to-hand fighting, which he enjoyed. The warriors were coated, so was he, with ornamental paint, which made them slippery to get away.

Try to take them captive, and they wriggled off like eels.

There, too, Guerrero could think of things to do no native would have thought of doing. Reaching for his opponent's nose rod, he yanked. The man gave a grunt, stumbled, and fell. He turned out to be the leader of the uprising, so Guerrero had a string of victims to hand over to the priests.

Suitably bound with tufted cord, they were sacrificed the next day. Not that the priests, the people, or even the idols were bloodthirsty. It was merely that, like Aguilar, whom he had almost forgotten, and perhaps the Saints, they went through the proper forms. At the head of the pantheon there were deities so remote that, like God, they were never worshipped, for what was the point of it; they had no interest in human affairs.

After the affair at Bacalar Nachancan created him a noble and warrior of the first class. Since the high priest performed the ceremony, it was a little like being baptized by an archbishop, the distinction was so great, the event so trivial.

Yet it was a rite of some importance. They dressed him as a warrior and painted him a sacrificial colour. He remembered, for the first time, that cage in the plaza at Tulum, with the difference that now this was his world, whereas before he had merely gone to feed it.

He crossed the flagstones of the plaza with Nachancan's son on one side of him and the high priest on the other. That the high priest, who was very old, should officiate now was a mark of especial favour.

He was taken not to the temple altar at the top of the pyramid, but to another, on a landing half-way up. There he had to lie on the curved sacrificial stone, head up. He saw the intense sky above him, his head swam, his legs trembled, and he thought of Valdivia. No assistants held his wrists and ankles, nor was he painted that mortal blue, but no doubt Valdivia's heart had pounded in much the same painful way. He tensed himself, determined not to cry out, but felt so dizzy, that he seemed to fall down into the sky.

The priest held his nose and jabbed swiftly through the

septum with a large bone awl. The pain felt hot, Guerrero's eyes smarted and began to weep, but he did not cry out. There was not much blood. Dead cells swam in his eyes, and he saw all the gods in concentric circles in the flickering sky above him. It was a vision, but it was not insight. The man who has lived in more than one culture, can believe only in a God beyond the gods of either.

The priest whipped out the awl and inserted a temporary plug. For a few days the wound smarted and seeped with ichor. Then it began to feel itchy, natural, and pleasant.

On the seventh day Nachancan gave him a gold nose rod, elaborately carved, from Guatemala. It was of a material seldom seen in Yucatan, old, valuable, and rare, and for a few days it annoyed him, by intercepting his line of vision. Then he began rather to like it. It showed who he was.

Life went on. There was some question of finding him a wife. He must have children. Children gave life a continuity that otherwise it lacked.

Then, in 1515, without warning, came the great plague. It was their first benefit from Europe. The natives called it *mayasimil*, the easy death, for they were an old people, and so enjoyed irony. But there was nothing easy about it.

They had had plagues before, the worst in 1480, but none so bad as this. It raged from one end of the peninsula to the other. There was no mistaking it. Great pustules broke out over the body, the legs and arms seemed to rot, and in four or five days the victims died surrounded by a great stench.

Guerrero had only to look to know what it was. He had seen it often, though never in so bad a form. It was smallpox. Yet he did not think that he or his party had brought it, for it had occurred too long after their arrival. Those traders who went everywhere must have brought it back from some other Spaniard or infected Indian.

The traders had always bothered him. They were bound to attract the Spanish some day. It was extraordinary that they should move about undetected. But then the Spanish were not observant, only the smell of gold, well worn, faint, like the smell of dirty linen, would bring them on, and the merchants had no gold.

He tried not to think about the Spanish.

He lived in one of the courtyards of the palace now. He was awakened by a great wailing. It seemed to come from the royal apartments. He went there, and found Nachancan alone and weeping. That in itself was usual. The Maya had a terror of the dark. Yet Nachancan sat in it. His son had just died of the plague.

They sat there together, alone in the midst of all that necessary and terrible commotion. Lamps sprang into flame everywhere. They were a people terrified of death, perhaps in this flat rain forest they found it all around them, whereas in the mountains from which they had originally come, the fact of it was better concealed. They were healthy, they were careful about sanitation, but their world was damp. A little of it rotted away every day. Some people find one thing before the parable of life, and some another. They found death, and that left them with a passion for children. If they could not live for ever, perhaps their children could, for children know nothing of death.

At what age does that moral necessity make itself felt? To the childlike, perhaps never.

But Nachancan, an adult man, by some accident, and through no fault of his own, had had only one son.

The body was shrouded, with jade beads placed in its mouth, and then burnt, an honour reserved for warriors. It was a great loss. He had been a pretty and agreeable boy.

Nachancan did not appear in public, but at the end of the mandatory eighty days of mourning, he married one of his daughters to Guerrero. He must have grandchildren, and he must have them quickly, in order to see again what life looked like.

It was a good marriage, for among the Maya, love came after the event, so that instead of dwindling into familiarity, it had the chance to grow out of it, and Guerrero had reached the age when we want permanence rather than novelty, though he had not realized that before. He began to discover his own ability to love, and found it larger than he had known. His wife was so fine.

For two more years the world left them in peace. They had children.

Indeed, when the news came from Ecab, Guerrero had just returned from the high priest, who had named his second son and cast its horoscope. The boy, it seemed, was to be a warrior, like his father, but not a ruler. He was to be called Hun Imix, after the day on which he was born.

Nor was Guerrero called Guerrero. He had taken the name Ah Ceh, because it was the name of one of their ancient heroes and pleased him, a man who had gone down to the other side of the sea, as in a way he had done. It also meant "the deer", an animal which to them was a sign of departure and loss.

And who, watching a deer alert at the edge of a clearing, would have thought that it could mean anything else?

He walked through the courtyards of the palace rather slowly, seeing things intensely, as we sometimes do in moments of stress. For now that the Spaniards had at last come, though he knew what he would do, he had yet to know exactly how he would feel. About his loyalty he had no doubts, but loyalty is not always what we want to do. If, in the act, we discover that it is, why then that is recompense enough.

Yet he had been Spanish once. He wondered how he would look at them, if he ever saw them, and knew how they would look at him.

That made him angry. To have anyone dispraise what we love always makes us angry. And Nachancan was such a wise man. He saw everything and said nothing, and somehow that made you love him, at least it was the sort of wisdom Guerrero could love.

Between them they plotted what was to happen at Champoton.

TWO

IX

It had never occurred to the Spaniards, since they were provincial, that any world could exist but their own, and since they had so recently put down all opposition to themselves in their own world, they did not expect much resistance from the world outside. The Moors had made them carpet-baggers for so long, that they were always indignant when anyone attempted to prevent them from stealing what they wanted, and what they wanted was to go home rich, for they thought no wider than their own native village.

When baulked, they turned vicious, if only out of sheer astonishment, that anyone should not accept them on their own terms, for after all, were their terms not the only ones?

Besides, they had Charles V behind them. In time he would retire into a monastery, leaving behind him nothing but a few Titians and an enigma, but at the moment he was an ambitious boy of seventeen who needed money. He could not get it all from the Fuggers, and so anyone who could give him a fine cow to milk would soon rise in the world. He loathed Spain, though he had invented it, but his subjects did not know that. Then, too, carpet-baggers are always looking for a cow to milk.

They had not found it in the Caribbean. Therefore they searched on. They found the Caribbean unrewarding.

For twenty-five years they had lived in daily expectation of the Indies, despite Darien, and the brutality of finding only an empty ocean on the other side of it. Yet the Pacific might still be the China Sea, and did not the Orient have islands as unprofitable as these, but close to the jewelled East? Like most people they were always waiting for someone else to find something worth taking away from him. In the meantime they ran their ranches, an occupation which suited them, for a gentleman is permitted to run ranches.

In their own eyes they were all gentlemen. In Spain anybody who owns a horse is a gentleman. A few of them would even have passed for such at home, in Estramadura or Castille, which perhaps was why the others had emigrated.

And went right on emigrating.

Now, under Fernandez de Cordoba, they were out on the Caribbean, in search of slaves, for Indians did not make good slaves, they died off too quickly, and since no gentleman ever did his own work, had to be replaced.

Secretly he hoped to find the Indies for himself.

A storm caught up his three ships. The horses whinnied and tried not to fall down. The men were terrified. They prayed to St. Nicolaus, who like the Diving God of Tulum, of whom they knew nothing, swoops heavily out of the clouds to save the faithful. Waterspouts they had heard of, those fabulous snakes which hissed up out of the China Seas, but a hurricane filled them with dread.

They knew nothing of navigation. That they left to the Portuguese. Their own means of self-preservation were more primitive. When there was something to shoot, they shot it. When there was nothing to shoot, they prayed.

The storm caught them up and then released them. They spun out of it, with the sunlight before them like a carpet, and saw that low, shoaled, limestone coast, with Ecab shining white and colourful before them, one of the coastal cities, topping the jungle with its pyramids. They thought it a mirage.

There was nothing in Spain so grand nor so unexpected. In our time, only explorers of the Antarctic have seen a new world for the first time, its storms, its glitter, its lichens, and its miraculously open little lakes. We cannot know what they felt. But they were ruled by cupidity, and cupidity is incapable of wonder, which is selfless. Their only standard of civilization was that of the people they had destroyed.

Luxury to them was Moorish. On the spot they called Ecab El Gran Cairo.

Naturally they expected no difficulties. Now they had driven back the Moors, good Christians were welcome anywhere. They prepared to go ashore.

Taxmar's son was ready for them. His father had kept Guerrero as a source of wonder stories, but the son had a firmer grip upon reality. There was some prophetic nonsense about gods who were to come from the sea, he believed it, but he did not believe it now, and he also knew that these were not gods, but only another kind of enemy.

He acted accordingly.

It is strange how the Spaniards, who brought nothing but sorrow, expected to be greeted everywhere, even in the older and more sophisticated Orient, which they thought this was, with joy. That these fine nobles, with their jewellery, dignity, and plumes, should set out to meet them seemed to them altogether natural.

Perhaps it was because to them sorrow was life's best and most enduring joy.

Yet they sensed that something was unusual. These people seemed too hospitable to be anything but savages, but they must know they were worth robbing, for the more richly dressed of them wore ornaments of gold.

The Spanish prepared to march into Ecab.

They never reached it.

Taxmar had them ambushed, beat them off, took one captive for the fattening pens, and sent a messenger to Guerrero at Chetumal.

The Spaniards, knowing nothing of Guerrero, got back to their boats and put out to sea. Though wary, they were pleased at what they saw. Surely such large stone cities must mean wealth.

They did not put into shore. Protected by low forested sandbars, the shore did not seem worth putting into. Thus they passed the hidden cities of Conil, Dzilum and Yobain, and on St. Lazarus' Day, came to Campeche. Campeche fought them off, so they thought it better to go on. "Castilan," they had said at Campeche. "Castilan," but it had not altogether sounded like a compliment.

Guerrero had had time to prepare.

Thus they came to Champoton and dropped anchor there, in the mouth of the estuary, near what they took to be a carved rock.

It was not a carved rock. When Kulkulcan, the Maya Quetzalcoatl, god of wisdom and the morning star, promulgated by the Lords of Xiu, had left Yucatan he had built in the sea off Champoton, so legend had it, a temple, for he was also the protector of fishermen and Champoton lived off the day's catch. The Spanish ignored it. No fanatic knows how many things in this world are sacred, and therefore dangerous, so they were doubly blind, being fanatics both for God and gold.

The Couohes of Champoton were fanatic themselves. They loved war, and their temples always needed victims. Guerrero had known he could count on them, and he had not been wrong.

The Spaniards saw before them only a large rich city set back from a shallow bay collared by white beaches. They put ashore to get water and supplies, their boats clumsy with long casks.

When they landed they found the beach deserted. It was unmarked by so much as the footprint of a bird. Beyond the beach rose the scrub forest, beyond the forest, Champoton itself. A stream of sweet water meandered down aimlessly into the sand. They made for that.

The Couohes blew their conches, separated themselves from the forest, and attacked.

The Spaniards had scarcely time to drop their barrels and prime their guns. It was the first time they had seen these devils in battle formation, and devils is what they thought them, if only because they were not easy to defeat.

The beach had a slight camber and the sand was loose. War being a ritual matter, the Indians were painted black, while their plumes and ornaments waved over their heads in a ripple of colour. They did not fight to kill, except to save themselves. They wanted Cordoba, for sacrifice.

The guns either misfired or did not fire at all. The Spaniards had to use their swords, as they fell back towards their longboats. The Maya made straight for Cordoba, who thus had the experience, rare in a military commander, of having to fight for his life. He was wounded thirty-three times, though not fatally, since the Couohes did not wish him dead.

The boats finally got into deeper water. The Maya, being a short people, could not follow, but their arrows could. The firing of musketry did not seem to disconcert them. It was almost as though they had expected it.

The Spanish had to row past that rock to reach their ships. They could see now it was no rock, but a building swarming with warriors. Cordoba received another wound and two men died at their oars. Somehow the Spaniards reached their ships.

Their last glimpse of that beach was when the sea of feathers parted, and they saw that two of their number had been captured. The Indians had stripped them naked, painted them with black and white stripes, tied their hands behind their backs, and were prodding them up towards the jungle and the temple towers beyond.

The Spaniards did not know about blood sacrifice yet, but they found the scene bitter enough. They were all wounded. There was nothing to do but to return to Cuba. The bay they named the Bay of the Losing Fight.

Its real name was Potochan.

X

Nachancan, when he received the news, was delighted. He thought the matter over with. Their own wars were frequently won so.

Guerrero said nothing, but thought not. He stood there, blinking in the light, while the messengers from Champoton told their story. They told it well. It was almost as though he were seeing what had happened. Indeed, he could see what had happened, for the messengers had brought with them a picture roll.

It depicted the sacrifice of the two Spaniards who had been captured. The painting was painstaking, ritual, and exact. The little flat firmly outlined bodies lay over the sacrificial stone. They were painted blue, but to show they were Spaniards, had been drawn with their casques on and their beards neatly spaded. A lot of white showed to the eye.

The drawing startled him. There they were, as the Indians saw them, and as he must see them now, as nothing more than foreign oblations to one's own gods. In a way he did see them that way, but with a twinge of bitterness, he did not know about what or against whom.

They made good victims, struck down by a god of whom, and to whom, for once, they could not make an excuse. He liked that, and yet an echo sounded at the back of his mind, the sound of home, which, whether we like it or not, is always the sympathetic overtone to what we do now.

He had never had a home there. His home was here.

He caught Nachancan's eye, and thought: how can you trust me if you do not trust me. But he said nothing. Nachancan did trust him. Therefore he would have to set to work to teach these people a new use for war. It would not be easy. They had lived in anarchy now for too long to unite against anyone not like themselves. It was something they could not imagine. Even the Mexicans who had conquered them for so long had not come from an alien world. They had certainly not brought another world with them, as the Spaniards did.

Nor would it do to trust allies such as the Couohes of Champoton, just because they were bloodthirsty and had owed Chetumal a favour. The favour was now paid back. It was Guerrero's turn now to repay a favour.

It was what he longed with all his being to do. But that would not make it any the easier to rouse the peninsula.

Yet that picture roll of the Spaniards had unsettled him,

and made him uneasy. He needed to see what he did believe in, in order to remember what he did not. It was as though his own life had suddenly become nothing but a *masque* in front of him. He looked down at these little painted strangers captive on their sheet of paper, over the blurred outline of the nose rod that barred him inside what he was now. It was the life he had chosen, yet he felt sad and angry, not so much about the Spaniards, as about all those who love life but not the world they live in, and who so do something wrong. He needed reassurance. He went to see his children and his wife.

His wife always made him feel gentle. They spent the long slow evening together.

Her name was Ix Chan, and she was Nachancan's daughter, which made her a princess in this country. At any rate she was a gentlewoman. She could not help treating him with a loyal courtesy which followed a tradition so ancient and alien that he could scarcely comprehend it. For what would seem to a westerner spontaneous affection, was to her only a matter of form, whereas those things which to a Spaniard would in her seem cold and impersonal, actually sprang from the shy wells of a controlled but passionate regard. The Maya were not physically demonstrative. What they really felt they showed only by the way in which they held a dish or twirled a flower. In the midst of sex they were never there. They were off somewhere, remembering a tenderness, glancing at what their own bodies were doing over their shoulder.

It made them intangible and silvery, and made him ache with love. It was a little art she had, to make the now endless, by that being somehow somewhere else.

It had taken him a long time to find out how much she loved him, for when she said she was proud of him, he thought she was poking fun, or when she massaged him, that she was being kind. He was at first a little in awe of her. She was so fine, and in Spain he had been told that he was not. In any fantasy about a woman of such quality, and he had

had them, he had been the lackey let up the backstairs. So it took him longer to love her. It took him until he realized that here he was what he was, which for once was the part assigned to him, rather than the ill-cast thing Spain had made of him.

He was only playing at being one of these people. It was not until he had to help to take care of them, not until right now, after Champoton, that he realized that simply because he never could be one of them, therefore he would be nothing else.

To him life was still marvellous. He had that nature, but he had also had that luck. If it had not been for that storm, he would have been wallowing with some peasant until she wrinkled, and he ran after camp-followers and cheapjack tarts, though wrinkled before his time himself.

Yet here he lay with Ix Chan, who was soft, and undulant, and kind, in a stone room, lit gently by lamps, while they talked of simple matters as they had always done. Sometimes, in the night, when she thought he was sleeping, she would get up and walk erectly away to look at the children.

Tonight he got up to follow her.

The children, their two sons, were huddled up to each other asleep, dark haired, tired, and plump as hairless puppies. The boys stirred. He saw how the Maya derived such endless pleasure from watching children. Ix Chan gave a shy, contented look, and they went back to their own room.

Daily things can become the most precious. He knew he must have spent a restless night.

At dawn the priests began the day with pink-lipped conches. The sound rumbled out across the bay, on which there was not a single canoe, let alone a ship.

Nevertheless, as he knew, that ship would come. He must prepare against that day. It was time now for envoys and diplomacy. But how can you rouse a people against an enemy they have never seen? Men always prepare to fight their last enemy, not their next, and their last and habitual enemy had been themselves.

XI

He was right. In a few months that ship came.

Cordoba had died of his wounds, but not before he had had time to report the land rich, on the strength of the few miserable and unknown to himself imported gold trinkets he had stolen from Campeche and the Isle of Women. He had to justify himself in some way.

So did the Governor of Cuba, who therefore reported the discovery to the Crown, and then, in order to get to the land first, in case it should be rich, authorized and sponsored another expedition, under the direction of a man called Grijalva, whose chief recommendation was that he paid for everything. Everything in this case consisted of four ships and 250 men.

Not knowing the borders of that deceptive sea, the flotilla headed for Cozumel, of which they did know. A few days later, in the spring of 1518, they sighted it. That island, which is now merely a beach resort for expensive Mexicans, was in those days holy.

When, three or four days later, news of their arrival reached Chetumal, Guerrero swore.

The Spanish had taken possession of the island, which had offered no resistance, for as was their habit when a town was taken, the inhabitants, not wishing either to be sacrificed or enslaved, had fled. A few, too old to honour the gods in that way, had stayed behind, but the Spaniards, being raised on Xenophon and Plutarch, thought that desertion their first victory, ran up banners, and had taken possession of the land in the name of something called Castille.

What, asked Nachancan, was the meaning of that word, Castille?

Guerrero knew very well what the name meant, but found it difficult to explain. How could he explain it was a country as disunited and as anarchic as this, and yet so much worse? How explain that thirst not for hearts, but souls? That intolerance, and that greed bred of insecurity, whereas here there was some gluttony, yes, but no greed, some lust for power, but almost none for possession. How can you explain intolerance to the tolerant?

Yet life in Chetumal went on as it had always done. The same was true of northern Yucatan, so far as he could judge. There was no attempt at defence, but only curiosity and a certain sacerdotal foreboding. These strangers fulfilled a prophecy. True, they did not come at quite the correct time, but they did come from the right direction. And then they were so few. The gods are always few, and if they were not gods, then it takes little effort to remove a few, and life then goes on again.

He could not explain, even to Nachancan, the juggernaut of Europe. These people had no knowledge of a juggernaut, and less than none of Europe. Nor, unlike Christians, could they understand the awful power which derives from doing one thing in the name of another. They were not fanatics,

Messengers now came in daily. The strangers had turned south.

There was no end of messengers, for life is very like Greek tragedy. The chief events which change our lives, the chief events, therefore, in them, always take place offstage. We ourselves are reduced merely to discussing the moral impact of what has been done to us, of what we have become, to a chorus of the inevitable I told you so.

The Spaniards drew closer.

They passed Zelha and Tulum.

"We followed the shore day and night," wrote the Spaniards, "and the next day, toward sunset, we perceived a city or town so large, that Seville would not have seemed more considerable, or better; one saw there a very large tower; on the shore was a great throng of Indians, who bore two standards, which they raised and lowered to signal us to approach them; our commander did not wish it."

Having no comparatives of their own, for they had created nothing, naturally they thought of Seville, that

Gothic, quarrelsome, and futile city, which only the Moors had been able to ennoble, and which already, after so little time under the Spaniards, had become a vainglorious borrowed shell with quagmire streets and open drains, which once had been spotless and serene, where fountains played all day.

At least their ships were slow, and at least Tulum had taken warning. Guerrero began the building of breastworks, a science of which the Indians knew nothing, and planned the strategy of the bay. So much was dictated by loyalty, but he had yet to feel the rage of desperation.

He was watchful, but he thought that the Maya would naturally win. Yet, at the same time, he dreaded the engagement. He did not want to be reminded of that world he had discarded.

Then the Spanish turned back.

Guerrero sighed with relief. Though he did not know why they had reversed course, that they had done so gave him a little more time.

They had done so because they thought Yucatan an island. For twenty years they were to think so, and no Maya would tell them differently. Why should any Maya tell them anything? They had entered what is now called the Bahia de Ascension, hoping for a passage to the other side, and finding none, had decided to search out the richer cities of the west coast some other way.

News came they had touched at Cozumel again, and that they had been sighted off Ecab, Dzilan, and Conkal. It was therefore obvious where they were going. They were going where Cordoba had found those pitiable dull gold trinkets.

Guerrero had an interview with Nachancan, said good-bye to Ix Chan, and his sons, and set out with an embassy across country towards Champoton and Campeche.

It did not surprise him that he could accomplish nothing at Champoton, for they were warriors there, who had yet to see equipment that could defeat them. They refused to be alarmed. But at Campeche he did somewhat better. At

Campeche they were less sure of their own strength and much closer to danger. The ships had been sighted, and the priesthood was alarmed, for the strangers were desecrating the temples.

The night he arrived the rain was thick enough to make the air one solid cube of water. The Maya were used to that, used to watching the rain and the thin, ghostly creatures who lived only in the rain. When it was good, it brought the crops; and when it was bad, it brought the rot. One had only to sit cross-legged, until it parted, to see which was on the other side.

Their whole approach to life was like that, which made them difficult to organize.

When it parted, towards morning, they saw four ships on the other side. They did not like the look of ships, and they had heard of guns.

Guerrero had the war conches sounded. Angrily that sound eddied out over the sea. The warriors assembled. But the Spaniards stayed in their ships all day.

The CanPechs, who had been frightened, now felt better. Apart from the taking of slaves and victims, wars were won by feinting. Therefore they had won a war. That night they slept.

Guerrero knew better, but it was difficult to rouse them the next morning. He was almost too late.

For as soon as dawn hit the water, Grijalva put out boats, and these now rowed gently towards the shore, their landing parties armed.

Guerrero watched from the edge of the scrub, and suggested strategy. Nothing he said had any effect. The CanPechs had their own strategy and their own tactics. Every movement had behind it a tradition, according to which their warriors were well trained. They were proud. They would not fight in any but their own way.

The Spaniards had landed only to get water, which they needed desperately on that salten sea, so desperately that they were quite prepared to fight for it, and did.

The CanPechs cut down a few. But only a few. That was because of their strategy, for though they admired the gods and knew they had to be placated, they had no desire to have their own hearts ripped out unless that were unavoidable. It was useless to tell them that the Spaniards were not interested in their hearts, but only in everything they owned that made having a heart worthwhile. When the CanPechs began to lose they ran away, instead of pressing closer. That was the Maya way. They would have to learn by experience that not all men had the same gods. Guerrero could not hold them.

The Spaniards, who had only come for water, marched into Campeche instead. They were not opposed, for they found an empty city. Its inhabitants had fled so swiftly, that Guerrero had been left behind.

The cacique of Campeche had a garden menagerie. It was extensive, but far from neatly trimmed. Guerrero took refuge there. It was his duty to stay alive and unknown. But he did have a curiosity to watch.

As he had thought, Grijalva and his captains took up their residence in the cacique's palace.

Fortunately for Guerrero it had begun to rain again, which did not bother him. He was used to it. But the Spaniards would risk neither their velvets nor their helmets and cuirasses to the damp and rust. They had no experience of living with the weather, for like all Europeans, they lived against it, rather than following its rhythms. While it rained they stayed indoors. But they were restless; they came and went in the rain, in the empty city, a little apprehensive, even a little awed. They were, after all, only 250, and to them luxury meant power, as indeed it does, and in this case, since the inhabitants had fled, an unseen power. They feared an ambush.

Guerrero saw all of them.

It was the first time he had seen Spaniards in eight years. He shifted on his glistening hams, hidden by foliage, and hungry. Yet he stayed. Even if they found him, they would take him for a native, he would take himself for a native, but they did not find him. Grijalva was a cautious commander, and besides, it was raining, so no one came outside.

He saw that yes, he had not been wrong, they were, as they had always been, strangers. He had never belonged in that world. He was lucky to have found a place in this.

They were having some quarrel among themselves, whether to stay, turn back, or go on. He had almost forgotten Spanish. It now sounded as a partly porous, almost meaningless, alien tongue. He found they were strangers to him. To the poor, men in power, swaggering around in fine clothes and with unpaid debts, are always strangers. But now he was rich, he found them doubly so.

He saw the real difference that reinforced that difference of circumstance, but was still there, naked, now that they were equivalent. He shivered, but he went on watching. The rain now was a solid vertical wall.

As they peered out of the heavy masonry doorway into the garden, cursed, quarrelled, and spat, he saw all their great ones. It was, though he still believed they could be turned back, a preview of the conquest.

There was a young man with a white face and a black beard, a certain swagger and a cruel look, the look of a hooded hawk, who sits there waiting. His name was Pedro de Alvarado, though Guerrero had no way of knowing that. He only saw an ambitious, wild man, very proud, very cunning and therefore a little stupid, the future Conqueror of Guatemala. He would make a name for himself, but what is a name? Spain had many such younger sons, who, since they could not rise on the shoulders of their own countrymen, must find some other country to grind down. Like all the *conquistadores*, caught in the cage of his own success, like a proud animal, he would die not of natural combat, but the mange. For though suicide is impossible to a Christian, still, the cage of success makes every man a Bajazet.

There was Davila, the man without qualities, who looked like a gentleman, and was one, but who just for that reason would fight a good war for very bad money, and never know, but sometimes be disturbed by, what he had done.

The third man looked as though he would have been happier in a counting-house. That was Francisco de Montejo, who wanted this land for himself, for he was the sort of man who thinks he can turn a better profit on the second best, and often does, than the first comer makes of his advantages. Even now, scenting a bargain, he wanted Yucatan for himself.

Grijalva, whom Guerrero did not see, had heard rumours of wealth somewhere else. He was a man to chase butterflies, and unlike the Maya, did not know they were made of obsidian and signified nothing but the death of the soul. In two days he led the party off, uneasy and overweaning, and so going back to their boats in a tight defensive clump.

Guerrero was left alone in an empty city. That gave him time both to see the serene order and the futile weakness (for weakness is not always futile) of this world of which he was from now on a part.

Then the CanPechs came back. He had nothing to say to them. He was stiff with exposure. It was all he could do to keep his temper, let alone tell them that they had not won a world by flight, but lost it. Yet he saw how these flights, if only he could teach the Maya how to fight, might be turned into ambushes. He saw a great many things.

And on that trip back to Chetumal, he had a lot of time to think of them. They sobered him. They made him sad. For though he would go on fighting, something inside him, to which he refused an ear, yet told him that he could not, that they could not, win. Never mind. They must.

He gave it up. It was all a little too much for him to think about. Meanwhile he was going back to his wife, his sons, and Nachancan.

It did no good to think about such things. It was better to be a healthy body, vigorous and wily, and to do what came next. It was better to trust to that. Yet he found himself gazing at the vivid wild greens of the jungle, and at the other members of his embassy, as though both might vanish overnight.

He was determined that they should not do so, if only because he now had sons.

What he needed was a respite. He was not to get it. For unknown to him, Grijalva had sailed on to the Empire of the Aztecs, and at Tabasco had at last discovered gold.

As soon as he heard the news, Valazquez sent out an expedition under Cortés. And under Cortés there was to be no respite for anyone.

XII

The two men never met, and being so alike, could not have met, which is a pity, for they might well have understood each other, though we find it difficult to understand them.

About such great rapacious leaders, Alexander, Cortés, there is always something ambiguous. We know what they looked like, what they did, and what they said. But that is not the same as knowing anything about them. They are riddle, sphinx, and Oedipus too. At best we catch only the ripple of their well-oiled thighs, as they hunch themselves to ask the question. About those who have the smile of success, the smile of the sphinx, we know a good deal. But about those who drove her to her death, and whose expression is somewhat different, nothing, except the later fate of Oedipus, which those who have driven her to that extreme have always shared.

With Cortés there was no nonsense. He came from Spain's dustiest province, and though he could lament the destruction of much beauty, that did not prevent him from destroying it. So when he arrived at Cozumel, he let those priests his government had foisted upon his expedition destroy the temples and pull down an idol or two. Though he was not a bigot himself, such actions upped the morale of the men and cost him nothing. Patrician by nature, he was above such things, but precisely because he was above them, they meant nothing to him, and it was important to keep his men content.

Besides, he was a lord. He looked a lord. Though he always dressed with care, stripped naked, he would have looked one, because he was one. And the natives recognized that. He was the first foreign lord they had ever seen, except for Kukulcan, or Quetzalcoatl, in whom they believed, but whom none of them had ever seen, that legendary ruler who had conquered them before.

It left them curiously relieved, who had fought among themselves for so long, to see a lord. Knowing only a two-class society, they had been puzzled by those uneasily ostentatious bourgeois hidalgos who were the only Spaniards they had seen before. Now they felt the difference at once. This man was a ruler.

Not that they were submissive, but like very old cultures and middle-aged men, there was about them something feminine. Even at their most manly, they still wished to be dominated by the father of them all, against whom they could rebel, only to learn in the end, from some odd ancestral gesture of the elbow, some way of holding the head, that it was the same pattern they repeated and that life went on. They were a people who proceeded by precedents. With Cortés they thought they knew where they were.

With its idols overturned, the life went out of Cozumel. One by one the natives came back to make their submission. And from these, Cortés learned of Aguilar and Guerrero, not by name, but as bearded men who had come among them from the sea. He guessed who they must be at once, and since he could do nothing without an interpreter, sent for both of them, and even posted a ship to patrol these shores, until they should appear.

He did not for a moment doubt that they would appear. Were they not Spaniards?

It was Aguilar, first, who received the news.

He was still alive, and still in the harem at Ecab. He had spent so many years in servile bending, to save his skin, so he claimed, for God, that it took him a while to straighten up.

But then he became very straight indeed. He still had his notched stick: the year was 1519. He had suffered indignities. He said a mass for himself. He wished revenge.

As Cortés' interpreter, he would have it. A priest could do much.

But would the Maya let him go?

Of course they would. This foreign lord had, in the proper way, sent a ransom, two bags of round stamped golden disks. They meant nothing to the Lord of Taxmar, but they could be turned into gold ornaments, and gold ornaments were rare. He liked ornaments. Aguilar was a nuisance. He had ceased to be amusing years ago. He was just an oddity in the harem. Taxmar did not put much value on people who would rate such an idiot so high, when a dwarf would have been so much more entertaining.

Who would have thought he would have been worth so much?

The women of the harem took a new interest in him. They even asked him to tell them again about the Virgin Mary, some kind of goddess his people had, who could beget without men, and whose labour was never referred to. It seemed so odd.

No one had ever made much of him before, but he knew why they did so. It was because he was leaving. Nor did he expect any kindness of Cortés, or any man, that he could not extort. It was not as a Christian he was being ransomed, but as a possible interpreter. That left him with no real love of Cortés, for he foresaw difficulties. He did not speak the language well, first of all because it was a heathen language, and second because he had no curiosity.

He was also asked to summon Guerrero. He had not known Guerrero was alive, and would have preferred him dead. He did not admit to himself that this was because Guerrero, if he came, would supplant him. He preferred to believe that it was because the man was a renegade.

Yet he complied and sent a message to Chetumal. Compliance was one of the prices of his manumission. But he did not wait for an answer. Nothing could have made him do so. Guerrero was a heretic. Guerrero had seen him at a disadvantage. He could only pray that the man would not come.

The man had no intention of coming.

Rumours had reached him from the north, and he had sent out spies. He realized what manner of man he had to deal with this time, and that now the Conquest would go on in earnest. Those first invaders had been ineffectual, but now, he could tell from the natives' reports, that with Cortés there would be no turning back. Even garbled in Maya, that name had the sound of authority, the sound of a man of honour.

But gentleman or not, Cortés would have to make use of the Aguilars of this world, who were without honour, and therefore without mercy.

Guerrero also knew why he had been summoned. He would be a useful man on that expedition, even though the invitation made no mention of that. He was exhorted as a Christian to do his duty, he was commanded back into the fold. But when the wolf calls the sheep back to the fold, do they answer?

That sort of thing he would leave to Aguilar, and much good might Cortés make of him. Somehow he did not think Aguilar would be of much help.

He had forgotten the wretched man. But now, remembering him, he felt only disgust.

And yet he was unsettled.

When he had sent back his answer, he watched the messenger until he was out of sight, not so much to call him back, as to be sure that he had gone. Then, not wanting to see anyone, he had wandered about the city.

There it was, spread out around him, at dusk, white, gleaming, peaceful, clean, and orderly. His two sons, his wife, his father-in-law, were here, somewhere, going about their familiar, quotidian affairs with that good-humoured gravity which was their approach to life. There was no ordinary detail of this daily life that did not give him a warm and customary thrill.

He was upset and angry.

What did they mean, to call him back to his duty as a Christian? What did they understand of such things, from Aguilar, with his crouched hatred of the world, to the great ones, who bought on Sundays the right to do whatever they chose during the rest of the week?

Did it mean they wanted to tear this world down, and needed him to help? Was that what their pious summons, what Aguilar's revolting hypocrisy, meant? That he should go unshaven, spitting through the jungles, shooting down a culture they would not even comprehend, because they could not comprehend it, and because they thought it might be rich? That spoils system which led every illiterate foot soldier to believe he could become a millionaire, meant only that one or two grew prosperous by creating a universal squalor.

Cortés, yes, might be a gentleman, but a gentleman can at best ride unsullied on that universal wave of filth which is man's hatred and ambition. Even he, in time, if he is not careful, will be sucked under by it.

These people loved life. No Christian does that. How can he, saddled with the ultimate impiety called Original Sin? There is nothing original about it. It is merely the same old irrational vindictiveness of those without the will to be good.

And yet he found himself shaking.

He could have sent no answer, but that was not his way. He did not like to leave decisions unmade. That was not the honourable way. And yet he could not help but feel cold, for though he was a grandee here, he had been born there.

It was not a matter of loyalty. It was not a matter of having anything to regret, of ever having had any desire to return. And yet a man is a little lost in any place where he was not born. It is a piece of the earth he carries around with him, and gives him something to stand on.

The city, lit by hundreds of lamps, was reflected in the Bay of Chetumal. He saw the lights of a fisherman's canoe on the water. Yet he also, for the first time in years, saw the bleak yellow landscape of his native place, Nieto. It made him blink. He had never felt at ease there, as he did here. And yet he had had a father and a mother, brothers, sisters, and as a child, those native hills to play in.

He had said no. He had meant no. And yet there was something about the sheer weight of the jungle behind the city that oppressed him, something about these people he would never understand, simply because he had not been born here.

Never mind, he had been reborn here. And there was Ix Chan. There was Nachancan, who would say nothing, but understand.

Who among the Spaniards had ever done or would ever do that?

At the top of the pyramid, someone had cast incense into a brazier. He looked around him. No, this was the world to fight for. We fight for the world we have. Only a fool looks back, for no one can fight time.

Meanwhile there was much to do, but only because it had to be done, and he was the only one who could do it. The motives of hate he left to Aguilar.

But he did not underestimate them.

Aguilar had worries of his own.

He had learned nothing during those eight years, except a little, a very little and that ungrammatical, Maya. In despair he went over his irregular verbs, but could find nothing but a series of uncouth infinitives. At least, no matter how little he knew, his redemptors knew still less. That was something. He hurried towards the coast, unable to believe that this ransom was not some kind of trick. He had never, in all his life, been able to believe that everything were not some sort of trick, even God. And perhaps he was right. Perhaps it was.

The harem had made him flabby. He sagged over his loincloth, and had never got over the shame of going naked, which made him move more awkwardly than ever.

Now he found himself in a canoe rowed by five slaves. It was how things should have gone, from the beginning, to have those five strong backs in front of him. Fingering his rosary and breviary, he baptized them at once. It is so easy to make converts if you only ask them about what you want to believe.

There was no ship at the coast, but he did not dare to turn back. That was unthinkable. He ordered the rowers on to Cozumel. At dawn he drew up alongside the boats of the Spaniards. But how could he present himself? He was naked. That showed the degree of his long martyrdom, but a European is nothing without his clothes.

He fingered his breviary. His Spanish was rusty, but his Latin was in better repair. The soft water lapped at the boats. He had himself announced to Cortés.

Cortés was a modern man, as all men who know how the world goes and say nothing live in the same now. He had his own amusements and recreations, but they were not those of a long voyage, and could come later. Meanwhile, he saw himself anchored off a low coast, of whose language he knew nothing, and whose strength he was beginning to perceive. He had also to impose order on several hundred avaricious men who, though they could be terrorized by their priests, in actuality respected nothing. Yet he himself could leave nothing to his descendants, and keep little for himself, unless he had this New Empire to offer to the Crown. Therefore he meant to have it. And for that an interpreter was indispensable. Therefore, when news came that Aguilar had arrived, he prepared to make himself agreeable.

That turned out to be more difficult than he had expected. He was disappointed. He had hoped for Guerrero, who by all accounts was more competent.

Instead he saw nothing but an Indian with a black beard, and not a very savoury Indian at that. Aguilar prostrated himself and began to creak Spanish. He claimed a distant Cortés cousin in Seville, a sixty-fourth cousin, but still, a cousin.

Cortés was taken aback, and tried not to show it. It was a little startling to hear this loinclothed Hottentot claim a cousinage in disjointed Spanish. But he did seem to know how to speak to the natives, and he was a priest. That would mean a lot to the men. Cortés sent him away, ostensibly to rest. He would hear his story tomorrow.

But he already knew what his story was. It was obvious. But it was also incredible. You gave men like that the wealth of a new world, and they said nothing except to complain that it was not the pottage they got at home. It was because they had no position, no rank, and no initiative. They were born slaves, and it is the servants of this world who keep the standards up. They cramp even their betters by doing so, demanding so much formality from people who have outgrown such things, that one complies only because it is so hard to get dependable servants any more.

And then, there are so many in this world who long to be servants. It makes the lot of their betters far from enviable, for how can they provide all those places, when in their innermost hearts they cannot bear to be waited on? Besides, servants are spies. They gossip among themselves. And if they serve one master, it is not out of loyalty, but professionalism. No valet would ever descend to curry-comb a horse. He would lose face. No priest would behave with common sense for the same reasons.

This was the wrong man. It was the other man he was after. The other man, by all accounts, had done well in this world, therefore he must understand it, and would have been worth the having.

For Cortés, like Guerrero, had no illusions. He belonged to the little company of those who are sane, even though they may have to change worlds in order to remain so. That little company has been piped away a thousand times, but thank God, it does not matter whose, it always comes back again.

While Aguilar slept the message from Guerrero arrived. It was hard to interpret it, without an interpreter, and yet "no" is never hard to interpret. The other man would not come, and perhaps Cortés respected him for that, knowing that the men worth having are not those so easily to be had.

He must do with Aguilar.

Aguilar knew very well he was the second-best choice. He had to raise himself somehow in his own estimation, and now that he had borrowed a Franciscan robe, and had something to justify him, he had his explanation ready. Guerrero, he explained, had had his hands tattooed, his nose, lower lip, and ears pierced, and was living in sin with the natives. No doubt he had been ashamed to show himself.

Somehow Cortés did not think so. Men such as Guerrero, if what he had heard of Guerrero were true, were never ashamed of themselves. Nor did he believe what Aguilar said.

But he could not loiter here. He weighed anchor and swept north, and then west, around the peninsula, bound for Tabasco and his place in history.

As a matter of fact, Guerrero had had his lower lip pierced. It was the ultimate honour, and the honour was a heavy one, made of gold, in the Aztec fashion, a serpent with a flickering tongue, held by a stud on the inner side of the lip. When nothing was worn there, one could press one's tongue in and out of the hole, which helped one to think.

It also made certain other things possible. When Ix Chan was pleased, she had so many gestures to prove that she was so.

Meanwhile, he settled down to await developments. He waited, first, until 1521. It was a respite, after all. His sons were growing up, and Nachancan was growing older. He kept himself informed, but also he had his daily life to lead. It seemed the more precious now, that perhaps it was in danger.

XIII

He learned the news, the Maya learned the news, in September of 1521. At first it frightened all of them. But then, should they not rather rejoice in the destruction of their hereditary enemy, and was not Mexico very far away? Surely what happened there, could have nothing to do with them?

Guerrero could do nothing to rouse them, nothing to put them in a state of defence. Yet even he had heard of the glories of Mexico, and that they could be swept away so easily filled him with despair.

It was the traders who brought the news: on the 13th of August Technoctitlán had fallen.

It was the chute of a world.

That city of the robber barons, that great city in the middle of its lake, that city of the eagle on the cactus, who holds the snake, that city had been swept away.

A few years ago it had glittered there, white, polychromed, and secure, its altars fed on human hearts, smoking to heaven, the greatest city in the known world.

Now it was gone. And those people who had come from the dark bat-hung caves of the north, perhaps in Sonora, who knew where, with their wooden hell and their hell on earth, they too were gone. The Spaniards had marvelled, but knew no mercy. Aguilar was with them, somewhere. Faced with a culture higher than their own, they could think of nothing better to do than to destroy it.

The traders said it was terrible. The Maya were not impressed. Guerrero, looking at the intact temples of Chetumal, swore, but listened to the traders' tale.

Once we know how bad things are, then there is hope, for then we can begin to plan.

The Spaniards had levelled the great temple and the city, and ignorant of sanitation, had filled the drainage canals with the massive carved blocks of an alien world.

They were ignorant of so many things. It gave them, as it gives all such, a dreadful strength.

Moctezuma, the Great Speaker, had been stoned by his own people and then tortured by his conquerors. That, too, was the way the world goes. What they wanted, said the

Spaniards, was gold. Moctezuma did not understand. Gold was only an ornamental mineral, of no value in itself. Would they not rather have jade?

Bernal de Diaz, being prudent, took a little jade. It was to ransom his life later. But the others wanted only gold.

Moctezuma II, who had never doubted his own pre-eminence, but only the survival of the world that made his own pre-eminence possible, died, was succeeded by Cuitlahuac, and he, in four months, by Cuauhtemoc. As usual the Indians had fought among themselves. That was what had, as usual, defeated them, until Cuauhtemoc, that true and supple hero, had nothing left to defend but his own four acres of palace in the desolation of Tenochtitlán. Again and again these hairy savages attacked him, across the raped boulders of the city.

The traders made a chronicle of it, that Guerrero had no will to hear. He had heard of none of these people, but a rehearsal is a rehearsal.

Finally Cuauhtemoc had fled, with his favourite wife, across the shallow lake, by night, in search of allies. Since he had none left, the Spaniards had taken him easily.

All around that lake, the subsidiary cities were empty, deserted, and smoking, He had the bitterest fate of all, the one war gives us, unless we are careful to die: he survived his own world.

Guerrero quite understood that. He knew it must not happen to him. His boys were now seven and six, and he had had a daughter. Men not male want sons, but men most male, once the continuance of their name is assured, a daughter. For women are the conservators. They could not make something out of nothing, like men. They needed something already there, to rearrange and pass on in order. Hence his daughter, who would be beautiful, no doubt. Ix Chan was so pleased. They had not the habit of kissing, and yet he kissed her.

Somehow, by some miracle, though he was alert to trouble, they lived in peace for three years. He knew the dangers of that peace, but could not make even Nachancan understand them. The Maya had been conquered themselves. It meant no change in the order of their days. One treated with the conqueror to keep one's place, that was all. That far Nachancan could understand, but no further. Even the old tales the travellers brought from Mexico could not dissuade him from a belief that the world went on as it had always done, conqueror or not. Chetumal had been secure for too long, and besides, the Maya could conceive of a moderate hunger, but the immoderation of Europe was something beyond their ken.

There was nothing Guerrero could do, except wait, and undertake a certain modest diplomacy. So much of his time, during those three years, was taken up in travel and the effort to make allies. But allied, the natives wanted to know, against what, and to what advantage to themselves?

He could not make them understand that the advantage was their own survival. Had they not always survived?

Yet, if the whole peninsula was to be some day one battleground, at least he had the opportunity to learn the topography of that coming war.

And then, in 1524, came the terminal event, the event that stunned even Nachancan. The event which proves that even the noblest man cannot avoid one fatal error, the event that, in proving each life a tragedy, improves, somehow, the sense of comedy, for without tragedy, there could be no comedy.

When a man does something against his own nature, he begins to fail. That is what happened to Cortés.

In 1524 he started south, through Guatemala and Honduras. He had no choice, and was a little tired. In order to maintain himself, he had to find out new worlds, for the demands of Spain were insatiable, and had to be satisfied. Guatemala and Honduras were rich, so they said.

So they had been, a thousand years before.

Cortés marched into those treacherous uplands through Chiapas, with six hundred men to carry the baggage, and, as hostages, the Lord of the Province and the Emperor

Cuauhatemoc. The latter he could not leave behind, lest he become the centre of some uprising.

After two and a half years of confinement, surrounded by a mockery of attendants, Cuauhtemoc was probably glad enough to go anywhere.

At first all went well; and then Cortés began to lose his luck. But then, that goddess, if personified, goes off blandly upon her own affairs at once. Thus found the Caesars. Thus Cortés.

The rains were a solid assault of water. Savannahs became quagmires, and quagmires, lakes. Most of the region had been abandoned centuries before, so that they had to hack their way through tropical jungle and met no-one. The men were for turning back, and so were the priests. There were quarrels. There was always whispering behind Cortés' back.

That had never been so audible before. They were waiting to pull him down.

With Cuauhtemoc he played chess. It was a game Cuauhtemoc had learned easily and played well, for it was like his native game of Potelli, but more subtle. Potelli was a game with four fields but only one kind of counter. He had always felt its limitations as a symbol. But in chess one played with the world, and the whole game was a parable. In the beginning the king could do nothing, and yet he directed the pieces. He was the object of the game. In the end one did not capture him. One merely made it impossible for him to escape. He could appreciate the irony of that.

They played not on the board we know now, but on that circular Hindu board the Spaniards inherited through the Arabs. It is the peculiarity of that board that the king cannot castle, but goes to sanctuary once during the game, and only once. He is safe for the moment. Yet he knows that on the next move he must come out and face the game again, on a slightly changed board and himself changed, by that same move into sanctuary, which destroyed his immovable sanctity for good.

The king was defeated by the ineptness of his own supporters.

Potelli was sacred to Macuilxochitl, the Five Flower god of youth and games, but also a god of the south, the unlucky direction; and were not he and Cortés playing out this game in the south? He understood the parable all too well, and defeat has certain advantages. One can fill up one's days by playing the whole game out again, unblinded by self-interest.

Cortés would find himself staring into those polite and knowledgeable eyes. It was, after all, a royal game, and Cuauhtemoc had lost it. But sometimes, on that damned symbolic board, Cortés lost it. Cuauhtemoc would then quietly smile, but somehow that smile lingered in the mind, for he was a vivid man, fearless, and quite as capable of irony as his captor. He had a special little grimace when he was checkmated, particularly if the board had been swept clean.

He had also a special offensive, when he won in turn, which was not to sweep the board clean, but to trap Cortés behind his own pieces, so it was they, rather than Cuauhtemoc's, which checkmated him.

He must be doing that deliberately, and lately he had done it too often.

Something rather peculiar happens if you play chess, not mathematically, as we affect to do now, but skilfully, thoughtfully, as though the pieces were only something to twiddle with. We pretend that the pieces are not symbolic, but the game is a communion and a rite. One is soon swallowed up by that parable and becomes part of it. Suddenly, three or four moves in, plotting five or six moves ahead, as you reach your hand forward, the board vanishes, the pieces vanish, you and your opponent vanish, and you are off in some other place.

The board then becomes whatever your real quarrel with the world is about. The game becomes a test of strength between two wills. As you move, so are you judged, not personally, but essentially, neither by yourself or your opponent, but by those judges of the secret court whose sessions never cease. It does no good to plead before that tribunal. Eloquence means nothing, for they have the documents in the case, and there is no jury. They are far, far worse than Atropos, Lachesis, and Clotho, for they ordain nothing, they reach no conclusion, they administer no punishment. They simply know.

That is the worst punishment and the worst fate: that anyone should know, except ourselves, when even we prefer not to know.

The game then tells you things about yourself, you should not know. Cuauhtemoc was content to lose. He did it more and more cleverly, it now took more of an effort on Cortés' part before Cuauhtemoc's will snapped and he allowed himself to be beaten.

Outside their tent it rained. It became harder and harder to discipline oneself to make that effort, while Cuauhtemoc sat there, a graceful man, somehow not defeated at all, and sadly smiling. One had only to look at the board, to see that he knew too much.

Cortés hanged him.

There must have been something else. And yet, though the official reports make mention of an Aztec plot against the Spaniards, apparently there was nothing else. Cortés had disgraced himself. The Judges of the Secret Court exchanged glances, and that, too, he saw. He looked at the man's wilted body, the way a hunter looks at the body of a pheasant one more than he had meant to kill. The dignity and the rebuke were of the same quality. The standards of the world mean nothing, but once fall from our own, and we never again feel the same certainty. We begin to fall apart. A dishonourable act is irreparable. We become indign.

After that there is nothing to accept but defeat. For though outwardly we may prosper, inwardly we shrink. We lose authority because we no longer have it ourselves.

He marched on, but it was the end of him. The natives could see that. He had the look of a man whose luck has changed. They breathed easier. He had been a great man, and a great man is difficult to deal with. Now they would not have to deal with him at all. He was no longer great.

But though difficult to deal with, great men can be dealt with. Having a two-class society, they had no concept of the inexorability of the infinitely small, those men in the middle, who take from rich and poor alike, and who, since they have not the courage to face their own appetites, can never be appeased.

In the world of honour there is no place for the middle class. Therefore, the world of honour must go, in order to make the world safe for those who have none.

So Cortés, so God, so beauty, and so Yucatan. One cannot defeat an enemy of whose nature one is unaware, and this race of lawyers and small clerks was so recent that as yet no-one knew anything of them, nor that to them the world was a department store, in which they could safely shop, since every man had his price, and if he had none, must be thrown away.

If one is a gentleman or a peasant, one does not throw such things away, for if one does, one has nothing left, for the one has too little, the other too much, ever to be taken in by that modern mass delusion that the meaning of life can be deposited in a bank.

Yet this old order of things, being swept away for a time, this immutable order of the soul, had one advantage over its conquerors. It had certainty, and so the poise to die.

But not unless death were unavoidable, for like all those who accept the fact of mortality, it also had an immense joy to live.

XIV

It did not take long for the news of Cuauhtemoc's murder, for that was what it was, to reach Chetumal, for those uplands through which Cortés was marching were so thinly settled, that news came all the swifter through them for being ungarbled along the way.

Cortés had turned back at Tayasal. That he had reached it at all was sobering enough, for Tayasal was the sacred last redoubt. In all Guerrero's years in Yucatan he had seldom heard it mentioned, for it was not mentioned. For it was there, when they were beaten back by the Mexican Invasion after the league of Mayapan, that the Itza had retreated, going back to the place from which they had come, to await the preordained end of the Maya world, at the final return of Katun 8 Ahau. For they were a determined people. No matter what disasters might overwhelm them in the interim, they had the piety to conform to their own calender, and to survive to see the end of their own world, rather than to have that end imposed upon them. And since that world was not to end until 1697, they maintained up there their palladium. That there should be Itzas at Tayasal was their palladium. It was the whole centre of their being not to pass away before the proper time. They would neither commit that impiety, nor allow anyone else to do so.

Even Nachancan, who was himself of the Itza, never mentioned Tayasal. But you could see in his eyes, as you could see in the eyes of all the Maya, that it was there, waiting, an extensive lake, surrounded by upland jungle whose roots were steeped in those waters, with in the centre the city on its islands, like Technoctitlán, but without the causeways, the tombhouse of the race, furnished for that last journey with everything they had ever done or believed in, ready for that day when it would close on the race, which would then go completely furnished back into oblivion.

There was something a little sad about that, but then about grandeur there is always something saddening. It lasts such a little while, and is yet so noble.

Now Cortés had penetrated there. It filled them with despair. Unlike other foreigners, he was comprehensible. He arrived on the appointed black days. He went into the evil directions. He was that secret clause in that pact they had made with the gods, who can never be trusted because we can never help but suspect that there is a secret clause. A bargain among equals is one thing, but a bargain with one's superiors means nothing. They are always breaking it. It is because they know everything, that the gods never tell us the truth, for they cannot be bothered to shrink themselves down into anything so limited as what we call truth. Even the calendar is only a moment in oblivion, endless though for the Maya that moment was. There are other calendars. Perhaps they had calculated the wrong one. Perhaps they were to end now.

Even in Chetumal the priests were busy in the temples now, like surgeons in an emergency, turning panic into a last moment efficiency. Nachancan, himself, went often there.

Then Cortés turned back. They found out what he had done to Cuauhtemoc. No god would have done such a thing, and no instrument of God, for it was inconsistent with his virtues. He had betrayed himself, therefore he must be merely a man, as much a victim of his destiny, which was to say his nature, as they were of theirs.

It filled them with relief.

Guerrero could not understand that. He knew so well what was happening, for he had seen it happen, when he was a child and then a young man, in Spain.

When they had displaced the last Moors, when they carried on their brutal wars with Catalonia, what then became of all that dynastic grace, that charm, those people who should never be touched by any but equals? The Moors, like the Maya, had been a little decadent. And yet they too, like the Maya, had been much concerned with tradition, with grace, with beauty, with some way of filling up the time, as pleasantly as possible, between now and the end of life.

His wife, Ix Chan, that beauty in her own world, with the soft confiding grace of her nights, with so much beauty expended, and how happily, merely in bending over a cradle, with her gravity, her breeding, and her mental reservations about everything, her cleanliness, and her little humour, must always be allowed to go on as she had always lived. He adored her. He found her touching. Like the last flower on any vine, she was determined not to wilt. She kept her youth a little longer.

He did not want to see her the victim of some coarse savage in steel armour, who would not understand her. Like any civilized person, her wits might go swift, but her body went slow. She had great dignity. But what would that mean, in war, carnage, and rape?

And Nachancan. Nachancan he loved as one man loves another man, not to ask anything, but simply for being there. Love, the passions, marriage, they are transitory. They are real, and not real, all at once, so that we never get to the end of them. If they are there, why then they are there for life.

But friendship and admiration are more excruciating virtues. For we feel them for someone we cannot touch, we cannot lie with, who yet touches us more than anyone or anything could do. He had found a father.

Did he want to see such a man strung up, as Cuauhtemoc had been, his body slowly turning above the ground, after that last involuntary gurgle in the throat had turned to the silence which always precedes death.

Did he want to see, from the ground, the slightly soiled pattern of his feet? It is not the murder of a man we mind so much. Once he is dead, that is the end of it. There is nothing to say. It is is the overthrow of everything we respect or cherish, represented in that murder, by those who respect and cherish nothing, that turns the knife in us.

It is not so much that we die, who minds that, if it be inevitable, as that everything we love and live for can be overturned by the greed of those who love nothing, that we find horrible.

He could see Nachancan, twirling in the air, twisting at the end of that rope. And it made him furious. Take everything from us, he wanted to say. "Kill us, if you wish. But leave us at least our dignity. Otherwise death is not worthwhile. Better yet, take me, but leave him his dignity." Then it would be worth while.

But since Alexander, no conqueror has done that. For more than anything the conqueror wants, he wants dignity, which he thinks he may have by taking it from the conquered.

Whereas dignity is innate. Either one has it, or one has not. Like honour, it is not to be acquired.

And what he hated most, was to see a new look in Nachancan's eyes. Not, certainly, a look of fear. A man like that was incapable of fear. But a look of defeat, even though Nachancan would fight beyond even the limits of fighting. But yet, it was the look of defeat.

For no man should ever dangle at the end of a rope, even with the saving courtesy of a blue silk thread in it, at least no real man ever should.

He could see Nachancan dangling so. And yet Nachancan said nothing. He was perhaps a little quieter than he had been before. And he watched his grandchildren with a slightly different look, a look that tore the heart out of Guerrero.

Guerrero wanted someone to fight. He wanted the enemy there, to be dealt with. But there was no enemy to deal with. The defeat would be by a creeping paralysis.

It was the first time he had ever faced the fact of defeat. And he knew there could be one. One must either die or win.

Where was the enemy to fight? It made him restless not to have one, for the forces against them were somewhere gathering in. Why would they not appear?

And Nachancan, as he bent over his grandchildren, had such a curious expression on his face, that it made Guerrero doubly love this world of which he was only outwardly a part and which made him curse aloud.

For why, out of what hunger, must you others tear this

ancient, grave, hieratic, and not by you to be understood world apart? Five hundred years from now, when you have reduced everything to barbarism, and are trying painfully to build again, you will look back and be sorry. You will make a romance of it. You will learn to be rueful, as conquerors always are, about the defeated. You will want to save something out.

But by then it will be too late. We shall be dead, and beyond all power of sorrow. But you will feel sorry. You will want it back. You will want anything to keep you from that awful cold knowledge, that having destroyed what you wanted, just because you could not have it, you must now, painfully, make it all over again, to be destroyed by somebody else, and so time goes, the awful war between the hungry, who have forgotten the taste of food, and the well-fed, who have forgotten hunger.

Where was the enemy? Whom could he fight?

Could they not come forward and identify themselves?

And so he fell into a bed, felt incompetent, loved Ix Chan, wished always to protect her, wanted to see her grow old, wanted to go through all the stages of love's ageing, but loved Nachancan even more, as a man loves a man, not as a body, not even as a person, but as an embodied principle.

Nothing must ever happen to that wrinkled, knowledgeable, and austere old man.

Nothing must happen to Ix Chan.

And of what was happening to him, he was not even cognizant.

It was, if you like, a Passion, such as all religions and all lives have. But a Passion with different symbols, and so, to any Christian, to any, as to him, non-Christian, unconscious and unintelligible. It could only be endured.

There was also Aguilar. Where was Aguilar? Aguilar, not these soldiers of the conquest, not even Cortés, who in his failure of himself, hanged Cuauhtemoc, summed up the inexorable quality of the world. For Aguilar thought himself a saint, and the man who thinks himself a saint is only a fury in disguise. Saints are not among the living. They are only what we remember of those among whom we move. Saints among the living are, by example, a Torquemada to all true belief.

He had only to go out into the jungle, he had only to look at the fields of tasselled maize, to realize that life has a meaning which brings tears to our eyes, a meaning holy and exact, that none of those who search for meaning and tell us what life means would ever have the dignity to respect, the pride to love.

For God, the gods and we, nothing is possible, without a mutual respect.

Which no man will allow possible. For Christians grovel, and that is not the way, either of God or of a man.

It is because men cannot bear to be defeated.

And yet defeat, on honourable terms, is the only honour we can have, in such a situation. Oh yes, he knew that. He had felt it always.

As the Moors went away, to Africa, but remembered what they had been, and therefore knew what they were, so would he. So would they all. The vain man cries, gives us back our world again. But the man of honour says, you shall not have it.

It was, for Guerrero, so beautiful a world. And therefore, these people insensitive to beauty, they should not have it.

And looking at his father-in-law, looking at his wife, he said, no man shall pull them down.

For those who do not understand love should never be allowed to see it. Better suicide, than to allow another man to pull such beauty down.

XV

Two anxious years went by.

For the moment there was nothing Guerrero could do. You cannot help people until they realize they need help, and the Mayas were not yet alarmed. Until such time as they were, he could only send out spies and watch.

Besides, perhaps the Mayas were right. Time had gone by, and in Chetumal they were secure enough. It was easier to believe so. He pretended to himself that, like them, he did not know better. When the time came, they would fight.

But when is it time? To the losing side somehow it is always a little sooner or later, to the winning the time is always now. Yet it is sidereally the same time.

It was a problem to leave to the astronomers, who in this world were priests. It was something he did not wish to think about, for to him this was an important day.

Still, if they had founded a town, no matter where, that was dangerous.

His elder boy had come of age.

Chetumal had a special brightness, as though it had been burnt white between the twin mirrors of the sky and bay. He went early to the temple to make sacrifice, a matter of jabbing blood from the upper part of his ear with a thorn, and from his tongue. The contrived pain jerked him into an awareness of things such as others got from religious drugs. Too much time had made them sleepy. These imported Mexican rites helped to wake them up. It made familiar things new again, and there is nothing that better reassures us than a walk through the same dewy world again for the first time.

He liked his world so much. He got such relish out of it, for way back in memory, he had something to compare it to. It is a good thing, sometimes, to have these reminders of the scale of things, a person we once were, like a child, by which we can measure the extent of what we are now.

This boy would be a warrior. The younger one, as often in their ruling houses, would be a priest. It was a little like Europe, that arrangement, only better, for here, if you were born at the top, you stayed there. The ruler might change, few rulers were dynastic, but the ruling class itself was small. Like any secret society, it could not afford to lose a member. Now it had two more, for though he himself might still be an exotic, his sons were not.

He might not say anything, but it pleased him very much to see them there. Being vigorous himself, he did not envy youth. It touched him, like something fondly remembered.

Also, already, the older boy could fight. He was quite promising. And that was as well, since he might well have to.

The rite was simple, but took all day. Nachancan, who was growing old and portly now, was delighted to stand as sponsor. His chief duty was to give the feast, and he delighted in feasts.

The ceremony was held in the courtyard of that wing of the palace in which Guerrero still lived.

He found the patio swept out and strewn with fresh leaves. The boys of Chetumal were lined up on one side of it, and the girls on the other. His son was the fifth in line. A godparent was chosen for each sex.

Four priests sat at the four corners of the court, with cords held taut among them, to form a square, which the priest then blessed. It was a new high priest. The former one had died. Guerrero's younger son was already apprenticed to him. An offering of incense and maize was made by the boys and girls. Guerrero thought his son held himself very well.

There was then an intermission. The court was swept out again, and again floored with fresh leaves. The evil spirits had been dispelled. It was now time for the blessing.

The priest returned, in a jacket and mitre of scarlet quetzal feathers, tall and wavering. An assistant handed him an aspergillum of holy water, which he flicked about with a stick trimmed with rattlesnake tails. They were a people who loved anything that rattled. They could sit hypnotized by the sound of gravel in a red fired pot, and who could tell where that rhythmic shaking took them? He had been among them now for seventeen years, he too found that something happened when he heard that rhythm, but he could not say where they all went, even he, when they left themselves. It took them back to an antiquity that was around and then behind their gods.

They lived in the fourth creation of the world, and there would be others. They had been here before and would be back some day. It made everything curiously familiar. It also made them a little sad. They knew everything repeated itself. Their history went in cycles, and they kept full records. At the beginning of each new twenty-year period, they would open the records from the last recurrence of it, 260 years before. And one day, they knew, they would open them and discover that this time their world was about to end. It was only a matter of filling in time. They knew they had passed their apogee. That was already written down for the benefit of the next future but one.

Still, they were not sad today. They were never sad *now*, and it was always now for them, for after all, if one is getting on, it cannot be helped, therefore one makes the best of it. Age has its compensations.

The four attendant chacs came forward and placed a piece of white cloth, woven by their mothers, on the head of each child. Ix Chan was adroit with a loom. The white cloths sparkled in the light. A few of the older children had sins to confess. That took time.

Guerrero found it difficult to believe in that fatality of cycles. He would have preferred to cut his way out. And yet he was content today himself.

Those dangerous invaders up there, to the north, in Mexico, even if they sacked whatever stood in their way, or found favour at Court, would not do so well as he.

As a child, in Spain, in Nieto, he had stood outside while the local count gave festivities in the courtyard, or in the aisle, while princes of the church pranced through whatever it was they did in the choir, behind the reredos, or in the sacristy, afterwards. Anyone who owned a horse in Spain, was at least a count, but you were never allowed into the closed circle of the great ones, which was the ultimate secret society, the inner council that planned the whole mummery for what it was, and yet even so, had a mumbo jumbo of its own. In Spain there was a way up, but no way in.

He had wandered through those turreted and whitewashed courtyards sometimes, when they were empty, as a stable boy, blinded by the mica in the walls. Then he had felt a hopeless awe.

The priest finished his sprinkling of holy water made of cacao beans and the attar of flowers, dissolved in rain water, and cut from each boy's head the white bead that he wore there from the age of five.

His sons were now one with the Maya; Guerrero did not feel awe, or even gratification. He merely felt at ease.

The ceremony was followed by the feast. Nachancan presided well at a feast. It was a diet of deer, peccary, and turkey, smothered in rich sauces, salads, the avocado, and fruit, and there was a certain amount of drinking. It was hot, spicy, and savoury. He had never lost his taste for these good things. He knew how much they meant. He knew how much Nachancan meant.

The women ate separately, as they always did. It helped them to keep their glamour, not always to be there. Ix Chan was almost thirty now, but still wistful and gay. The boys would move away from home, for training; until they were ready to marry they would live with other boys. She would miss them, and he wanted to go to her.

It was late before he could do so. The moonlight was a spectral shade of blue and eddied over everything, for it was windy. The lamp guttered. The black frames of the night trees seemed to gutter too. The curtain in the doorway rustled and shook.

It would be six years before the boys could marry. Their wives had already been carefully chosen, but nothing could be done until the couples were of age.

A lot could happen in six years, but they must be able to go on. The Spanish must be driven out of there.

He began to think of them as the Spanish now, almost as though he had been born among them in exile, somehow gotten back, and knew from that captivity how dangerous they were.

It was so slow, that process of alienation, that he scarcely realized that it had taken place.

Ix Chan must have known that he would come. She must have gone to great trouble, to wake so gently and be so exactly as he would wish. It was that little imitation of surprise and spontaneity that moved him more deeply than could have any new experience. It made him feel worthwhile.

It is so charming of a woman to be clever, just for a man, and not because she has to. Usually a marriage is not so good and delightful a game. So few players realize the point of any game is not to win, but play.

He was so content.

And yet, there were the invaders up there, to the north. A man called Montejo had arrived. He was a little man, and no Cortés. He should not be hard to beat.

There Guerrero guessed wrong, and for a reason he could not know. The world was changing. Montejo belonged not to the old world, but to the new.

Therefore, ultimately, he would be impossible to beat.

Meanwhile, Guerrero set out, with a party, to make embassies, and to unite, what could not be united, that culture against the invader.

THREE

XVI

No-one could have united against Montejo. And the reason was simple. He was not a *conquistador*. He was not even, except in the counting house, a man of honour. He could not be fought on those terms. For he was that new thing in the world, a creature beyond values. Of his species he was one of the first, south of the Germanies, and the men there as Charles V had discovered to his chagrin, even while he bankrupted them, were only usurers. Montejo was an improvement on that plan. He was a business man. He, too, aspired, as Cortés had done, to title, but he saw his title less as a great house, than as a dynastic bank. As banks do, he had branches. There was not one Francisco de Montejo, but three, for his sister's son, and his own illegitimate son, all bore that patronymic, and all entered Yucatan, so to speak, to learn the business from the ground up.

He had seen other men take Honduras, Guatemala, and the other lands. There remained Yucatan. No one else wanted it. He saw no reason not to have it for himself. He gave no thought to its real owners. Their title to it, because not Spanish, was not valid. He came from Castille. What other civilization was there?

His flotilla dropped anchor off Cozumel in September of 1527.

It was now sixteen years since Guerrero had been washed up on Yucatan, and eight since Aguilar had gone away for good. A good many things had changed. There was now a world around them, the Maya knew that, but they still thought of that world in terms of their own. And their own world was in its usual state of anarchy.

There were many states, some peripheral and impregnable, such as Champoton and Chetumal, but the two great states were Mani and Sotuta. Mani was ruled by the Lords of Xiu. In Yucatan now they were the oldest house. They had ruled the country once, until the league of Mayapan, and were proud to have come from Mexico, and to trace themselves back to the Toltecs, long ago. But they knew what had happened to Mexico. And they remembered very well for how many generations they had been prisoners in Mayapan, before they revolted and destroyed their Mexican overlords.

Sotuta was ruled by what was left of those overlords. They hated the Xiu as much as the Xiu hated them. But in their continual jockeying for advantage each left most of the rest of the peninsula in peace. There were those, too, who wished to be allied to neither, and who would therefore accept protection from anywhere, without asking about its nature.

Montejo found himself amiably received by Naum Pat, the cacique of Cozumel. He even behaved well in return, going so far as to refuse to allow his friars to smash the idols in the temples. For one thing he needed rest, supplies, and information. For another, they could do that later.

In those days men did not have either our sense of the holy or our sense of the beautiful. All holy objects were Christian, religious not because of what they were, but of what they depicted. As for beauty, that was anything made of the best materials in the latest taste, which was usually the Italian, and all the portraits were done either by Titian or the next best man.

Not all the priests felt the same way. A priest is a professional. He sees things from the inside. Gregorio de San Martin was a Carmelite friar. Such men are not aesthetes. But Montejo's own chaplain was like those later colonial bishops, who kept a record of what they destroyed, in part out of scholarship, as an attaché writes a monograph on the country he is attached to, but in part because they were sorry. There was Landa, who wrote the Things of Yucatan, and Sahagun, who diligently got the Aztecs a little mixed up as he wrote them down.

Juan Rodriquez de Caraveo wrote nothing down, but he was curious and peaceable by nature. He was also, in so far as the time and the place allowed for that, a sensitive. He could feel Cozumel was thought to be holy, which was almost as tolerant but not quite so wise as to know that it was.

The great temples it was unwise to approach. There was too much that was waiting and unknown at the top up there. But he wandered through a few small outlying shrines. Of those gods he could make nothing. Saintliness was a cooperative venture. He was used to the iconography of saints who had been martyred by their fellow men. But these gods seemed to have martyred themselves. They bristled with the attributes of animals, and like animals, they crouched there waiting by the watershed. The great gods of Christianity became so only when they died. But these were not dead. They were right here, all around him, and they did not intend to die. They would have to be destroyed.

He could see that. Perhaps if they no longer had any images, they would no longer lurk out there, in the rustling dark.

But he found a clay figure that pleased him. It was nothing but the first unfurling leaf of the corn plant, tall, pointed, and slim. Inside it sat a little benign spring goddess, like the Buddha on his lotus, though he had never heard of the Buddha, or Brahma popping out of the bud and sleeping on his lily pad, on the world ocean, but he had never heard of Brahma either.

It was so very vulnerable that it touched him, so he never said anything about it. There are a few things belonging to the enemy, even of the True Faith, that should not be destroyed, for they are our things, too.

These people, like their gods, had the matter of fact reality of farmers. It was both their wisdom and their wealth. You saw it in the fields of tasselled maize. It made them fatally complacent towards an enemy. An enemy was not something to defeat, but to survive, like a plague of locusts.

Perhaps they were right.

Next day Montejo crossed to the mainland, and founded a town, a few miles north of Tulum, on the coast. It was called Salamanca. He was to move it many times, but it would always be called Salamanca. That was where he had come from, and what he understood, so of course somehow he must have the same thing here.

"España, España, España, viva," cried the new mayor, and raised the royal standard.

The natives were not impressed. The site was unhealthy. It was only a foolish little invasion. It would not last long. In time the strangers would get tired of it and go away. España was the name either of their home or of their God, something like Quetzalcoatl, only feminine. There were so many gods.

Meanwhile the priest Caraveo wandered happily about in the mud, for he had discovered that first word of a language which is the key to everything, and with his monkish neatness he was busy labelling a world. The other Spaniards would not have thought to do that. They preferred either to give their own names to things or else destroy them.

"Machu cava," he would ask, What is it? What is it? What is it called? and the natives, amused, for it was what children said, told him. It was a pretty language. He liked it.

Montejo approved and set three of the brightest men to the same task. They were not like Cortés, passing through. From now on they must be their own interpreters.

XVII

Guerrero was misinformed. He thought Montejo only another conqueror, like other men. And the principles of conquest were simple.

What one had to do was to fight back with better weapons.

He would have given anything then for a few cannon. But he had not the art to make them, and perhaps in that land, they would not have been efficient, anyhow.

Chetumal was so far away from the centre of Yucatan. It was the reason for its security, its happiness, and its complacency.

Now complacency might endanger everything.

Looking at him, Guerrero could not decide whether Nachancan was complaisant or not.

Looking at it, we see Yucatan as rather small. But to the invader it was not small, and to its inhabitants, it was an empire, an empire fallen into a series of anarchic states, but still, perhaps the more extensive for that fact, for though it had nothing so large, neither had it anything so small as the ferocious Germanies of that day.

Nachancan seemed very much disposed to let the rest of the peninsula fight as it would.

Guerrero wanted to send out embassies. He wanted to rouse the whole peninsula.

"And do you think you could do that?" asked Nachancan sceptically.

"It has to be done."

"Which is not to say it can be." Nachancan looked round the stone room in which they were sitting, sighed, and peered at the bright sunlight outlined against the open door. "We live well here. We always have. It is because we are out of that. For a thousand years we have fought against each other. Been invaded by the Mexicans. Thrown them off. Survived. And it is written that we will survive. No, you can do nothing with them."

"But you don't understand. I know what these people are. There is a great empire overseas. It can send supplies. They will never give up. They have to be beaten now."

"But if they will never give up, then they cannot be beaten?"

"You don't understand. We've got to drive them out."

Nachancan smiled. It was a wistful smile. "Oh yes. I

understand. You have taught me a great deal. But what can one do? One plays greed against greed. And what do you have to play with? It is all we can do to hold our own provinces. And you will see. They will be driven out. For a little while. And what can we ever have of life, but a little while? Then we will be driven out. We are so old, you see. And the old can never fight the new. They have not the energy. Only the skill. But if the enemy has a different kind of skill. . . ." He shrugged his shoulders. "Why then. . . ."

"But you must do something."

"That is not something to say to someone who is powerless," said Nachancan. "You forget. We have been waiting a long time."

It was not something to say to the young, who because they are young, think the world they live in also has the vigour to fight back.

"Very well. Send out your embassies. You must learn that way. But we get what we deserve," said Nachancan.

"You don't understand."

"We only understand what we know. How could we understand anything else?"

"But *I* know them."

"You would not be here, if you did. If you really knew them, you would be one of them. So you must only know about them."

"It isn't any time for philosophy," shouted Guerrero.

"Can you think of a better one?" Nachancan went to the doorway and looked out, across the courtyard, at the temples and the jungle. "Oh yes, we shall fight them when they come. But not to win. Only not to lose. That is all our world can do."

And Nachancan looked out across the city as though he had never seen it before.

"I don't want you to leave," he said. "I want you with me. I am an old man, and we are an old people. It is dreadful to think ever that we might see the young for the last time. And in a way you are my son."

"But if the Sotuta and the Xiu knew the danger, they would drive them out of here."

"But we never do know the danger," said Nachancan. "We are too busy turning it to our own advantage. And then, we never believe we can lose, until we have lost."

There was nothing Guerrero could do, but fret. There was nothing to be done with Nachancan. The man was too used to too much security. Yet was that because he knew too little, or too much?

Guerrero was a forthright man. He was not accustomed to doubt. It made him uneasy. He preferred action. Action cancelled doubt, and even if the action were the wrong one, at least it put an end to uncertainty.

He wanted the Spanish out of there.

Therefore, despite Nachancan's advice, he set out across the peninsula, both to spy out the Spanish and to try to unite the Maya against them. Being a fighting man, he had no knowledge of diplomacy. So he had much to learn, all of it saddening.

That was what Nachancan did not want to have happen. He did not want to see him saddened so. Now there would be no choice. They could only hope that he would return safely, for he would be needed soon enough. That being so, he was foolish to risk himself on the field, but there was nothing to be done about that either. He must learn this way.

They did so want him to come back. They wanted everyone to come back who had ever had the privilege of living. For they found the world well worth the burden, which it would not have been, if, once having laid down that load, one could not pick it up again.

Hence their calendar, and hence their character. It is only your Christian who wants to live once, and as a reward for that condition which is reward enough in itself, were not every Christian too much a Manichee to see it, be given heaven. Whereas to them, the thirteen heavens, though honourable, were only a poor substitute for life, a consolation for mortality, but nothing more.

XVIII

The Spanish were driven out of there, but not by him. The country had its own revenge on them, for that plague that they had brought, the easy death. For Yucatan had deaths of its own, and they were not easy.

They had come at the beginning of the rainy season. In that part of the world it was almost always the rainy season. They had had a vision of white skies, white cities, and rich fields whose corn was every colour from champagne to gold. But now that view was cut off from them. They were surrounded by rain that glittered as though they sat at the hub of a roll of steel mesh.

It cleared every two or three days only long enough for them to see where they could not go. And the rain rattled like those musical instruments the Maya loved, now an angry shake, and then the double incessant boom of a two-tongued wooden drum.

At home, in Spain, they were accustomed to drought. Now they understood why the worst of these idols about them, Tlaloc, the god of rain, was in some aspects a demon who took your life. There is more than one way to drown.

But to Guerrero, the rain meant nothing.

It was strange, since he was born in a yellow landscape, how he took to this, which was every shade of blue and green, which slithered with life, which was never still, and wherein a Cattleya burst out of a tree like a sour trumpet voluntary, shocking in the Byzantine mosaic of the jungle, where there are always glitters in the gloom, as though the vegetable world were a damp building, holy not to any idea of goodness, but to life itself, which is neither good nor bad. Decorated piers of mahogany, buttressed with liana, and a choir screen of snakes and vines, on which the monkeys perched like patron saints, lit some green fuse in him, which burst into an explosion of pleasure, despite a scorched youth.

Perhaps it was because, if one relaxes into the rhythms of nature, one finds one has a double strength, and he liked to be strong. He liked his body. The two of them, himself and it, they were good friends.

It was what had never made him give in and be a Christian, that enthusiastic collaboration, for no Christian ever loves his body. He was older now. His skin no longer had the sheen of youth. His biceps, his pectorals, the fan muscles of his back, were no longer all of him. Maturity makes us shrink into thought, which does not fill our shape the way emotion used to do. But the body was there, he liked it, it had its graces, and if we accept the fact of mortality, then each age has its pleasures, and since we have it no longer, but love it, then we love youth in any shape or form, the youth of the world, our own children, the dew at dawn. And that, given that attitude, still makes the world agreeable.

It is only your ascetic who hates the world, because he never had the courage to accept its conditions, and therefore despises himself. But to Guerrero, what he was, and what he had become, was an infinite source of amused curiosity. He sat in himself and watched. It is the best we can ever do.

He was one of those people, they are always neglected, always overlooked, and despised by the articulate, who are not verbal, who do not express themselves in concepts, and so all their philosophy goes ignored. And all their insight too. For they do not talk about it. Maybe they do not even know it is insight. Yet, they have something that takes them out of themselves, some parallel activity, to the life they lead, which makes them selfless. Insight made him happy in the world, even in its bad occasions. So few mystics can ever say so much. So padding through the forest, at an agile forty filled him with an endless, impersonal, and yet personal joy.

One could not go from Chetumal to Salamanca de Xelha by boat. The currents were in the wrong direction. He had first to go to Bacalar, and then through the jungle and its cleared states. He did not know all the diversity of that peninsula. He began to learn it now. And travelling now as an honoured member of this world was far different from fleeing through it, as he had done over fifteen years ago, as a fugitive.

In a week he came out at Tulum. Salamanca de Xelha was near Tulum. He had not seen that city since his captivity there. He saw at once that something had gone wrong with it. It had died a little more, more of its palaces were empty, the weeds were thicker in its streets.

For the pilgrims had stopped coming. Cozumel was desecrated by the foreigner, and so no longer, though it still was holy, efficacious. And there was also less trade than formerly. The conquest of the rich land of Mexico had everywhere disrupted trade. It was no longer safe for the merchants to set out on the Ocean Sea, and so they did not stop at Cozumel to pray for good commerce, nor at Tulum, to pray for a safe passage there.

Guerrero went to the temple of the Diving God. For in the absence of the nobility, it was the priests who would receive him now.

The square where he had been held captive, where the priests had danced in a dead man, the altar where Valdivia had been despatched to a Valhalla unknown to him, they all had their ghosts. But the worst ghost was perhaps the Diving God himself.

Blue and immense, he hurtles down, through a knotted rope of sacrifice, immune to currents in the air or sea, for the saviour descends like a pilgrim hawk. Then he soars up and away.

As light from the sea made ripples on the ripples of the murals, so in that ghost of a temple, what they did only gave a flickering life to what they were.

But the priesthood, unless its prerogatives are in question, is always a hundred years behind events. He could do nothing with them.

Yes, the foreigners from the sea had built a town. They discussed them as a man would discuss a cancer. It may destroy us. It may interfere with our natural functions. But it has nothing to do with us. That nodule is only the body's guest, in the groin, at Salamanca. There was nothing to be worried about.

"There wasn't, was there?"

Their assurance had a question in it. And that was ignoble. He did not want to see that.

He set out for Salamanca de Xelha. That town, the original Salamanca, which he had never seen, wrested from the Moors, a university in a sea of mud, and a cathedral bland above squalor, meant something to Montejo. Otherwise he would not call his new towns always after it. But what did it mean? The middle classes are always trying to invent an aristocracy, even while their basic cautiousness prevents the existence of one. They want a title. But how can they know what a title means, when they will not even accept the risk of pre-eminence. For property is only half the story. Property gives one the right to be free, but the acquisition of it makes one a captive for life.

No, such vaunting gestures could never vault the bar, if only because those who made them would not let go of the pole. And therefore they could not land where they wished, with that special ease of the ankle, that spurt of dust, that shows where one has been, up and over, but which leaves one unchanged, unmaimed by the experience, and eager to try that sport again.

It is exhilarating, so, to raise the bar, and yet never, out of what one is capable of, to shake it loose.

That sort of thing was beyond Montejo, as it was beyond the middle class. The middle class never dares itself on. For it does not love the game for itself. It only wants to win.

Guerrero came to that town, and squatted in the weeds, to watch, his legs slim and bare. He watched everything, and the posture did not bother him. Always in Spain, he had watched his betters so, from hiding, as any man who sees through them must.

But here, now, he had something better than a hut to go back to. And therefore he could see them plain.

He summed up Montejo and his efforts very well.

Salamanca de Xelha was nothing but a name on either side of a muddy swamp some men might call a street. You can live on a name, the noble Spaniards did, but you cannot live in one.

Besides, it was a town, and these men were no colonists. They were *conquistadores*. In those days men had certain limitations. No matter how ambitious they might be, at best they were only good for destroying each other. They did not have the means to destroy the world they lived in as well. Therefore, when the world fought back, they found it unfair. It made them fret. The world did not play according to the rules men devise. And so the Spanish were frightened. They were frightened of the full weight of the world itself. They were accustomed to winning, but you cannot win against the world. Either it annihilates, or else it waits.

Heat, heat, despite the rain, it steamed with heat. Their armour alternately sweated and then rusted. But heat has advantages as well as particulars. It served the peninsula of Yucatan very well.

Having no one else to destroy, they began to plot among themselves.

Montejo made things worse. He was not a coward. He was not stupid. But he was an administrator, looking desperately to find something to administer. And an administrator does not appear. He does not chat with the men. He issues directives. He was courageous in a battle, but he thought the real battles were fought indoors. He thought of Yucatan as an office in which one intrigues, according to the rules, for position, and is rewarded at last.

Yes, Guerrero, by watching and by sending for messengers, and taking their reports, could see that very well. He even saw, one day, Montejo. The man was pale. He seldom ventured out in the sun.

He seldom ventured out into the world at all. It was not necessary, though he had bravery of a kind. But this was the bravery that defends its investment, the bravery of a vixen at the end of its earth. And his burrow was his desk. He was one of the first to see Heaven as a sort of bureau, with God at the end of His desk, and Montejo, as deputy, at the end of his. Salvation and sanctity were investments, like any other. Everything was an investment. It paid its per cent. That was not usury. It did not involve the lending of money, which was, of course, accursed. But it did involve the giving of money, in return for a *pourboire*, which was not.

And to Montejo, one had only to see him squinting to the sun to know that, the world went that way.

Guerrero belonged to the older dispensation, the one the middle classes despise, but always have to come to terms with, when they come conquering in. But Guerrero was no conqueror. He did not have that greed to possess which makes the conqueror congenial to the entrepreneurs of this world. He was fighting for what he had, not for what somebody else wanted. It was perhaps a fatal point of view. But it was his.

Watching Montejo taking his outing, around the sloughs of that pompous, meaningless, transitory town, he felt nothing but disgust. Did that cautious, parsimonious, watchful, economic little blob of fat actually think it was a man?

He overlooked that other kind of courage, the courage of tenacity. And so he did not see the better, and therefore, the more dangerous, side of Montejo.

He had not the knowledge to see that Montejo was ahead of his time. He would have made an excellent Colbert, but in his own day men murdered and stole for what they got, and murdered and stole to keep it. The world had progressed once more to the extent of having lawyers for afterwards, which was a gain for lawyers. But his *conquistadores* had not yet reached the afterwards. They were living now. They wanted not a vice-president in charge of the board, but a commander.

And even the bravest commander cannot very well lead his men against the rain, when he does not know what lies beyond it.

If a man has the same stubborn thought, that rhythm makes it grow to an obsession.

A few of these men had been with Cortés. They could make comparisons, and did. The country felt wrong.

Montejo had his problems. Some of them he knew. Some he did not. He was a city man. The country was inimical to him. He did not understand the country.

There was first of all this plague, to which the natives were immune. They took baths every day. They knew how to build a drain. The Spanish never bathed and had seldom seen a drain. They began to sicken and die. To a man called Luzan fell the honour of being the first Spaniard to be buried in that place. It was an honour the others deeply felt, for it is difficult to bury a man in the rain. Over his grave they put a cross made of two stripped palm leaves. The cross blew down.

Very strange things sometimes live in palm trees. At first they did not know what was the devil of their death. But the men had little wounds that oozed, and made them feverish, before they died.

There are so many devils in the world. Even the true believer is not protected against another man's gods, which, since they are demons, serve him, not us.

Or were there men out there waiting, with some magic weapon of their own?

The wounds multiplied. The men were too delirious to tell what had struck them down. At last, one of them saw it, a fluttering, timid, but voracious ball of fur, with very sharp teeth, red pig eyes, and an avid expression, its half-folded wings rumpled back, sitting on an arm or a neck, biting greedily, and sucking up the blood. Then it whirled squeaking away, and they could see there were others, chattering around the palm trees, as they set out to feed, swerving haphazard but sudden through the dense night air: vampire bats, something they had not heard of before, and did not want to see. They left an awkward wound.

There were also blood-suckers, fleas, ticks, chiggers, mosquitoes, and gnats, centipedes and scorpions waiting in the warmth of an empty boot, and elaborate spiders, of which all men are afraid.

The weeks went by and Montejo did nothing. There was nothing he could do. Food gave out. All this time the Catalan merchants had waited in their ships off shore, with only the soldiers for customers. They did not make good ones. Perhaps when the rains lifted, Montejo would get them customers.

He seized their stores and fed his men. That might not have been so bad. He was a rich man and gave them letters of indemnity. But in their holds their fine cloth trade goods were rotting away. There was in particular the cloth of Courtrai. It was already mildewed and fallen to holes. Who here could buy the expensive cloth of Courtrai? It was no good for armour.

The chief merchant was Juan Ote Duran. He began to plot. He wanted to turn back. There was no profit here.

Guerrero saw his chance, he knew how desperate and how narrow-minded men such as Duran could be. The local natives did not like such strangers in their midst. Guerrero went to work. He did not have to work very hard. It was a new kind of war, the war of attrition, a war he was not adjusted to, but he learned fast.

Quite quietly, the local Indians cut off supplies. Montejo was forced to send out raiding parties to scrounge for food. At first they stole it. Later they had to be more cautious. The Indians were clever at ambush. A few of the Spanish were killed or led away, and not heard of again.

Guerrero enjoyed that. He used Indian strategy. It seemed to work here. And he waited, and he watched. Cat and mouse, spider and fly, had never impressed him before as being the games of an honourable man. But he found he enjoyed to see his former countrymen suffer. Let them die piecemeal, then. And slowly. They had so many sins against the world to expiate, that they might just as well take their time.

Patiently, outside the stockade, in the jungle he waited.

Half the company was now ill, or mutinous. Fifty of the soldiers had died in two months. Duran could do better at Veracruz. He planned to seize the *San Jeronimo*, man it with discontented soldiers from Salamanca, and sail away.

Davila found out and talked. Montejo filled a boat with crossbowmen, and bribed the captain of the *San Jeronimo*. The little party set out across the stormy water. From the jungle the Indians watched. A report was sent to Chetumal. The Spanish were fighting each other.

It seemed an excellent solution to everything.

The rain cleared and they had an excellent view. Montejo scuttled or burnt both ships. They burned for a long time against the sky, and the smoke from them made the afternoon sky look green. The crews he added to his own company. They might not be willing, but at least they could fight if they had to.

That suited Guerrero very well. He was not impressed. It was what Cortés had done at Vera Cruz, but Montejo could only ape the gestures of a larger man. Being himself small, he would not know what to do next.

It was a miscalculation. But then Guerrero was between worlds. He still thought initiative was in the hands of the individual, who wants this or that. He had no knowledge of the world's new conquerors, the little men, to whom personal integrity means nothing, and possessions at no matter whose or what cost everything.

Montejo marched north, leaving forty helpless invalids behind. He had been lured, as Guerrero hoped he would be, by false promises, into the interior.

The Indians had not the courage to attack. Cortés had left prestige behind him, and few men will attack prestige, for it is an evasive enemy. Very well then: let them be picked off, Indian fashion, a few at a time. It would make them suffer, and they deserved to suffer. Suffering was all of the world they understood. Perhaps to endure it would make them saints, and that, surely, should please them.

Guerrero saw them now as the enemy. Perhaps even as a child, he had seen them so. He followed. And he made his preparations. That was when he began to understand Nachancan's quietism, for sometimes he could rouse the natives, and sometimes he could not. He found it difficult to suppress his rage before those who would not help. Did they really want to give away a world which, even if it plagued them, was still their own?

He went ahead, failed or succeeded, and then came back to watch the Spanish. They had the fascination of the horrible.

Montejo's progress could not exactly be called a march. The rain forest grew quickly during the wet season, and no one would show them a path. They had to cut themselves through.

In addition they had no idea where they were going.

Eventually they reached a place called Pole. The Indians so far had left them alone. But now they were close to inhabited parts of the country. They had to advance with more care. Twenty more men had sickened. These Montejo left at Pole. The Indians there seemed friendly. He went on towards Xamanca, which was on the coast. He was himself ill. At night now they let the horses wander loose, for if Indians tried to attack, the horses would whinny and sound the alarm.

It was impossible to tell anything about the Indians. In these parts each town seemed to have a policy of its own. There did not seem to be any large unified states, as in Mexico.

That was what Guerrero had found out. But they did not, as yet, even imagine the existence of a Guerrero, and would have thought him a renegade, if they had.

Sometimes the townspeople came out to meet them, bearing gifts of maize, turkeys, and jars of honey. But sometimes they would not appear at all. Between the trees and the vines they would instead build palisades called albarradas, at an angle to the line of march, and disguised as underbrush. From these they could shoot down the

Spaniards with arrows, lances, darts, stones, or anything else that came to hand.

It always meant a few men hurt. The Spaniards took up the quilted armour of the country, and cast aside their own. It was made of cotton, and in that weather, clung heavy, treacherous, and damp about them.

Guerrero, who had made many improvements in the albarradas, now judged the time the right one, and sent a message along the rear of Montejo's line of march.

As a result, at Pole, the Indians swept down on the Spaniards, killed the weakest, and hauled the others off for sacrifice. So even a coward makes a good ally at the right time. It meant a few Spaniards the less. Guerrero was not displeased. It was obvious, now, that Montejo was desperate to reach the coast. That meant he would have to pass through Xamanca.

Guerrero sent off a message to Naum Pat, got no answer, and then went to see the man himself.

Naum Pat, ruler of Cozumel, controlled Xamanca and the coast. Meeting him, Guerrero began to understand Nachancan's polite despair.

The man was middle-aged and quite immoral. Already, tired of sensation, at fifty, he had begun to tipple, a self-indulgence the Maya approved of only in the very old, who might be presumed to need that alcoholic screen between themselves and life.

There was nothing to be done with him. Since he believed he might die tomorrow, and was an elegantly selfish man, he made no plans for the future. The future for him did not even exist, for the world to him was himself, and for himself it was always today.

Oh yes, he admitted the evil in their midst. But it was not his business to deal with it. Besides, he was bored. He would do anything to be amused. Prudence, perhaps, is always short-sighted. Strangers often came to Cozumel. It was better to treat them well until they went away.

So he would not even listen to Guerrero. He was on the

way to the marriage of his sister, at Ecab. He departed, encountered Montejo, saw what he was, and befriended him. It pleased him to arrive before his brother-in-law at Ecab with such an exotic company. He became benign. He gave the Spaniards gifts, as one would reward a dwarf or a zany.

Not to be outdone in splendour, the Lord of Ecab presented the Spaniards with gold necklaces encrusted with jewels. It was a fatal mistake. The Spaniards had no way of knowing how rare such things were here. They took heart and began to preach Christianity at once.

The Indians listened politely and went away. It seemed a professional matter for priests, not the subject for a public harangue. Of course if the strangers preferred their own gods they might keep them. There was nothing wrong with being devout.

Guerrero, anonymous in the crowd, could only curse. What Indian in that crowd could make anything of it? It was both naïve and horrible, naïve in its greed, even more naïve in its hatred of the world.

His Spanish was rusty. And yet he could follow the argument. But more than ever it had done, once, it now disgusted him. What awful pride these people had, to see the world in their own way only and never perceive the diversity.

He set himself to foment disorder. He had not much trouble.

Though reduced by death and disease, the Spanish were expensive guests, and difficult to get rid of. The Lord of Ecab decided to pass them along to the nearest border. It was amiably done. They were even shown a little more treasure. Montejo was afraid to take it, and told his men not to do so.

"I found many signs of gold," he wrote home, "but to prevent the natives from gaining the impression that we came to find it, I did not dare accept what they offered me. Rather, I pretended to hold it in little value, because my men were few and ailing, and because the Indians, if they believed I desired gold, would deceitfully conceal it."

You cannot do anything with a mind that works that way.

But then the Spanish could not do anything with the way the minds of the Indians worked, either.

They removed to Conil, another prosperous city too large for them to attack, where they were well received. Down by the sea, they found fresh springs bubbling up through the gentle tide. They rode the horses out there to drink, and counted it more of a marvel than anything else they had seen. But then apart from greed, they were a simple people. They could only marvel at simple things.

Guerrero was ahead of them, but could accomplish nothing at Conil. He moved on to Chuauca. It was on Montejo's line of march, and Chetumal and Chuauca had, as it happened, excellent trade relations. Guerrero did better there. An ambush was planned. He supervised it himself. He was beginning to learn diplomacy. Since the Spanish spent two months at Conil, he had ample time to plan.

From Conil, confident that the country was within his grasp, Montejo moved to Chikinchel, and from there, to Chuauca, which lay on a fresh-water lake.

Guerrero was ready for them. So were the Chuauca. They were a proud people, sure of themselves, and therefore difficult to shock. Yet the Spanish did shock them. They had that naïveté of the truly rapacious which takes one's breath away: it is so oblivious of all values but its own, and therefore so rude.

However the Lords of Chuauca were not ones easily to lose their poise by giving way to fits of temper. They saw how that bland assumption of superiority might be turned to some advantage.

The first thing to do was to provide an adequate welcome. They provided well. The welcome left nothing to be desired. The cacique himself greeted Montejo in the plaza in front of the palace. Montejo took him for an effete dandy, and relaxed. He should not have done so. Effete dandies can be extremely dangerous. They also lay their plans well in advance, and the cacique had had the best advice. He did not care for foreign men-at-arms wandering about. For the present he fed them well, assigned them lodgings, and made himself as agreeable as possible.

He even managed to show a polite interest in their vulgar and appealing little gods. He stood respectfully through evening prayer. Then he put them to bed drunk.

The Maya retired early, as did all men in those days. Lighting was bad. There was only the moon, and on that particular night the moon rose late.

The priests had provided a few omens, all favourable. They were, after all, members of the ruling house.

It was a very large city, built of stone. The moonlight made it sedate, full of scented flowers and gardens, platforms and terraces. But though soldiers may marvel, they do not admire.

It was Caraveo the priest who gave the warning. He did not drink, and if this white world was to die, at least he wanted to see as much of it as he could. Besides, he could not sleep. He stood in the doorway of the room assigned to him, high on one of those terraces. It was a little before dawn.

Then slowly he became aware of things. Shapes fluttered in shadow, and though feather head-dresses do not reflect much light, gold ear plugs and lip ornaments do. Here and there in the quiet he heard a jewelled tinkle.

A sense of beauty is of some use after all. He went to give warning.

But it was hard to wake drunken men and harder still to round them up from the various houses where they were lodged. The Indians attacked at ten o'clock, while the Spanish were still buckling on their armour and trying desperately to build a barricade. They came from everywhere, without their customary shouts and drumming. There was not even the sound of a conch. They came in silence that was more frightening, and they filled the world. And when they were close enough, they attacked.

Though the Chuauca cacique could dispense with the ritual of war, he could not dispense with the idea that war was one. That notion was too ancient, and unlike the musicians, could not be ordered away. The Indians made straight for Montejo.

Montejo was no coward, and he had not only to save himself, but also his men. If he did not whip them into a victory, they would be hunted down one by one, and he had been to Yucatan before. He knew what happened to the leader of any engagement. He knew he would not be killed. What the Indians would want was capture, and from his horse he could see the temple stairs up which his captors would lead him, painted blue. He dug his spurs in and charged, slashing with his sword.

It did not take him long to learn that he was wrong. The Indians were too furious to bother even with their own religion. They merely wanted their invaders dead. That is why they had left out the customary music. But by then he could not turn back. He fought on.

By afternoon he had them beaten to a standstill. They had already evacuated the city. Now they fled themselves, leaving their dead behind them.

But they also left ten Spaniards dead behind them. The Indians used obsidian arrows. These shattered when they entered the flesh. Those Spanish who were not dead, soon wished they were.

The next day the Lords of Chuauca sued for peace, swore allegiance to the Spanish and the Spanish king, accepted Christianity, let the friars smash a few idols, did everything if only they would go away.

Perhaps a defence in depth would work better. Once the Spanish were inland, the Maya could heal over them like flesh around a wound. There were a great many Maya and very few Spanish. Even picking them off a few at a time might do.

So they induced the Spanish to turn inland to Ake, a rival state, and gave Montejo bearers. They then sent messengers to Ake, announcing the Spanish were come to conquer them, and to Montejo, to say that the inhabitants of Ake were coming to conquer him. It was a standard Maya ruse. It had worked before against the Mexicans, why should it not work now against a small force? It was impossible to make them understand why a people would come four thousand miles, across the ocean, just to destroy them. They had no concept of an alien culture or of a lemming-war.

Guerrero alone of all of them knew that. Yet even he approved.

As usual in such wars, the Akians evacuated their city and prepared an ambuscade. The Spanish marched right to the town and fortified it.

That was what everybody wanted. The Chuauca burden bearers and allies sacked the city and made off with the plunder, leaving the Spanish to be killed. The Akians moved up their ambuscades, surrounded the town, and prepared to kill them. Night fell, and then came day.

The Maya were satisfied. They were also extremely angry. But they had no doubt that they would win. They had had time to follow all the proper forms. The conches were blown. The whistles were sounded, and the drums. They put on their war paint, and all their nose, lip, and ear jewels. They marched out in orderly fashion, and then they attacked.

The sight of those decorated demons, following their own arrows over the ramparts, and eager for human hearts, was supposed to be unnerving. It was unnerving.

Unfortunately the Spanish won.

It was a great victory. They did not lose a man, though one or two were wounded. Above all, it was a diplomatic victory. The surrounding pueblos swore friendship and loyalty, having decided to temporize. There were other stronger states. One of those could defeat the Spanish. For the moment they had done enough.

The Spaniards began to march for the coast. That, too, pleased everyone. Perhaps they were leaving.

Whatever they were doing, though they might be good fighters, they were quite contemptible. All the tribes agreed to that. They had no manners.

Guerrero, by now, was desperate. Who would think it

would take such an effort to kill so few men? It made one believe that perhaps they were invulnerable. Not because of their nature. They were men like himself, and their nature was contemptible. But because they were the new thing, that always overwhelms the old.

There remained Loche. He went to Loche. Perhaps Montejo could be ambushed there.

The cacique of Loche would not even see him.

It was his usual procedure with anyone not of his own family. He could not demean himself by fraternizing with those of inferior rank, and who was not inferior to Loche? It made no difference that his province covered at most a few square acres, or that those outside it did not honour his pretensions. Since he never travelled, he was not faced with such dilemmas. He was so eaten up by the pretensions of his house, that he scarcely regarded himself as a person. He was Loche. That was enough. There was only himself and the gods. To whom else would Loche speak? No one else was sufficiently exalted.

He sent Guerrero away. Nor did he receive Montejo either. He was of very high rank. He was of very old family. Why on earth should he deign to see such people? For the sake of diplomacy, he had to receive them, but he did so lying in a litter, protected from view by gauze veils. True, he had a certain curiosity. They were odd-looking men. It was easier to answer directly than to speak through his aides. But he answered from behind the veil, with a fine verbal contempt.

Unfortunately the Spanish did not know the language well enough to catch the cool insolence of the phrasing. But they were amused. They had gotten their confidence back and they were amused. They named Loche the town of Grave Doings. Two systems of snobbery had at last met, both indefensible, and therefore dangerous.

Guerrero when he heard about that was far from pleased, if only because he understood it. It exasperated him. Such behaviour had fifteen hundred years of precedent. How could he possibly make them afraid of the might of an enemy they did not even know the name of? He looked round Chetumal and wondered how long it would be before the Spanish heard of it.

It was not to be very long.

Montejo was marching for the coast. He had heard of other states, Mani and Sotuta, that were stronger than anything he had yet seen. He was not without prudence, and he had learned much. Besides, he had not yet found the ideal site for Salamanca. For several days he passed through heavily populated country, and then entered a band of forest where there seemed to be nobody at all.

It disturbed him. He feared some sort of ambush. And he now had only sixty men. He would need reinforcements. He tightened his lips, drew his party defensively together, and marched on.

The jungle began to grow yellow and porous, and abruptly the company marched out into the plaza of an enormous city. He was wary. At first he thought that the enemy had fled into an ambush, as before.

He had stumbled on Chichen Itza, abandoned for a little over three hundred years, in one of the returns of Katun 8 Ahau, but still sacred, and still the object of pilgrimage. It was kept in repair. The circular Temple of the Snail was still standing. The light of Venus could still be sighted through its precisely aligned windows, and the rise and setting of the sun. It was like a clock that goes on ticking out the days even after the family has left. The vast shadowy colonnades of the Temple of the Warriors and of its plaza were still in place. In their own deep shadow, they looked inhabited. Grass grew up through the paving, but the little temple above the Well of Sacrifice was in good repair. It was still used once a year. The gods in their temples were undisturbed.

It was too big and desolate. It seemed to swallow up a mere sixty men. They found themselves whispering, and glancing fearfully around them.

Half-heartedly they smashed a few idols, But the idols only shattered into silence, or rolled down the steep stairs of a temple they had climbed as a lookout, and came to rest at the bottom, staring up at the sky. There were too many of them for sixty men to destroy.

They looked down into the Well of Sacrifice. There was no surface water in this land. The horses suffered as a result. The water welled up from underground, or rained into the cenotes. The cenotes were damp and dark, traversed by watersnakes, their walls heavy with ferns, and the men did not like to go down into them, even to get water for the horses. The water was thick and black. They could not know how many generations of the sacrificial dead lay down there, nor even with what treasure.

They stayed the night but they did not like it. It was like being in a cathedral without a roof. It gave them a glimpse of something too big for them.

It was too big for Guerrero, who had followed them. In that vast city, the most sacred of the New Empire, and deserted now, in which desertion there was some meaning which bothered him, but he did not want to think of it, he had been able to keep out of sight, and yet he had heard their voices. Those voices sounded lost and insignificant, echoed back by those waiting buildings. It sobered him, that sound.

For there was something abroad in the world he had never understood, even in Spain, a new spirit, an approach to the world that was not his. And the world he had joined was an old one. It had no new spirit. It sat surrounded by its own ruins and its own traditions, which these new men rendered meaningless to anyone but those who shared them.

Well, he shared them. But still, this past was too big. It overwhelmed you. It left you no room to move, let alone to fight.

And yet they must fight, if only to prove something which, because it was no longer true, would always be.

But how? But how?

Next morning Montejo marched out along a sacbe which seemed to lead towards the coast, the last procession that would ever tread it, though neither they nor the Maya could know that. Even the sacbe was too broad for them. It swallowed them up. It called for confident plumed processions, not an anxious and irritable company of sixty tattered and ill-kempt men.

Montejo had the drummer set a beat, and there was a flute player in the company. But that did not help much. Around them the jungle creaked, and the sound was not merry. Cortés, on his march to Honduras, had taken an entire orchestra, complete with violins. They hurried on.

At last they reached Salamanca. Those at Pole were lost, but Salamanca was safe. The men were dissatisfied. Their six months' forage had killed most of them, but that was not what was wrong. What was wrong was that it had not made the survivors rich. They could not even hope to become rich, even in land, unless they got reinforcements.

Even Montejo could not hold them.

Then a ship appeared in the roadstead, sent out in search of him. It brought both men and supplies.

Montejo gave no one time to think. He went down the muster roll, and split all malcontents into two parties. He was still looking for a place to put a city, and from the Indians he had at last heard of Chetumal. It sounded ideal.

Davila was to march towards it along the coast. He himself would take the relief boat, and sail down the peninsula. At the Bay of Chetumal they would combine forces and seize everything.

The worst disaffected of the men he left behind, with instructions to build a small boat and then follow. That left the choice up to them. If they did not build a boat, they would die of fever or be starved out by the Indians and then picked off. If they did build the boat, there was nowhere for them to go, but to follow their commander. They had neither the knowledge nor the means to face the open sea. He was well pleased.

So was Guerrero. It was a relief to face the enemy at last, and besides, he now had a plan, for unlike the Maya, and unhampered by precedent, he could improvise.

But the man Davila made him thoughtful. He had seen Davila often during those desperate weeks. And Davila was his own kind of man, unaccountably in the service of this pusillanimous weakling, to whom he would, because he was that sort of man, despite his own interests, be loyal, and that made him an opponent worth bothering about.

Montejo was not worth bothering about. Guerrero hurried overland, to prepare Chetumal against the invader.

XIX

They were glad to see him back. But they did not like what he had to tell them.

Nor did Nachancan care for what he had learned. It was so plain to see that disillusionment in what before had been always interested eyes. When that special sparkle goes, in a man of confident maturity, even though he does not know it himself, one can see it, and it is as distressing, as futile. to be touched by that, as by the look children have, who, always having seen the world for the first time, no matter what we do to protect them, no matter how we love them, no matter how they love themselves, then see it for the second, and though they are still delightful children, still that look which turns a knife in the heart, which makes us tremble for the safety of the joy of being, is never quite the same again.

At that age, six or seven, they first learn about the Performance, that imitation of life with which we solace ourselves even when we are gay and most absorbed, for the impossibility of life itself. It can be very beautiful, the performance, but it is never quite the same thing as life itself, as those first years of experiencing our future lines, which then seem reality, but are only the rehearsal.

And yet that is why we admire a good performance, because we also went through the rehearsal, we feel for the players, and know that in their parts we should not have done so well.

But if a man of forty learns what the world is, particularly if it is a world in which he believed, that is different. That is a little sad.

Guerrero had been young so long; and Nachancan, so long old. They had been father and son for so long. But now experience had made them equals. It left them with so much not to say. It made them father and son the more, in that collaboration which is possible, only when we have learned enough of the world not to hate our parents. When and if that point has been reached, a man and his son may be blood brothers.

That point had been reached. And it saved them time. They found that they agreed.

Guerrero had found the disunity of the peninsula a shock, but there was no time to indulge in such a thing as shock. Montejo was on his way. The city would have to be defended. The strategy of the bay would have to be planned. And, since he could not hold the natives against a determined force, he sent out messengers every day and planned a ruse. It might work and it might not. But if it did work it would give him a little more time to intrigue among the provinces.

Montejo was coming by sea, Davila by land, and they expected to meet at the Bay of Chetumal itself. Montejo, though willing to fight, would not fight unless he had to. He had not that nature. But Davila was a fiery man. He was what in those days was called a man of honour, that is, a man without prudence, who having no thoughts and few ambitions, could justify himself in no other way than by always taking the offensive. But such men are happy only in a world which contains nothing but people they can beat and people they cannot. Confronted with the world itself, their nerves snap and their self-assurance begins to change into something a little more desperate.

And the coastal landscape between Salamanca de Xelha and Chetumal was so desolate and inhospitable, that even the Indians themselves, who knew how to maintain themselves in such places, avoided it, a low, feverish coast, reptilian and rank, full of sluggish waters, salt lagoons, quagmires, sandbars that heaved out of the sea, at low tide, with a flabby flop, and almost no vegetation that was edible.

The people of such lands would obey Chetumal, and small bands of natives could be sent in, as decoys. Guerrero first had Davila's food supplies cut off, not entirely, but capriciously, so that he could never know whether he was to eat that night or not. Let him paw in the sand for turtles' eggs, which would make him sick, and drink brackish water which would make him double over with pain. Dysentery was no way to calm the nerves.

Between friendly natives who had no food, and hostile natives who picked off his men, but never came close enough for an open battle, Davila began to sweat. His eyes would have a different look now, a worried, irritable look. He did not know the language. He could not therefore know where he was, or how far he had to go. And in particular Guerrero shut off any messages from Montejo, coasting comfortably down the coast.

Those of Davila's men who had picked up a little Maya, were beginning to ask questions about Montejo along the coast.

Guerrero judged it time for his stratagem. He did not send a messenger to Davila. He had a more convincing plan. He let the Spaniard come up on a small group of natives, fishing at the shore. They tried to flee but Davila caught them. That, too, was part of the plan. Then their carefully rehearsed story came out.

No, Chetumal was at least a week's march away, over difficult territory, heavily armed.

And a ship? A big thing that looked like this? They inspected a *graffito* drawn in the sand with a stick, and then beamed with comprehension. Yes, they had seen such a thing. They had been out on the ocean, in a canoe, fishing. The thing, what was it called, a ship?, had appeared on the horizon, coming towards them. Then, suddenly, the sea was rough, it had foundered and gone down. They had not dared to go too close. They were too busy saving their own lives. But yes, they had seen it. There was no doubt.

There was nothing for Davila to do but turn round and go back to Salamanca. He could not persist in this country without reinforcements. The lagoons and sandbars and shallows cut off all sight of the sea.

That taken care of, Guerrero settled down to deal with Montejo, for whom he had planned other surprises.

The ship had been sighted off the long bar which protected the Bay of Chetumal from the open sea. That meant it would arrive in the morning.

That night none of them slept. Even Ix Chan, who was usually so deliberately placid, seemed astonished to find herself uneasy. If they were careful, they could destroy Montejo. But life from now on might be a series of Montejos, one could not hope to destroy them all, and besides, suppose they failed.

Guerrero was determined not to fail.

At dawn he and Nachancan went to the temple. It was the highest structure in the area, it topped the trees. From its platform they could see the orderly fields, thinned forest, and prosperous villages. The light struck the surface of that ominously empty bay. A breeze was blowing up the water.

Nachancan had never seen his own land invaded. Indeed it never had been invaded. It lay below him, perfect and familiar, and now, suddenly, somehow, at a touch it might vanish, as perfection does, instantly. His face was full of a bewildered astonishment. But he said nothing.

Together they waited. The world was absolutely silent.

The colours of the world came up a little more clearly, as the sunlight struck the forests and the fields.

It was the creaking they heard, even before they saw the ship. It was the sound of canvas and tackle, which Guerrero had not heard for over fifteen years, and yet as soon as he heard it, it brought back memories.

On that bay, which had never heard the sound of sail, the sound was ominous.

Nachancan shifted uneasily, while Guerrero pointed at a spur of forested land, at the end of the bay, which hid the channel.

Behind them, a priest threw copal into a brazier on the altar. It hissed. It made a little cloud.

Half-rigged, moving cautiously, the clumsy ship moved steadily but ungainly into view; the sun caught glittering on what must be helmets. The air was so clear that they could see everything.

Nachancan had never before seen a ship. He looked grave.

Though it plunged and had no grace, the boat came on, until whoever was watching on it could see Chetumal itself. Guerrero could pick out distinct figures now.

One of them, rather thick-set, stood alone on the poop.

The ship moved into the centre of the bay, the sails came down with an exhausted rustle, the cable ran out, and they could hear the splash as the anchor hit the water and then plummeted, unseen, to root in the mud.

The enemy had arrived. Nachancan now knew what it looked like. The two men went down into the town, to await developments.

There were no developments. Montejo was also waiting. Perhaps he did not like the silent emptiness of the bay, for Nachancan had had it cleared of canoes.

Darkness fell.

Montejo sent out the long boats. Guerrero had expected that, for the Spaniards would need water.

There was a brisk skirmish. The Spaniards retreated, unfortunately with two prisoners.

Thus, at last, Montejo learned of the existence of Guerrero.

He was delighted. He had thought the man dead by now, but that he was not was excellent luck. He would be as invaluable to this conquest as Aguilar had been to that of

Cortés. He would receive the man well. He would even pay him well, since he would be well worth paying.

Really things could not have gone better.

Early next morning he sent off a messenger to the town, returning, perhaps rather incautiously, both the prisoners.

When they arrived, Guerrero was supervising the fortifications. In particular he prepared the narrow strip of land that was the only access to Chetumal except by water.

It was hot work, and he was already sweaty when Nachancan sent for him, and handed him Montejo's letter, unopened. He had the liveliest interest in seeing what would happen next. That Guerrero would prove competent he had no doubt.

Guerrero knew what the letter would say, for the letters of would-be conquerors are all much the same. He took the sealed and folded piece of parchment. It was years since he had seen such stuff, and he had never received a letter with quite so massively aggressive a seal. The seal, somehow, showed the pomposity of the man. And those who act out their little game not for their own time, but for posterity, are of necessity unapt to conceive of anything but praise for their performance.

With a wry smile Guerrero wrenched the letter open.

There would be, of course, some sort of exhortation to return to the Fold. Such men, since another would not have justified them so well, could imagine no religion but their own.

Indeed there was.

Montejo had a fussy and flamboyant hand which betrayed a slight tendency to wobble. Since he was so sure of the verdict of posterity, which to him was a sort of secret court of the mind, best influenced by documents, since unfortunately he would be unable to address it in person, he had written at length and kept a copy for the family archives. It was quite true he needed Guerrero. But he was not also saving a Christian soul? That was how the conquest sounded best, as a saving of souls. That way it was entirely justified. He had the precedent of Charles V for such an attitude.

On the other hand, he was also, of course, speaking to an inferior. This man was merely a common sailor.

"Gonzalo," he wrote, "my brother and special friend, I count it my good fortune that I arrived and have learned of you through the bearer of this letter. I can remind you that you are a Christian, bought by the blood of Jesus Christ, our Redeemer, to whom I give, and you should give, infinite thanks." (It was well to keep on the right side of the clergy. Cortés, to his ruin, had not.) "You have a great opportunity to serve God and the Emperor, our Lord, in the pacification and baptism of these people, and more than this, opportunity to leave your sins behind you, with the Grace of God, and to honour and benefit yourself." (One must also mention the Emperor, and it did no harm to remind the man that the Spaniards were bound to win. He could not live Indian fashion for ever.) "I shall be your good friend in this, and you will be treated very well." (The man would be invaluable. Later when the country was pacified he could be given a small farm.)

"And thus I beseech you not to let the devil influence you not to do what I say, so that he will not possess himself of you for ever." (Apparently the man had gone over to the natives, according to Aguilar, tattoo, ornaments and all. He must be a curious sight.)

"On behalf of His Majesty, I promise you to do very well for you and fully to comply with that which I have said. On my part, as a noble gentleman" (the common people always trust gentlemen), "I give you my word and pledge my faith to make my promises to you good without any reservations whatsoever, favouring and honouring you and making you one of my principal men and one of my select and loved groups in these parts." (One cannot repeat these things too often.)

"Consequently I beseech you to come to this ship, or to the coast, without delay, to do what I have said and to help me carry out, through giving me your counsel and opinions, that which seems most expedient." (Flatter him.)

Guerrero read the message twice. As the chronicler Oviedo said later, "As for this evil person, as he must have been from his origins, brought up among low and vile people, and uninstructed in the elements of our Holy Catholic Christian religion, his friendship and his words were such as himself was."

Indeed they were, As Oviedo also said, "He placed the Spanish in such a situation that all the Christians of that land were ruined." But first he took a piece of charcoal, and scrawled across the back of the note that he was a slave and had no freedom, even though he remembered God.

Indeed he did, but he was not without irony. Position had given him that. For irony, after all, is only worldly insight with enough to eat. "You, my lord, and the Spaniards will find in me a very good friend," he added.

And that also was true, since he did not say to whom. He sent the messenger back and stayed to lunch with his father-in-law. He could not help but feel angry. These ex-countrymen of his were so impertinent in their use of God, as a convenient excuse for everything. Not even the Indians thought that God fought on either side. They took captives to sacrifice them to the gods, as one caught flies to feed a toad, but that was only so that they might be placated. Unlike Christians, they did not suffer from the vanity of believing in a full collaboration with the Deity.

He would have liked to see Montejo's face, when he read that answer, and hoped Montejo would at least allow the messenger to return safely to Chetumal.

For a wonder he did.

Montejo shut himself up in his cabin and fumed. It was an insult to God, to the Emperor, and to himself. Of the three it would have been hard to tell which was the worst offended, but since Montejo saw that trio as a Trinity, perhaps to insult one was to insult them all. More than that, it was an insult from a common sailor.

Not only was he angry, but life on shipboard had made him a little overconfident. He decided to march on Chetumal at once. But he was not that overconfident. He marched at night. He expected no difficulties. These people always ran away. When they understood he wanted only Guerrero, they would hand him over at once, and then he would put the man in chains.

Guerrero was ready for him, and had a report on every movement Montejo made, for the Spaniards were surrounded by spying Indians they could not even see, who flickered in and out of the darkness, making their observations and reports.

He had not been wrong. A man that pompous had been easy to goad into a trap.

By the time Montejo and his horses had reached shore, it was an hour before dawn. He kept his company in good order, and outriders had brought him the lay of the land. He advanced over that little isthmus which connected Chetumal to the peninsula. He sent the horses in first. They behaved well. They did not whinny. He wished to surprise whatever sentries might be about. He told the men to move quietly.

The path was dense with forest debris, but the natives had levelled the trees. It seemed an odd strategy. Usually they preferred to fight like cowards from behind their trees.

Montejo rode back along his little line. It was just as well he did.

The front horses gave a terrified whinny, screamed, and fell through the forest floor, with their riders on top of them. Their riders also screamed.

Guerrero had dug pits, lined them with spikes, points up, and covered them with debris. There was time only for one quick glance. Two of the men were spitted down there, and were being kicked by the desperate horses. No wonder they screamed.

Montejo retreated in a low continuous volley of well-aimed arrows. It did not much wound the men, for they had the remaining horses between themselves and the barricades, but it drove the horses almost insane.

An hour later he was back on his boat. After all, he had with him only ten or twelve fighting men, and what could be spared of the boat crew, and of the men, he had lost three.

The men in the pit had not been killed. Guerrero turned them over to the priests. It was dawn by now, and the altars were hungry. He did not go to see the sacrifice himself. He had not yet reached that point of desperation. But he knew that Montejo could gather what was happening from the ship. The ceremonial music rolled out across the bay.

In silence Montejo and his men watched. They knew by now that at the actual moment of sacrifice the music stopped. It stopped now.

He cursed, but there was nothing he could do until Davila arrived with reinforcements. Those pits were a European trick. If Guerrero was behind that, he would have to be cautious, and of course the man was behind it. He settled down to wait.

Since it had not been possible to destroy him, it would be necessary to get rid of him. Guerrero had prepared for that also.

Late in the afternoon a tattered messenger got through from the north. Davila and his company had been ambushed and destroyed. Naum Pat sent the message, therefore, since Naum Pat was an ally, the message must be true.

There was nothing for Montejo to do but weigh anchor and depart, pick up the men at Salamanca, and rephrase his campaign.

Guerrero watched the departure with satisfaction, having speeded it alternately with gifts of food and showers of arrows from canoes.

But he knew he had accomplished nothing. He had only gained a little more time, that was all. Somehow, he must rouse the whole country, against the moment when the Spaniards returned. He could not know when that would be.

It turned out to be two years.

Yet, though he did his best, he could not feel confident that his best would be good enough. For there was one thing he had reckoned without. For more even than the ambitions of the Lords of Xiu, and the lack of unity among the provinces, the Maya were the victims of their own calendar.

And when Montejo struck back, it was from an unexpected quarter.

XX

It was a curious contrivance, that calendar. No one but a priest could grasp it. It was a system of interlocking wheels so vast no Christian could understand it, for Europe believed the world was built in 4004 B.C., but the Maya dealt directly with the stars, and reckoned by such units as 23,040,000,000 days, all of which ceaselessly came back again. Thus mounted, time rolled over them like a juggernaut, and bound to its wheels, they were crushed. Everything had happened before and everything would happen again. But since everything that happened today had also happened the last time this day had occurred, one had only to open the sacred diary of the past, in order to find out what to do. On some days one could fight and win. But on other days, even though one had to fight, because one had done so last time, one did not make too much effort, because one knew one would lose.

It was impossible to plan a campaign on those terms. No Maya, of course, would attack on the wrong day, but the Spanish were another matter. The Spanish did not even know what day it was. Even his own younger son, the one training to be a priest, stood against Guerrero, who wanted to decimate the Spaniards at Salamanca de Xamanha. It could not be done. The last time there had been invaders in the land on this day, such an attack had failed. To choose another day, they would have to wait until the katun bundles applying to it were ready to be opened. Besides, there was nothing to be worried about. The nation would not be destroyed until the next return of Katun 8 Ahau, and that would not occur until 1697.

Guerrero looked at his son with exasperated disbelief.

And yet even he could see the irony of it. He had wanted his sons part of this world, and they were, so like that world that they would go down with it. But not, they said, until 1697.

1697 seemed far away.

Still, he could not sit there and fold his hands. He thought of a way out.

Surely, at some time in their history, some priest had forged the katun records?

His son was shocked.

Nachancan's attitude had more dignity. Yes, of course they would fight. One always fought against fate. But only because it was the thing to do. Even he did not believe you could replace the inner cogs of time.

To forgery he would not agree, but only on the grounds that it would not work. It did not matter what one said. The records were true.

Their only hope lay in the fact that not every Maya state was doomed on the same day, not, that is, until 1697. If they sent emissaries to various states, they might to that degree play with time. But to which state was the question. No-one could tell until the katun bundles had been opened at their appointed times. And history, too, was kept not by months or years, but by the twenty-year periods. The new period was still several years away.

Guerrero could do nothing.

In Mexico, Montejo counted time much faster, he had to, for he could see it running out. Unless he established himself in Yucatan rapidly, there were many who would want to take even that place away from him.

So one morning there appeared before Acalan, not Montejo, who would have been bad enough, but Davila, who was worse.

It took the whole peninsula by surprise. The way to Acalan lay across quagmires and swamps which, in this rainy season, were treacherous lakes. In Acalan they knew they were safe. Until now they had never doubted it. And now here was Davila, assuring them that no harm would come to them.

The Maya were not reassured. Cortés had been there, and taken away their cacique and six hundred porters, none of whom had ever returned.

In two hours the city was deserted. The food still bubbled in its cooking pots, incense still rose on the altars, but the people sat in the jungle, watching.

Davila was undisturbed. Since it was the rainy season, five thousand people could not sit in the rain for ever. The next morning the cacique decided to become an ally.

When he appeared before Davila, he brought with him the usual gifts of bright birds and bales of food. But Davila was now sure that he would conquer, therefore such efforts to temporize were nothing more than disobedience, a little before the event, but all the worse for that, in so far as disobedience before the event sometimes prevents it from happening.

He put the cacique and his nobles in chains. The Maya had not seen chains before. It had been Davila's inspiration to bring them. Not even Montejo had thought of that, except for discipline among his own men.

At first the Chontal of Acalan thought it was some sacrifice. They saw the red-hot iron welded on. The nobles did not flinch. At a sacrifice no noble would flinch.

But it was not a sacrifice. It was something far worse. It was an indignity.

The inhabitants returned to the town. It was anything to get rid of those chains, and in a few days Davila did have them struck off. They fell to the floor with a clink. The nobles rubbed their wrists and ankles, which the hammer on chisel had jarred, and said nothing. But they did not forget that sound. The Spanish would go. Unless they could find gold they always went. The indignity was another matter. That could not be forgotten.

At last they were roused. At last they knew what would happen to them, if the Spanish won. At night they sent messengers throughout the area, and one of these at last reached Chetumal. Acalan on the west, was much like Chetumal on the east, coast. It had seemed as impregnable, and had fallen as easily.

They wanted help. They wanted Guerrero. This time, even though Davila did march off, they knew he would be back; that the Spanish would never rest until the peninsula were stripped of everything that made life worth living, and those of the natives who survived, survived in chains, which this time, would not be struck off.

Guerrero left at once. Before he arrived at Acalan, Davila ran into a trap at Mazatlan, and narrowly escaped it. He too, had not forgotten Guerrero. He blamed the trap on him. For he thought the natives soft, they would not have dared to think of such a thing. There he was wrong. The natives were soft, but it was a softness made of wire. They refused to help him.

Davila was forced to torture them. He did not wish to do so. It was bad policy. He particularly did not want to do so in so far as he found torture enjoyable. It was enjoyable to see a body writhe. There was a special madness in that which made you feel competent. But it was useless. They would not give anything away. They had stiffened.

It drove the Spanish wild. They hated such stubbornness and malice. All they had done was to come to conquer the country. Why would the natives not co-operate?

Even when the soles of their feet were burned, the Maya only writhed and said nothing. They had made a special study of death, since that was what they feared most. They knew how to die.

When they did die, Davila allotted their lands to his followers. When they saw that, some of the local lords came over. As far as they were concerned, loyalty was a border they could cross at any time, and they did want to keep their land. There is more than one way of defeating the enemy.

Davila was not entirely taken in, but he was surrounded. He decided to march to Champoton.

It was a march he made alone. No Indian would accompany him.

Davila was a choleric man. Resistance only made him angry, and anger, competent. As for his men, since they could not have gold, they would have land. They were nervous and quarrelsome, there was something about the green jungle which sapped their nerve, but they did not rebel.

By the time Guerrero reached Acalan, Davila was already safe in Champoton.

It made him despair, to try to organize a campaign in this country. Acalan and Chetumal might now be allies, but the Couohes of Champoton co-operated with no one. They made the same mistake the Xiu had made, three hundred years ago, about their hired Mexican mercenaries. They believed that they could use the invader to conquer the country, then put him down, and rule the country in his stead.

Davila baptized them.

The Couohes were puzzled, but did not greatly object. It was a rite which meant nothing, and it did seem to please the mercenaries. True, the Spaniards were a brutal, uncivilized people. But if it pleased them to tumble a few idols down the steep temple stairs, one could always make new idols. It did not take much to please the invader, after all.

Then Montejo arrived. He entered the town in triumph. The natives could not do enough for him. And as they had foreseen, he moved on. It was time to found another Salamanca, which he did, at Campeche, a few miles farther up the coast. The natives did not think it would last long.

They were quite wrong. It was too late. The Spanish had come to stay. They were ready for conquest farther inland. But first they baptized everyone. They read the *requerimiento* to large groups. The natives must be loyal Christians. If they were, they would be forgiven their resistance to their conquerors.

The natives of Campeche had not seen those welded chains on their own nobles. They complied and waited. It was only a matter of waiting.

Both the Spanish and Guerrero forgot the priests who wandered ritually at the proper hours about those temple stairs and platforms. From the platforms they had an excellent view of what was happening. They did not interfere, but when they saw their own gods going down and that primitive little device of two crossed sticks going up, it made them thoughtful.

They were a small group, intermarried and interrelated with the nobility. Through the calendar, they ran the country. They ran it with a mixture of superstition and astronomy, but they knew what they were doing. Whether they believed in their gods or not, and most of them did, they meant to go right on running the country. The Spanish, being ignorant themselves, thought themselves up against superstition. It never occurred to them that they were also up against efficiency and a vast learning.

So Guerrero was to have an ally after all.

He badly needed one. He was back in Chetumal. The Spanish seemed to be succeeding everywhere. Even his own second son, the priest, said there was nothing to be done. The calendar ordained defeat. It made Guerrero furious. He had wanted his sons part of this society and they were. His younger son believed in the whole pantheon. The gods would save them. The gods would give a sign.

The older priests, however, began to treat Guerrero with more deference than they had done before. They wished to make certain plans.

Guerrero was tired of plans. He was forty-three. It seemed impossible to believe. It made the world more precious to have used up so much of it. He spent more time now with his wife. Now every hour seemed to count. But he was tired of waiting. As usual, he wanted to fight, and have the battle out in the open.

He did not have to wait any longer. News came that Montejo had founded his fifth and last Salamanca, at Campeche, his soldiers were discontented and disloyal, but he had four or five hundred of them. He was now ready to take over the peninsula, and there was even worse news than that.

XXI

This time the Spanish were determined to win.

Davila was marching across country towards Chetumal.

From Campeche to Chetumal is a distance of three hundred kilometres, across variable but nowhere easy country. There seemed plenty of time.

Guerrero knew better. There was now never to be time enough. And he knew what sort of man Davila was. Davila, like himself, would never give up, because he could always think of something else to do. Davila was wily.

As the messengers began to come in, Guerrero felt now hope, now panic, and again the stubborn will to survive. Nachancan was now very old. Guerrero directed everything, and that meant jealousies and suspicions to be dealt with. He dealt with them, but more and more he found his eyes turning east, as he despised one and worried about the other son.

The elder was out there, somewhere, with a raiding party.

He sent out envoys, but what good did that do? These men had the habit of quarrelling with each other. They could not trust anyone well enough to accept help.

He had never met Davila. He had never met Montejo, But he knew what kind of man the Adelantando was, and thought little of him. But men like Davila were another matter. He had seen a few such, among the raggle taggle of his Spanish years in Panama. When they win, such men are called great. But they are not great. They are merely lucky and dangerous, so avid for action they never ask the why of what they are doing, and therefore can only be stopped by force, or deflected by some trick.

He had no effective force. That left him trickery.

But what trick? He had had a plan, to defend in depth, but the Indians would never do that. And though Nachancan was a great lord, his vassals were not overawed by him. They wanted to be great lords too. It was useless to tell the old man that, for he knew it already. What Nachancan wanted to hear was something reassuring. He was sixty-seven now. He was unflinching, but what he wanted was his world put back where it was. He had not yet had a stroke, but he moved ponderously, and had developed a new mannerism, a rapid blinking of the eyes, whether the sun was bright or the sky overcast, the only indication that his self control was that and not ease.

Guerrero did not like to see him like that. No man should have had to be seen like that, and what made it the more heart-rending, was that there was nothing, except that nictitating eyelid, to see. Outwardly life went on as it always had.

But though life is best maintained by keeping up appearances, it can seldom be saved by the same means.

Everyone in that city came and went as they always had, but they came and went now a little nervously. It was a long time since they had had any enemy, and though that enemy was far away and unseen, they could remember the boat in the bay last year, the assault on the town, and under the surface things were not the same.

There was a diminution of trade. At first only the merchants noticed it, for at first it was very slight, and of course made-up luxury goods had stopped coming through from Mexico years before. Only the upper classes missed them, so though a few grumbled, none was alarmed. Then the supply of incense balls began to decrease, and the priests had to have incense. It came from the hill country of Honduras, where there were no Spaniards. The Spaniards therefore must be somewhere in between, though almost no-one knew exactly where.

They were in the state of Chuauca, marching towards Mani. There had been no resistance in Chuauca. Davila's strategy was hard to understand, from this distance, but his reception in Mani might not be so peaceful. Mani was ruled by the Xiu. Guerrero consulted with Nachancan, who had no direct heirs, and sent off envoys laden with gifts and promises.

He had never met the Xiu, but he knew their history. They

were an ancient and rancorous people, cold, harsh, and hard, whose sole desire was to burst back into their former glories, they did not care at what cost, or to whom.

To them their past and their present were the same thing, and of that past there had been a good deal, so they thought they loomed larger than they did.

They called themselves Toltecs from Tula, that real capital which had been legendary for hundreds of years. They had ruled all northern Yucatan, until taken prisoners by their own mercenaries. That yoke they had thrown off sixty years ago, but they had yet to slip their own back on. Like all dynasties who had once ruled, they wanted the old order back again, and would recognize no other.

It might be well to feed that vanity. Guerrero offered them inheritance of the province of Chetumal if they would destroy the Spanish. It was a secret offer, but Nachancan endorsed it. It demeaned him, but what else was there to do?

There was no direct answer. Instead word came that Davila and his fifty soldiers and thirteen horsemen had been greeted royally in Mani. There had not been enough that the Lords of Xiu could do for them. They regretted only that they had no gold. Gold was farther off, in Chetumal, or better yet, in Sotuta. Jade was a material they greatly preferred themselves, but if gold was what the invaders wanted, why it should not be at Sotuta?

Guerrero had miscalculated badly. He had forgotten the first thing those out of power desire is revenge. Sotuta was governed by the last of their former captors: by means of an alliance the Lords of Xiu could at last destroy that powerful remnant. They could then deal with their Spanish mercenaries, and have Chetumal as well.

It was the story at Champoton all over again.

Unfortunately the Spanish did not regard themselves as mercenaries. The problem of Sotuta Davila turned over to Montejo, which pleased the Lords of Xiu well enough, for Montejo had the superior force.

Then, taking his mining expert with him, and with maps

of the country provided by the Xiu, he entered Cochuah, a barren, thorn-covered, rocky state, towards Chetumal itself. Patently it was not gold-producing country, but Davila was following orders. He was to found a town at Chetumal. He knew what his men wanted, and they had to be driven on. The constant promise of gold farther ahead could be used as a carrot to a donkey.

Reaching easier country, he turned sharply south, and in a week, crossed the frontier into Uaymil-Chetumal. His goal was Lake Bacalar, forty kilometres from Chetumal itself, over country almost impassable by land.

When he heard that, Guerrero cursed. He understood what was happening well enough. Chetumal was a large confederated state, but no Maya confederated for anything but their own immediate advantage. They had no long-range plan for what to do next, for they needed none. Every twenty years the katun books were opened and told them what to do. They had only to comply with events, and improvise on those days which were governed by none. Nachancan was sixty-seven and had no heirs. His loyal vassals could well afford to remain loyal a little longer, but now that the invaders were here not even that might be necessary.

Politics are based upon fear, and now they had something new to be afraid of. No man could hold them.

The first to defect were the Lords of Chable, a prosperous town on the far border of Uaymil. They came to Davila of themselves, and Davila sent them to demand the surrender of Chetumal. Already, Guerrero could see, the Spanish had taught them something new. They had learned how to sidle. It was not a posture that sat well upon their panoply of plumes and servitors. Their dignity was cowed, and that made them respectful but venomous, for since they no longer had to look out for themselves, they took on a few of the pretensions of their new conquerors.

Guerrero looked them over, standing beside Nachancan, who sat cross-legged on his stone divan, giving them audience. The answer had already been prepared. The reception was only a formality. But it was also the last audience Nachancan was ever to give.

If he sensed that, he did not show it. His dignity was authentic. Nothing would ever make him show anything. It was perhaps only the impudence of these little lords, that made his hands tremble, and his blinking was the more startling, for his effort to control it.

He told them that Chetumal and its people preferred war to peace with such an invader, and that the only tribute they would make to such a man was lances instead of fowls, and arrows instead of maize.

It at least made the Lords of Chable look like fools, for in their first panic they had given the Spanish everything. They went back through the watchful city, still sidling, as though they could feel an arrow in their backs.

They saw a town prepared for war. Guerrero could only hope that would make them doubtful of their new masters. And yet perhaps not. Davila was clever. Perhaps he had not yet shown them what it felt like to go in chains.

Meanwhile, there was no land route from Bacalar to the coast. The only way was by canoe, down the rivers which emptied the lake into the sea. Destroy the canoes, and the Spaniards could be picked off one by one, in the swamps. Guerrero prepared to set out with a small party and do so. He had no illusions any more about the loyalty of Bacalar.

He was down at the waterfront, preparing to enter his boats with a picked force standing by, by the hiss and flare of torches, when news came that he was too late. The Spanish had been sighted paddling down Lake Bacalar towards its outlets, with an immense flotilla of canoes and Indian auxiliaries, including the Lords of Maçanahau and Ypumpeten. The watercourse they had chosen would bring them to a village three leagues south of Chetumal by morning.

Guerrero no longer trusted the army. Only one force could hold his men. He had Nachancan send for the high priest.

XXII

How does one behave on a last day? Ultimate situations by their nature have no precedents. We do not know quite what to do, we cannot believe it, so we do what we would have done anyhow, but a little differently, and perhaps with a certain apologetic incoherence of pauses, which we do our best, out of consideration for each other, to cover up.

One thing they did not want to do was go to bed. They did not want to face the dark just yet. Every night they expected it to be final, with less excuse than they had now. If a man must die, he wants at least to do it by day.

Certainly they expected to die. They had been a small ruling class for so long, that they did not even think of the people. They had a two-class society. It had a body and a head. And what body can do anything unless the head tells it to? But for the first time they felt a little cold. For the first time, like a man who has had a stroke, they learned that the body does not always obey us. It is the part of us that dies first.

There was no telling what was going on out there, in five times a thousand houses. There was only the terrible, dangerous, restless dark, and the flames from the temples and the watch-fires, burning like the eyes of a man who has lost everything but his intelligence and the knowledge of what he has lost.

They sat in the chief room of Nachancan's palace, which was bright with braziers and lamps. They had very little to say, and did not try to say it. Nachancan had done something exceptional. He had had his chief concubine come from the women's wing. He had preferred her for years, and he preferred her now. His daughter, who was Guerrero's wife, and the high priest, who was his brother, had also been there. They ate a little. They listened to music, or the low sound of the wicks drinking up the oil, the crackle of the rushlights. The rushlights were made of beeswax. They did not smoke.

From time to time conches, somewhere out there in the darkness, sounded the religious watches of the night.

Guerrero watched. The hole in his nose itched, and he tugged at it from time to time. There was so much they did not want to say, but his wife, he knew, was worried about their elder son, who was off with a military outpost to the south. That was where the Spanish would come from, the south. He was worried about Hun Imix himself.

His younger son was safe at the main temple. It was curious how priesthoods everywhere do somehow manage to be safe. Apart from wars he had no doubts. Except for his sons, his whole world sat waiting in this room, and at least they were waiting together. It did occur to him, vaguely, that it was so easy to die for this world, or even with it, when it had been so hard to live in that other that was now floating down the river to destroy them.

He did not intend to be destroyed without a fight. And he did not intend that Nachancan or Ix Chan should be destroyed either. But that could wait until morning. It was enough to be together now. As for his sons, there was nothing he could do.

From time to time news of Davila's progress came through. The warriors had been alerted, but needed sleep. There would be time to muster them in the morning.

At a little after midnight Nachancan decided to go to the temple. Guerrero did not wish him to go alone, and almost nobody could be trusted. He sent his wife off to her own rooms, under a close guard. He would join her later.

Nachancan was carried through the streets in a closed litter, bundled against the cold in two or three mantles. Guerrero walked beside him. Everywhere he could catch sight of burning lamps. There could be few, then, who felt confident in that dark.

As happened once or twice a month, there was a heavy fog off the sea, very low, that hung in patches over the streets and the fields. It was bathed in moonlight, and the stars were extremely bright. You could see the constellations marching slowly about up there, like the gods they were.

They reached the main temple, and the litter was deposited on the paving before the stairs. The fog was thick, but above their heads had a ruddy glow. There was no one to receive them. The priests were too busy up there. They were trying to evoke an augery, favourable, or even unfavourable, out of desperation, when they found none, just to know that the gods were still there.

For no one can stand the silences of God. It is like the death of a loved one one later came to hate. The hate vanishes and all the love pours back. Even the sceptic believes then, out of contrition, for no one wants to be a sceptic, really, and even the misanthrope cannot survive without at least one, or even the idea or memory of, a friend. There must be someone there.

Out of all those gods, did not even one exist, except perhaps that ultimate pair who were never prayed to, because they took no interest in human affairs?

They believed in the stars, and not in the world around them. The world around them was full of demons, but the stars were up there, subdividing time. Could not one star fall, like a tear, as an omen, to save them? Or were they really to be shuffled off down the prison corridors of merely human history before their time, an hour too soon, cut off thereby, from hope even of a last-minute reprieve?

It made them distrust the stars, which had told them so often their world had yet a hundred and sixty-six years to run. They worked rapidly up there, like surgeons when something has gone wrong. It could not be a mistake in belief. Not even the sceptics felt so. It must be some mistake in astronomy, made how many katuns ago; they must find out when.

Nachancan threw off his mantles and began to climb, with Guerrero beside him. The stairs of Maya temples have very steep risers and very narrow treads, so that one must go up tiptoe. This straightens the spine and improves the dignity, and besides, Nachancan was a very straight old man. They began to mount through the fog.

Still, one has thoughts as one mounts towards the gods.

Their plumes rose above the mist, and then their heads and bodies. The stairs were clearly defined above them. Every time the priests cast copal in the incense burners, the flames shot a little higher, dancing against the fog and the sky, and casting complicated shadows. They rose from the other temple, too.

Guerrero and Nachancan reached the platform. The high priest came forward and greeted both of them.

Nachancan had not really come to pray, but to confer. The place was holy, and he wanted to see it last, that was all. As for prayer, he knew better, for of course the gods do not really intervene. It is only that afterwards we like to persuade ourselves that at least they looked on. Somewhere under the foundations of these cyclically rebuilt temples some of his ancestors were buried. He had come out of a profound ancestral piety, nothing more. He wanted to say good-bye. Perhaps he had also wanted to get above things, and this temple was in the city the highest place. He moved into the shrine.

Guerrero did not follow, but remained there, in the cold air, looking out over the fog, the forest, the white city, and the bay, rather surprised that it was all still intact. It was a little like looking at what he believed in.

After a while he moved round to the open side of the shrine. In the flickering light he could see the statues of the gods, rippling in and out of the shadows. They were to him very familiar gods, and not nearly so terrible as men. Priests moved in the shadows.

He had thought that there were two statues in there, not three. Then the third took on colour, and became Nachancan. It was a natural mistake, but startled him. Nachancan's face had the same grave stone look, for after all, what we worship is something in ourselves, that is better than we are, which explained both the resemblance and why he, a Spaniard, had changed his allegiance years ago.

He had always accepted these people, but now, seeing

Nachancan, and the idol behind him of Ah Puch, festooned with bells, he believed in them as well, realizing that always, even in the beginning, instinctively, as he always did, he had. The Maya were sensible. The gods are beings whom we bribe in order to obtain the good things of this world, as well as certain information. Ah Puch was the god of death, and it had taken a little while to find the justification of his own death, that was all.

Something made the bells on the statue rattle. They were gold. So the Spanish would steal them, if they won. But the theft would not alter in any way the nature of the god of death.

Rattling that way, they made an almost welcome sound. He and Nachancan returned to the palace, perhaps to sleep.

Guerrero spent the night with his wife. It occurred to him as it often did these days, unexpectedly, and with a sense of helpless wonder, that she was still beautiful. She was also like her father. She said nothing, but felt much.

He wanted her very much, she wanted him, and even though cool by nature, her body was warm. They fell asleep in each other's arms.

When he woke she was still sleeping, a little frown on her face, even though she was smiling. The room was cold. He went into the next one.

The servants had not yet dared to run away. His little girl was sitting up on her mat, drinking cocoa. She held the bowl in both hands, like a squirrel with a nut, but the look on her face was so rapt that it made Guerrero shiver.

There was always a little doubt, even though he had always known which side he was on and why. But looking at his daughter made him angry. She was so beautiful. She had such tiny hands.

He went to Nachancan and the council of nobles. There were not so many of them now. There remained only those of Chetumal, and they were all interrelated. They were not cowards, but strategy meant nothing to them. It was their own family, now, they meant to save. All through those incessant wars, it was what they always fought for, and so often why they lost, for their soldiers were often nothing but family retainers. Nor would they go out to the barricades themselves. It was not their place. They would stream out in the forefront of their own warriors, in a battle. That was as things should be. But the manning of defences was something left to underlings.

Guerrero had to put heart in the men himself. And he could not be everywhere.

News came that Davila had reached the coast, unexpectedly by land, but that his horses and men had embarked in canoes almost at once. They were on their way. And as such news often does, it reached the city, as rumour, before it reached the council, as intelligence.

Guerrero's tactics were to hold the men on the barrier defences, withstand a siege, and pick off Davila with small foraging parties. That was one reason why his elder son was out somewhere to the south. The land between the south and Chetumal was mined and woven with ambuscades and hidden ditches.

Somehow Davila had found out. Men would have to be shifted to the shore front. Guerrero went to do so.

It was too late.

The flotilla had already been sighted, moving up the bay. In those circumstances the townspeople did what they always did. It was not that they lost their heads, but that they blindly followed precedent. When an army is on the way, you evacuate the town.

The flotilla was now so near, that they could hear the roll of Indian drums across the water. They left at once, taking the north road, which mercifully ran between fields high with maize.

Guerrero could not hold them, for they moved without confusion, and he did not even know what had set them on the move, or what had happened. Before him was the temple. He clambered as swiftly as he could up the stairs.

It was deserted, but from the top he could see everything.

On the land side the crowds had moved out the gates, destroying his barricades. They were streaming rapidly out along the sacbes, towards the fields and forests beyond. They had even taken part of the army with them. His men he could pick out by their nodding plumes.

In the other direction the sun sparkled off the bay. There was no fog now. He could see everything. Davila's flotilla was perhaps a quarter of a mile off, paddling swiftly towards the town. The sun caught the glitter of lances, and glinted off two cannon. The horses, swathed in cotton armour, stood neighing in sets of lashed canoes, and behind the party, came the more numerous canoes of a large Indian host.

Beside him, a priest stood there, holding in his hands two incense balls, with a look on his face Guerrero would never be able to forget. It was his son.

There was no one else there.

Grabbing him by the wrist, Guerrero plunged down the stairs and back to the palace. He found the slaves had already shouldered Nachancan's litter, but the old man had held them, waiting for him. Except for Ix Chan, his concubine, and other members of the family, the nobles had all gone. Even Guerrero's younger son had slipped away.

Nachancan did not even bother to turn around, as they left the city. Neither did Guerrero. It was his duty now to look after the old man, who was obviously bewildered, and to clear a way, for the road was clogged.

The city was still there, yet it might almost have vanished, this rout had been so swift. If they were to gain safety, it must be even more swift.

Fortunately, at the prospect of loot, Davila's Indian allies had broken away, and blocked him in their eagerness to enter the city. He could not follow.

Not everyone had been able to leave, after all. The sounds that floated across the air were not pleasant, and everybody knew what they meant.

Nachancan, at least, still commanded respect. After all, in his own person, he was the nation. The crowds let them through, and they entered the shelter of an untrimmed stretch of jungle.

Now they were safe, Guerrero knew what to do, and could turn his attention to other affairs. He had months ago selected and prepared their final redoubt.

XXIII

It was at Chequitaquil, a strongly defended, stone built village twelve miles north of Chetumal, so well hidden that for two months Davila did not even hear of it.

There they tried to put the world back together again.

It was like living in an armed camp. There were only three habitable buildings there, but at least they could depend upon the surrounding natives to feed them.

That gave Guerrero an idea. The corn was not yet ripe in the fields, and in any event, the Spanish would not know how to harvest it, or when, They scorned agriculture as beneath the dignity of an hidalgo. He had only to cut off supplies, to starve them out, and when they were weak, direct raids against them. He was not in a position to have his orders obeyed, but the priesthood was.

Nor did the priesthood raise any objections. From now on they were to be his most reliable allies. Now that he thought he had subdued the whole country, Davila was at last able to give the friars who travelled with him their head. It did not do to displease the Church, and besides, he was devout himself, once more urgent matters had been seen to. He too was eager to stamp out idolatory, once it was safe to do so.

For every idol that toppled, Guerrero had another Maya priest on his side. But he was not quite ready to move yet.

There was a certain irony in it. No Spaniard realized that in smashing the religion, they were also wrecking their own food supply. It was the priests who told these people when to plant and reap their crops.

For it isn't easy to put a world back together again from the top. For eminence is a shell. The longer one has it, the more hollow it becomes, for you soon find that the world has sucked all the substance out of it, the way one does with an egg. When it cracks there is nothing left inside to hold it up, except that tensile strength of the shell that is now diminished, because flawed.

To make matters worse, Nachancan had decided to fight in person. Perhaps he was tired of being bland. Perhaps he was angry with his treacherous princelings. Perhaps he preferred either to win or be lost, but not to lose and himself survive. He did not say. He still accepted Guerrero's advice, but in this matter he would have his own way.

There was nothing to do about it except caution prudence. If the old man were to be captured or killed, Guerrero would be without authority.

He kept his elder son by him always now. Him he knew he could trust. Of his other son, though he saw the high priest daily, he could learn nothing.

That worried him. His younger son had become a sanctimonious fool. There was no telling what he might do.

Meanwhile, though he sent out foraging parties. Davila seemed content to remain in Chetumal and convert it into the usual colonial slum. The only distinction of his newly founded Spanish town was that he called it Villa Real, instead of Salamanca.

Guerrero waited. He also prepared the army, for by now warriors were beginning to drift back to Chequitaquil, in search of Nachancan, and the old man had sent out messengers to rally them. They were well fed, and Davila, Guerrero knew from his own spies, was beginning to run short of supplies. His foraging parties wandered a little deeper into the woods, and seemed a little hungrier. They had the look of rationed troops.

He let his own men pick off a few, but mostly he was content to wait. He tried to hold the resistance back. But once again events got the upper hand of him. It was heartening, but inopportune.

On the other and west coast, Nachi Cocom, the Lord of

Sotuta, had learned what his enemies the Xiu had done. He moved at once. He in his turn was not so foolhardy as to move against the Xiu themselves, who were stronger than he. Instead he decided to destroy their allies, the Spanish. He was on the move through the forest to Campeche, with a force of 10,000 men.

No one had ever defeated Sotuta. Even the Xiu had not really been able to do that in the Great Revolt of 1461. Every lordling and city in Uaymil and Chetumal rose spontaneously at the news. They had got what they wanted, freedom from Nachancan. Now they wanted freedom from Davila, too.

All food supplies to Davila ceased.

It was both too late and too soon. Unknown to Guerrero or Nachancan, one of Davila's foraging parties had picked up hostages, and learned at last of Chequitaquil. He had moved at once, and unlike the Indians, he had no objection to the night. It was, as far as he was concerned, the best time for a surprise attack.

Guerrero had thought him at Maçanahau, whose lords had been the first to rise against Chetumal. He knew Davila was worried, for he had himself ordered to be killed messengers Davila had sent across the peninsula to Montejo. They had been struck down at a town called Hoya, while they were eating among people they still thought to be their allies. So savage had that sudden attack been, that the horses had been slaughtered too.

It filled them all with hope, to know just how desperate Davila must be, and how securely now he was cut off. Guerrero went to bed well pleased.

He did not know what waked him. At such moments he knew there was always a reason. He heard unfamiliar sounds, reached for his studded club, and went outdoors. Then, with a shout, the attack began.

The camp was on the alert, but even so, had no warning. At first he did not understand it. Then he heard the explosion of a gun.

Somebody shot a flaming arrow. It caught on a thatch roof, and the flames took hold and shot up in a vertical wave, casting a lurid glow everywhere.

Guerrero saw Nachancan, in full battle regalia, yelling his head off, and striking against some crouching figure that was not even a Spaniard, but an Indian mercenary, who was trying to escape.

The Spanish would not try to escape. He sent three men over to relieve Nachancan, told them where to come, and got his wife and daughter out of there. There was nothing else for him to do. The treasure of the temples and palace had to be abandoned. So did the men. His whole policy now depended upon Nachancan remaining alive.

With a few men, he fled for the wall of the jungle, with Ix Chan and his elder son beside him. Then he had to swerve. Some bearded, cuirassed, tattered Spaniard reared up in the darkness beside him.

His son cut the man's leg tendons with one swipe of an obsidian trimmed club. They ran on. All the jungle began to scream around them, wakened by the shouting and the glare. They dared neither to stop nor to look back.

The rendezvous was at a deserted temple, half overgrown, at some distance in the jungle. He knew that at least for the time being they would be safe there.

The hours went by, and still there was no news of Nachancan.

At last he was brought in, in an improvised litter, severely wounded. In that condition he could not be removed until he had had care. They had to stay where they were.

The temple, which dated back to the days, eight hundred years before, when the Itza had first colonized this country, was sacred to the rain god, Tlaloc, and stood beside a cenote, or natural well opening through the limestone into the water table below. The cenote had been deserted for a long time, and its walls were thick with ferns. These they gathered and stuffed into Nachancan's wounds.

The old man bore it without complaint. He even seemed

to rally. He seemed more determined to fight back than ever. And so did his warriors. During the next two or three days they began to gather there.

His body would not obey him, but he persisted anyway. His eyes had the bright look of doomed intelligence. He must know very well what was happening to him, but he had faced nothing before. It did not bother him. He kept his daughter by him, saw his great-nephew, whom he nominated his successor, with Guerrero to advise him, extorted compliance from his nobles, and asked for a cup of cocoa. They were still living in an improvised bivouac. By the time the cocoa was ready, he had died.

Guerrero stood there, with the hot cup the servant had given him in his hand, and stared at his wife. He had never before seen her weep.

He had never before wept himself.

These people had a protocol for grief and he did not.

He could not stay there. He had loved the old man too much. He wanted to be alone. He set down the cup and walked out into the jungle.

When he had stayed there long enough, he came back. He could hear the wailing from far away. When someone died, they always wailed, for to them death was the inexplicable event, which reminded them, who behaved always as immortals, that they were only mortal animals. It did worse than to cut them down to size. It cut them to a shape that did not suit them.

Yet perhaps all that noise was just as well. The chief thing about such honours is that they give the survivors something to do until life goes on again.

Next day they buried him under the temple floor. It was then Guerrero learned that the Sotuta had not won at Campeche. They had attacked on St. Bernebe's Day, hoping to pull Montejo down and sacrifice him. The Lord of Sotuta was proud. He would learn no new way of fighting. And so he had lost.

The people of the west coast knew their only future lay in

alliance with either the Xiu or Sotuta. The Xiu had been proven the stronger. They therefore joined the allies of the Xiu. For the moment Montejo was in a better position than ever.

Guerrero did not know what to do. He knew the nobles would not obey Nachancan's nephew unless they had to, and he had no way of enforcing either his or Nachancan's will upon them.

To his surprise, though they would not accept him or his son, they did want his advice. The defeat of Sotuta had hardened instead of panicking them. Such things sometimes do happen so. The whole province was ready to revolt, and they wanted him to direct the campaign.

There were only one or two who doubted his loyalty, for to those one or two, Nachancan was dead, and loyal only to particular men, they could not believe that anyone could be loyal merely to a principle.

Perhaps it was not a principle. But on the other hand loyalty need not stop with death.

Davila had moved up country, to Bacalar, in an effort to put down the revolt. He did not yet realize that for once it was too widespread for him. He was on his way to Hoya.

That soldier Guerrero's son had cut down, though he might never walk again, had at least told Davila what he had seen, and messengers said that the Captain was trying to find out if Guerrero was still alive.

Guerrero gave them orders to say that he was dead. It was almost true. Only he and Nachancan any longer remembered what he had once been, and that past had died with the old man. From now on he would never remember it again.

He sent his wife and daughter to a place of safety, a fishing village half hidden away on the relatively uninhabited coast, between Chetumal and Tulma. Then he set off across country, with his son, towards Hoya. It was right to say he was dead. To the Spanish, he was. They had destroyed a world, and he would serve anyone against them. About that, he had no doubts. It did not even matter whether or not the Maya won, so only the Spanish might suffer.

XXIV

Hoya was a small town, on the borders of Cochuah which before the murder of the messengers had been of importance to no one. It seems the fate of such anonymous places always to be the scene of some famous but futile last stand.

A few of them have even been the scene of great victories, as for example, Issus. As soon as he had arrived, Guerrero or rather Ah Ceh as he would always be now, immediately began to plan both the campaign and his defences, but in a day or two learned that the reason for that surprise and disastrous raid upon Chequitaquil was that Davila had marched swiftly on Hoya earlier, from Bacalar, only to be dismayed at signs of rebellion on the way, and to turn back to Villa Real de Chetumal.

In order to lure him into ambush it would therefore be necessary to trick him, and that soon, if the concentrations of troops round Hoya were to be held together.

Fortunately Davila tricked himself. He was worried now, and also very angry. He sent out more messengers, in an effort to reach Montejo, and these also Guerrero intercepted and killed, so that Davila found his position untenable, and decided upon a punitive expedition against Hoya. That would sound well, and whether he could punish Hoya or not, he did not intend to stay there, but to push on rapidly to the west coast and Montejo, before the Indians realized what he was doing and could rally in enough numbers to stop him.

He did not tell even his men what he planned to do, for it would be necessary to leave some of them at Villa Real, to keep up the fiction that he was not leaving for good. If he told them, they would not stay, and unless he got through to Montejo, they might all be slaughtered. As it was, those left behind stood a chance of being picked up by boat later.

He had an easy enough conscience about that.

Having decided what he was going to do, he next sent out

messengers to all the caciques of the supposedly conquered provinces. They were to assemble at Villa Real de Chetumal. Surprisingly enough they complied, first because their priests and advisers told them to, and second because the Spanish, whatever their present condition, had enormous prestige. One could never tell what they might be able to do next.

Davila gave them an harangue. It did not occur to him as ridiculous that they should meekly listen to him in the ruins of their own capital, a force of noblemen who by themselves alone outnumbered his own troops two to one, and who had never even entered such hovels as those which the Spaniards had built to live in, against the white plaster of buildings more complex to construct than they could have understood. It did not impress the noblemen as being ridiculous either, but they were not so docile as before.

Davila sensed that. As it happened, he did not even know that Nachancan, his chief opponent, was dead, but with Guerrero out of the way he felt much better. There was only one way to treat these men, and that was with a bluster of force.

The bright sunlight made him squint, but he had washed and trimmed his beard.

He told them briskly that he intended to avenge the murder of his messengers by the destruction of the Hoya. Those chiefs who had sworn fealty to the Spanish could best prove their loyalty by falling in behind. Apparently he had not even heard of the destruction of his latest attempt to get through to Montejo.

It was exactly what the nobles wanted to hear, and they had their instructions. They fell in behind in such numbers that Davila became suspicious, and whittled their number down to six hundred, and those mostly chieftains and their retainers. His official excuse was that there would not be enough water or food along the way to keep such an army going. That sounded sensible enough. In actuality he feared a trap.

It was one.

As soon as he received word, Guerrero began to make his final plans. He would need a great many men. And here again the priests helped him. They were eager to help now, for they too had received news. They always received such news first, for unlike the caciques, who were always at each other's throats, they maintained a sodality which seldom if ever failed or gave way.

Far to the north, across the border from Mani, lay Chichen Itza, one of their oldest and most sacred cities. It had been abandoned several times, in response to the prophesies and katun cycles, the last time in 1185, at the third return of the fatal Katun 8 Ahau. But it was still holy. It was still kept up. It was the city of the Sacred Well, and the city of ultimate prophecy, the home of Kukulcan, the saviour, and of the magic books of Chilam Balam, by which they foretold everything.

It was used only once a year, but they could not do without it. Once the Spanish had marched through it, to find even the ruins of this world a little too big for them. Now they were back, under the Montejo, the younger one, for like their own incomprehensible god, the Christians seemed to have three persons.

The books of Chilam Balam stated that eventually white-skinned saviour gods would appear from the sea, to impose a new age. But no one wants a saviour to appear, for his appearance would disturb the established order. What is wanted is only the hope that one will appear, which allows the established order to go on undisturbed and at the same time gives it something to wait for.

Besides, these men were not gods, and though the people might not recognize that at once, the priests had, instantly.

Now they had seized the city with two hundred men, defended it with cannon, and turned its most sacred shrines into a bivouac and a stable for their horses. They had subdivided the land among themselves, though it was not theirs, announced the levying of taxes, and informed the natives that though they were not slaves, still, each Spaniard owned 3,000 of them. Their new masters were the King of Spain and God.

The natives had heard of both and accepted neither. Even the local lord, Nacon Cupul, who had helped the Spanish for his own reasons, now for the same reasons helped them less. It was time to put the invaders in their place. They were ignorant and overweening. "We already have kings," Nacon Cupul told them, when the *requerimiento* was read to him, and with some sarcasm, "O noble lords," and named lords far nobler than they, the Kings of Sotuta, of the Pechs, the Chels. Had these invaders never heard of the Itza?

They had not, but Nacon Cupul could do nothing about it for the moment except wait, pretend obedience, and follow his own plans. The Xiu might follow the invader, for their own advantage, but few men would follow the Xiu, given the chance to do otherwise. The Spanish had one weakness. In their arrogance they took the word for the deed. They thought men loyal because they said they were. There might be some future advantage in that.

But the priests knew the Spanish could not be put in their place because, quite clearly, they had none. They could only be destroyed. And a priest can go anywhere. Guerrero soon found that he had a large force gathering, and many of the detachments appeared led by priests who knew how, and were armed, to fight. For the priests were the brains of the country. They married, they had children, they were interrelated with everybody of secular importance, and though they knew how to worship, they also knew when to kill.

There are advantages, it seems, to a theocracy, if everyone in it is a theocrat. Of his younger son he had heard nothing. He might be dead, but if he was, it was because, like all novices, he had taken the forms for the fact. His superiors clearly intended to keep instead the fact of the forms.

For the moment they allowed Davila to advance.

He did so, with amazing foolishness, but their plans almost went wrong at Chable. The caciques at Chable could not hide their contempt, even though their part in the plot was to reassure Davila of their loyalty. Davila seemed to hesitate. It was an anxious moment. But then, as they had hoped he would, he came on, and crossed the border into Cochuah. His native auxiliaries and their lords seemed restive, but he could not very well put them in chains. For one thing he did not have enough chains. For another, it would slow his march.

The first resistance to the Spanish was organized at Cochuah, behind a series of woven and disguised screens, called albarrada, which lined the road and were thick with warriors. Guerrero did not seriously expect to stop the Spanish there, but he did hope to disrupt them, and to give the Maya with them a chance to escape.

The albarrada was discovered by the advance party, and Davila soon came up to inspect for himself. He then tried to lead his men around the barrier, in order to attack it from the rear.

It was Guerrero's first sight of this particular leader of the enemy. He stared out pitilessly, and found that he felt nothing at all. He had seen Spaniards before. Clearly Davila was nervous. It would be a pleasure to tease such a man until he fell apart. It was a thought his visible arrogance evoked and deserved.

He gave orders for the Maya to put up a defence, but fall rapidly back. At the first volley of arrows, the Maya with the Spanish deserted into the forest, with a rustle of foliage and feathers, and the little party was left alone out there, confused by the absence of a path. The Spanish had crossbows. That meant some of his own troops were killed. But three of the Spaniards were wounded.

Guerrilla warfare was something at which Guerrero was astute. He told his men to fall back, and had already had the *pueblo* behind the albarrada gutted and its wells filled with earth and stones. It would make a good place for Davila to spend the night and think things over. The town itself, once the Spanish were in its ruins, he surrounded with warriors instructed to make their presence known, but not to attack.

Next morning, when Davila marched forward, two wounded men were strapped to the horses. That meant that the third had died in the night. It was at least a beginning.

The second albarrada was a well-concealed ambush, in the form of a hidden maze, whose perfectly camouflaged walls allowed the maximum of cross-fire. Davila could be seen advancing to the attack, towards that outer and poorly hidden stockade which was to act as a lure.

He was seen talking to the cacique of Uaymil, who had deserted him the day before, but had been hauled back by the two Spanish whom he had been unfortunate enough to stumble across in his flight.

He knew about the ambush of course, wanted to save his life, and was now obviously doing it. Guerrero had hoped the man dead, and if they won, he would be, but for the time being Davila deflected his troops, and circled around the maze, making camp in the town on the other side.

It was a setback, but Guerrero was not unduly worried. There are always traitors, and he had allowed for that. He called off his men and fell back on his third plan, which was to force the Spanish to attack. Indeed they would have no choice but to do so, for they had had no supplies for days, and must be hungry. He had also had his spies tell Davila that the Maya had risen to arms everywhere behind them. Therefore they would have to come on.

This they were forced to do, the next day, before the strong palisades and defences he had erected in front of Hoya.

Guerrero watched. The Spaniards came on again and again, Davila well in front. But by afternoon eleven of them had been wounded, and the others were worn out. To their evident humiliation they were forced to turn back. They now had only eleven able men and three horses. Guerrero ordered his men to shoot one of the horses, and it fell belly up, pawing the air and screaming.

He would have sent the Maya out to destroy them, but he did not dare. Maya wars consisted of one battle and then flight or loot. It was not that they were cowards, but that that was their method of fighting. If the Spaniards rallied, anything might happen.

Instead he planned to pick off the invaders slowly, as they had to retreat. But the Maya had other plans. They streamed out over the barricades and across the field, in the direction the Spaniards had taken, the priests well out in front, with a great roaring and yelling.

Guerrero shrugged. Perhaps it was better that way.

Unfortunately Davila had managed to make his retreat. Knowing he had no chance of getting through, he had decided to fall back on Villa Real, by secret or little known paths, and as a reward to the cacique who had told him of the hidden maze, threatened him with torture unless he showed him where such paths were.

The cacique showed him. To make sure of that, Davila kept him bound, guessing correctly he was not the man to lose his own life, by leading them into another ambush. There was also a captive merchant in the company, and merchants do what is expedient. In the end it was the merchant who got them through.

Darkness was falling. It was not until next morning that search parties managed to find Davila.

The Spanish floundered in swamps, lost another horse, cut their way through the brush, and had to scramble over huge trees overturned by a hurricane. The jungle was dense. If that hampered the Spanish, it also prevented the Indians from reaching them. They could only follow, loudly challenging them to fight.

And then, when at last an advance party did get through to them, because the Spanish were drawn up in a clearing, the Indians seemed uncertain and would not fight. Davila had prepared an ambush of his own. Riders on the two remaining horses rushed out of cover and broke up the Indians. They were still afraid of horses.

Exasperated, Guerrero drew a bow, and shot the treacherous cacique. But that was all he could do. He was forced to flee himself. Getting well ahead, he drew up a blockade across the route he thought Davila would take. Davila avoided it, and marched on the Chable. There he had a stroke of luck. He came up from the wrong side, and stumbled on the hiding-place of the women and children. Once he had taken them hostage, there was nothing the inhabitants of Chable would do to halt him.

Davila was in no position to fight. All his men were wounded, and most of them hungry. Somehow he evaded any contact, and reached Lake Bacalar.

There he was safe, for he could seize canoes and float back to Villa Real de Chetumal. There was nothing Guerrero could do about it.

It turned out there was nothing he had to do.

As soon as he had returned, Davila held a solemn mass in the church he had improvised, but he had only to look round that room, to see what his position was. The country was in arms against him. It was only a matter of time before the Indians marched against Villa Real. And he could not defend it. Eleven of the fifty soldiers with whom he had left Campeche were dead. So were eight of the thirteen horses. There was no food, and none of them knew how to grow any. They made plantings inside the town, but nothing would grow fast enough, and very little would grow at all. Of the forty men left to him, eleven were maimed.

And something else had happened, so unbelievable that at first he did not even notice it. The Maya were not afraid of him any more. That he was, after all, Spanish, seemed to mean nothing to them.

It made him almost afraid himself.

For two months he temporized. He had no way of knowing what had happened to Montejo. He could not go inland, and he could not expect a ship, unless he sent for one. Again he tried to get a message through.

It would take a month to get any answer, given there were

anyone on the west coast left to answer. It was not a pleasant month.

Guerrero had arrived in the region. He kept well out of sight, advised, and watched. It was easy enough to intercept the messenger, who had never intended to go in the first place. He was the cacique of Tapaen, and though Davila held his son as hostage, he had no intention of complying. He merely went home. The month went on. Davila must be almost demented by now. He seized the cacique and his nobles and tortured all of them, stringing them up over a beam and burning their feet and armpits. Then it came out. No messenger had been sent. It was something it was a pleasure to confess to.

Davila tried again, and again had to wait a month.

Guerrero had all the canoes around Chetumal, whether belonging to Davila or the Indians, burnt. He was well content to wait.

Davila was starving. He had to send out a foraging party. The Indians managed to kill two of them, before Davila could make a covering sortie from Villa Real.

That reduced their numbers to thirty-eight, which was not many. Two of those developed scurvy, and the eleven wounded found their wounds were slow to heal.

There was no word from Montejo, perhaps there was no Montejo to send word, and the Indians were closing in. There was nothing else to do but flee. Davila sent out small parties to seize all the canoes they could find.

Guerrero was away in the interior, but the Indians now that they were almost free of their tormentors, began to smart, particularly the nobles, under the impertinence they had suffered. It was a word Europe had not yet invented, for it is a sin that occurs only when barbarians manage to make their way into an ancient and established society, so rich in accepted answers, that it does not take kindly to the questions of the misinformed. As yet Europe had no such society. But that they had been forced to grovel before such a pigmy conqueror, now that they had the strength to straighten up, filled the caciques with an almost Byzantine rage, now that there were few enough of the enemy for them to punish.

They planned to annihilate Villa Real with their full host. That night the signal fires leaped up on every available hillock or pile of masonry, along the shore and far inland.

Davila knew what that meant. It was too late now to get any message to Montejo. He had the scorched but living bodies of the hostage caciques to show for that, and nothing more. He and the able men worked frantically through the night. The last thing they did was to dismantle their crosses and the church.

They did not even dare to wait for dawn, but set out at once. Some of the canoes they lashed together, to carry the horses. They had with them some Indian prisoners to act as guides, and these they shackled to the gunwales, for the sake of security, and forced them to paddle. In all there were thirty-two canoes.

As they shoved off from the jetty, the Indians were already streaming into the town, to find nothing but the smarting and hobbled caciques, and ruins everywhere.

Then, with a whoop, the canoes were sighted. The Indians piled into their own boats, and paddled after them down the bay. But by some miracle, and Davila was in such extremity that he believed it to be one, the pursuers did not catch up, and when night fell, were forced to turn back.

The Maya were cheated of revenge, but otherwise not displeased. Their countryside was in ruins, but at least the Spanish were at last gone. And they knew that coast and that ocean. Davila would die out there, somewhere, under the sun, with cracked lips, at sea. It was appropriate that he should, for death there was a protracted agony.

They had got rid of one enemy. But this time they meant to fight to the end. It was time now to uproot the others from Chichen Itza. Uproot them they did.

XXV

Guerrero was everywhere. He wanted to exult. But something had gone wrong with him. Perhaps he was too old to feel the passions any more. He could not exult. He could only feel a determined relief.

Though he arrived there too late to see Montejo driven out, he had complete reports of what had happened, and hoped that it had been a shock to Montejo.

For in 1533 Montejo the Elder felt he had every reason to be pleased with himself. He was quite sure that he held all northern Yucatan. Ceh Pech, Ah Kin Chel, Ecab, Chikinchel, the Xiu at Mani, Sotuta, the Taxes, Chakan and Hocba-Homun had all sworn loyalty.

He could safely turn his attention now to securing that of his own men, by one means or another. There being no gold for them in Yucatan, the means were chiefly other. He divided out the Maya lands, saddled the clergy on everyone, and sent for imported Negroes, since the Indians could not be induced to work.

The Indians were impressed. They had never seen black men before. The Negroes were also impressed. When they could they deserted to the native side. It suited them better.

He pleased no one but the clergy, who baptized thousands, desecrated a few more temples every day, and made enemies everywhere. Yet they were not bad men. They were not even bigots. It was just that they were Christians, and so did not understand.

The natives were quite willing to be baptized. They were not willing to see their temples destroyed. All the good things of this world they bribed from the gods, and now these strangers were cutting them off from the source of supply. Food was becoming more sparse. Baptism was all very well, it pleased the foreigner and seemed harmless, but these new priests could not tell them when to plant their crops.

Their own priests moved quietly everywhere.

The Christians explained everything. The gods had gone into hiding. They were now something called saints.

Try as they could, the Maya had not yet been forced to

see the resemblance. Their own priests told them differently.

One by one, the provinces rose, and now it seemed only Mani was loyal. But Montejo did not trust the Xiu. Nobody in all their history ever had, and with excellent reason, for they were not to be trusted. Yet there was an irony in that. For in that peninsula only the Xiu saw the Spanish could not be beaten, even though they might seem beaten for a time. The Xiu remained loyal.

Montejo took heart. But as soon as he did so, he had another problem on his hands. Lerma, the merchant who financed his expeditions, wanted to be paid back, while there was still time. He would take his payment in slaves.

That was the one thing Montejo did not dare to give him. Not that he either disapproved or approved of slavery itself. Slavery was a fact, and one never questioned facts. But unfortunately Charles V had forbidden the taking of slaves. If Montejo gave Lerma the permission, or the assistance he wanted, or even permission to act for himself, that transgression would give his enemies in New Spain the fulcrum they needed to swing him out of office. Yucatan was a poor province, but they could not help but suspect he wanted it for some reason, and besides, he was a rich man. Once he was a private citizen back in Mexico, they could soon devise some means to strip him of his wealth.

On the other hand, he owed Lerma a great deal, and might need, moreover, his continued support. He had made him Treasurer of Yucatan, but since there was no Treasury but the funds he put into it, that could scarcely satisfy Lerma.

There was one way out. Charles V might be a Christian gentleman of the best intentions, but he was also a realist, and to a realist no law could be considered useful unless it had a loophole. It had a loophole. Though his subjects might not take slaves, they were permitted, if they had to, to resell such slaves as the Indians had taken for themselves, and in the confusion of a raid, who could tell which was which? Though Montejo could neither spare the men nor run the risk of participating in such raids himself, he could at least suggest, though of course not openly, that if Lerma wished to make such raids, he would not interfere.

It left him with a bad conscience, but Negroes were expensive and Indians cheap. No one need ever know.

Before he had time to feel relief, news came both that Chichen Itza was in revolt, and that his nephew was cut off there.

If his nephew were murdered, then what was the use of turning Yucatan into a private holding company? There would be nobody to leave it to.

Not, exactly, that Montejo the Younger was taken by surprise, but he, too, had felt secure, and the Maya had been subtle. In the beginning they had told him only that supplies were difficult to get. The region, they said, had been disturbed. There was nothing they could do.

Then they smiled. They smiled so very agreeably that it was eight weeks before he learned that anything was wrong.

But one cannot hide hatred for ever, even in the interests of revenge. Nacon Cupul, the chief of the Cupul, could take insolence only for so long. He was a man of immense dignity. Montejo, he could see for himself, was not. He was common, coarse, and arrogant. In Yucatan he could never have been anything but a merchant. Here he thought he could buy and sell anyone.

One evening it became too much. Montejo, who had given him one order too many, turned his back. His sword rested against the wall. Nacon grabbed it and swung.

There were soldiers in the room, as always, and a cutlass is a heavy instrument. Nacon felt nothing, but staggered. Then he had time to see his right arm on the floor, bleeding, while the sword rattled away, and put his hand to the stump of his shoulder, before the soldiers moved in to kill him. Montejo merely watched.

On hearing that, the Cupul throughout the province rose at once. They knew they could not defeat him in an open stand, but they did not have to. They let him put them down. Then they cut his communications, refused either labour or supplies, and began to starve him out.

Montejo could get nothing to eat. He had to send out foraging parties. The Indians picked them off, and the more heavily they went armed, the less food they could bring back. The Cupul poured in from everywhere. Guerrero had arrived at Saci, their religious centre, and the revolt had turned into a religious crusade. They moved their men closer and closer to Chichen Itza.

Montejo tried to parley. He said he was willing to compromise with the Cupul demands. That pleased the Cupul. It meant he must be growing weak in there, in the sacred city. But there could be no compromise. They moved closer still.

Then they attacked, swarming towards the city, and killing ten Spaniards before warning could be given. There was no room in the defences for Montejo's Indian slaves. They could only hide. The Cupul ferreted them out and killed all of them, while the Spaniards watched.

It was all they could do. They lived in a state of siege, while the Maya taunted them from barricades and breastworks thrown up around the city.

The siege lasted five months. There was no reason to attack. The Maya knew the Spanish were starving. There was no need to risk their own men. Hunger would win for them.

There was nothing for Montejo to do but counter-attack. This he did, even if it meant his men would die in front of him. He tried to choose a favourable time. But no time was favourable, for Guerrero was watching on the other side, and there were too many natives. Reinforcements had come from Sotuta and the other neighbouring provinces. The Spanish came out of their barricade into a sea of obsidian and blue-green battle plumes. No matter how many they cut down, there were always more arrows, more Indians, and more plumes. It was as futile as to try to fight the jungle itself, and this jungle had sharp edges.

They were forced to fall back as swiftly as they could into the Ball Court which was their stronghold. Out of two hundred, they had lost one hundred and fifty men. Nor did all of those fall on the field.

Chichen Itza is a vast city, but the Ball Court is in the great court which leads to the Well of Sacrifice. In front of it is a skull rack, on its right, the Castillo, a considerable pyramid, but two hundred metres in front of it, on the other side of the square, is the Temple of the Warriors.

Tonight, by torchlight, that majestic building rising out of its grove of columns was used for the next to last time. From the walls of the Ball Court, the Spanish could see the company gathered there, as it went into the peristyle hall and then emerged, above the roof line, struggling up the stairs. At the top the priests of Saei were waiting, and the sacrificial knife plunged.

This time no one had drugged the captive soldiers, and their curses and screams were quite audible, even over the rattles and drums. There was not one of the weakened men in the Ball Court who could not hear them. It was useless to fire at the temple. They would need their ammunition to save themselves.

The Maya were in no hurry. The torches burned all night.

Montejo stayed in the Ball Court all next day. The Maya made no attack. They usually rested after a battle. That night the Spanish fled. Ignominiously or not, they no longer cared. All they could do was save themselves, and few of them believed they had much chance of doing even that.

Before they left Montejo tied a starving dog to the clapper of a bell, and placed some food just beyond its reach. It was a primitive stratagem, but it worked. The Maya thought they were rallying to attack, made their own preparations, and that allowed the Spanish to get away.

Not too far away, however, for the trick was discovered at dawn, and the Indians were soon on their trail. But though Montejo had been foolhardy, he was not foolhardy now. It is possible to learn wisdom at the last moment. He got his men through, and into the province of the Chel. He had expected a fight there, but found the Chel friendly. He soon found out why.

His father was in the province, near the ruins of an abandoned city called T-ho, with a party of 120 men.

XXVI

When he heard that story Guerrero merely smiled. It is something to get one's own country back again, when even you believe that the invader means to keep it. But it is not very much, for somehow nothing is ever quite the way it was before. The goods, though returned, have been damaged in transit.

There was a sacrifice of thanksgiving, in the Temple of the Warriors. He attended.

Chichen Itza was the most sacred city of the New Empire. Only long-abandoned Copan and Tikal were revered so much. And yet Chichen had not been occupied for well over a hundred years.

The costumes were splendid, but the panoply was hushed. Even he, treated with deference, himself rustling as gorgeously feathered as any of them, could not help but notice that curious hush. Captives to be sacrificed, copal, the attendants, everything was of the best quality. But the music was swallowed up by those immense masonry courts, the voices of the chorus sounded far away and lost, the steps of the temple were cracked and overgrown with weeds, the gypsum of the walls was no longer clean, and at dusk the bats skewed shrieking through the air.

Why had they let it fall into ruin? It could not merely be because they were too old any longer to manage it. And there was something wistful and furtive about the movements of these processions, something like the manner of someone who comes back, while the new tenants are away, to see the old house, rented out because it was too large and expensive to keep up, and alien to its original owners now.

No one seemed comfortable at Chichen. It was too big.

There were not enough of them to fill it, perhaps not enough life left in them to fill it. They seemed uneasily aware of that.

He remembered that night so long ago, in Coba, in the storm, and the joy of his lonely walk through it, the next day, when he had discovered a world.

What had happened to Aguilar he wondered?

Aguilar, set up in Mexico, had lived long enough to denounce Cortés to the world, for not allowing the basement of his house to be turned into a church, and had then died of buboes and ulcers, an embarrassment to his Church and a disgrace to himself.

But the world was full of Aguilars.

In the shadow of that immense portico, in front of the Temple of the Warriors, he looked across, towards the Ball Court where Montejo the Young had been cooped up. And it occurred to him, during all his time in Yucatan, he had not seen that sacred game of ball.

It, too, was not played any more.

The shadows on the plaza became solid. It was night. A thousand little lamps sprang up, here and there, but they could not push back the darkness. As the moon rose, the buildings glittered, distinct, exact, the assured relics of the world that made them.

In the jungle something chattered, far away, but the jungle itself was getting closer. It was growing back over the town, as the grass grows back over all of us.

It was a great moment for the Maya. And yet they were so silent.

At the Well of Sacrifice there was a single, solitary splash, and then once more the algae healed over the surface of that cyclopean, deep-socketed, sacrificial eye, in a cataract coloured green.

He tried to shake the mood off. He felt cold.

Yet, the curators of a world too big for them or not, now they were roused, they meant to fight.

The whole of the provinces were now in revolt, even Sotuta, of whom even the Spanish were wary. Montejo, it was said, had paid a visit to Mani, and had had a conference with Ah Dzun Xiu, the twentieth generation of that wily clan that knew what power was and meant to keep it. Nobody trusted the Xiu. They were not trustworthy. But it is sometimes easier to outmanœuvre the ambitious and the worldly than the contented and simple, for they have their own *naïveté*.

The Xiu would remain loyal, for they were now so doubly hated for conspiring with the Spaniards against their countrymen, that if the Spaniards were to be defeated they could not long hope to survive among their own people, and they knew it. Montejo no doubt planned to fob them off with a title, which cost nothing, and sap their power at his leisure. But right now he needed them, even as they needed him.

Indeed, they kept their title. They even got their provincial Spanish palace, in the end. But it was nothing to what they had once held at Uxmal, and the forty-first generation of the Xiu now lives in a wattle hut with a dirt floor. Time has its own punishments. It was a title nobody honoured but themselves. They could as well have hanged themselves in an empty room, as have expected any advantage from it.

But for the moment they were treacherous. They had to be watched. There was no telling what they might do, if they saw any advantage to themselves from turning on their fellows.

They were watched. But mostly the Maya watched Montejo instead. He had refounded Ciudad Real, on the coast, at Dzilum. With what was left of Montejo the Younger's forces, he now had 220 experienced men.

He also had Davila.

When he learned that, Guerrero was furious. For it frightened the Maya. It did no good to explain that Davila was no Cortés, that he was a man, and therefore mortal, that he could be defeated.

They did not take that view of men. And perhaps, being a realist, neither did he, which made his heart sink and explained his rage.

For yes, it is true, some men seem invincible. Nothing can turn the tide against them, except death. They had thought him lost at sea. Now, after two years of privation in Honduras, he was back again. He had not died. Perhaps he did not know how to die, and that was what kept him going.

Such a man is protected by his reputation. It is his luck. Rather than attack him, others fall back. No doubt that explains why most assassinations fail. How could they succeed, for how can one desperate and shaky murderer succeed, when he aims at the legend and not at the man?

With everyone around him but Lerma, who would not answer letters sent to him, and was seizing his last illegal catch of slaves, on the east coast, to be sure of a profit no matter what happened, Montejo, the land he held growing smaller around him every day, counter-attacked.

For a while he was successful. He was not a soldier of genius, he was not a soldier at all, but Davila was, and he had the Xiu as allies, who knew the country well. He soon had Champoton, Campech, Ah Canul, Ceh Pech, Ah Kin-Chel, Chakan, Hocaba-Homan and Acalan as firmly as ever.

It was Davila. The natives fell back before Davila. For he had about him some of the madness of a god.

It was a deadlock. The Maya held the rest of the peninsula, but neither side could win.

Guerrero supervised the seige of Ciudad Real. For a month he had had news neither of his wife and daughter, nor of his younger son. The elder son he had with him.

It was the elder son who kept him going. For though they did not understand each other, they understood each other well enough, and he wanted a world left for his son to live in, the world that Yucatan had seemed to be at first, when he had first arrived. Let it be rotten at the pith, given only that it still be. Given that his son might be.

He wanted that. He only wanted that.

And yet he could not seem to win. The Maya did not have the will.

Then something happened inside Ciudad Real. So Yucatan was saved, as men often are, not by their own efforts, but by something altogether outside themselves.

It took Guerrero a month to find out what that something was. And when he did, what could he do but laugh?

For greed had brought the Spanish there, and greed took them away, just as it lost Montejo everything. In Peru Pizarro had at last discovered not only the Incas, but the Inca gold, in Peru the temples were walled and roofed with gold, the garden of the Temple of the Sun had golden flowers.

The soldiers were ready to war anywhere. Yucatan was not to their taste. It was not rich, and they were not farmers. Montejo had evacuated them from Ciudad Real to Salamanca de Campeche. They had only to look around them, to see themselves in the same sort of poverty-stricken Spanish town they had come to the New World to get away from. They cast about for some means to escape, and soon learned that Pedro de Alvarado, the conqueror of Guatemala, was getting together an expedition to wrest away from the Pizarros the wealth that they had ripped away from the Incas.

They knew who Alvarado was. He was not Montejo. He was a real man. He could steal, and be stolen from, and what he wanted he got.

Montejo ordered them to stay. It was a futile gesture. He could not hold them, for they, in their turn, were the only means he had of enforcing his orders against them. They began to flee the city, at first in secret, then more openly, some overland, others along the coast in canoes.

Guerrero let them go. Indeed he did everything he could to assist them. Then he moved in closer.

There were only a hundred men left.

Montejo was desperate. He was sixty-seven, and a bankrupt. He could not afford to flee. Yet what else could he do? Now that he must lose it, he turned against Yucatan.

"In these provinces there is not a single river, and the hills are dry and waterless," he wrote. The inhabitants were abandoned and treacherous, never killed a Christian except by foul means, and never made war except by artifice. Not once had he questioned them on any matter but that they had not answered, yes, with the purpose of causing him to leave them and go elsewhere. In them he had found no truth about anything.

It was true enough, but what else could he expect? But he did not look at the matter that way. Yucatan had been given to him by Charles V, who had of course never seen it. He had, and it was his.

Against all hope he held out, with Davila, his son, and that small group he had given land, and who therefore had some reason for staying, or would have had, had they been able to hold the land against the Indians who stubbornly persisted in believing that you cannot give away another man's goods.

But the soldiers refused to obey them.

There was nothing to do but leave. Montejo embarked first for Tabasco, and then for Mexico.

To the Maya it was wonderful. They had at last driven the invader out. Their country was their own again. For a little while they could relax, before going back to their familiar occupation of fighting against each other.

It was the turn of the Xiu now, to look behind them everywhere they walked. It was they, now, who would have to go in fear, and hide that fear as best they could.

Even to Guerrero it seemed a victory. Who cared how or from what causes it had been won?

How was he to know in what manner the poor of this world, in the name of everything from social reform to God, will do anything to grow rich at the expense of their betters who, it is true, were once as they?

Of the gods of history, only Shiva informs us that for one to come, another must go, endlessly. So those who have no knowledge of Him, persist to believe that they rise not in response to natural process, as another goes down, but for ever, out of such little idiotic principles as truth and right. Neither Guerrero nor any other man in that world had any concept of such a thing as endless change.

His heart-break was to be more personal than any abstract truth could ever be.

XXVII

But for the moment he felt only relief and joy. It was unbelievable. But he had won. The Maya had won. The world therefore would be livable for a little while again.

He watched them go. Unlike the Maya, he knew they would be back. Montejo might give up, but in time there would be no more gold to find. Then they would try again, for even land in a poor country is better to steal than nothing there for the taking at all. Nevertheless, to see them go at all was a pleasant thing.

Campeche had no harbour and no port, but it did have a narrow white beach, between the jungle and the low, incessant waves. It was a day like any other, clear, sunny, bright, with the echo of a breeze that stirred the dry scrub forest only tenderly. The world had a scrubbed new look, and the white sand stretched untrodden around the slight curve of the bay. There was no one about but the Spanish, huddled close together, for the Indians had not come to say good-bye. The Spanish had with them a few slaves, that was all.

It took them all morning to load themselves and their effects on to the waiting ship. Only one ship had been required. It was a little as though Pandora had repacked her chest, with the difference that now it was hope who was let out, and the demons who were put back in. The Maya were patient. They had waited a long time to see them go, and it was a pleasure to wait this little longer. Drawn up just inside the forest, they watched.

The last boat put off from the shore. It contained Davila, the three Montejo's, and an old priest who had been lifted through the surf with his arms around the neck of a barelegged sailor, his rosary clacking at his waist. The boat rowed out towards the ship, it grew smaller, and no one in it looked back. Perhaps they felt too bitter to look back. The cities of Yucatan still stood everywhere, a little battered, but still white and splendid. But all they had built, even the wretched churches, dismantled and already cracking, would wash away in the next rains.

The sails billowed out, and the ship disappeared. The sea was empty again. It was as though they had never been.

Though he knew it could not be this way for ever, Guerrero felt a thrill run up his legs, and a lump in his throat. It was good to have the world back again. Nachancan was dead, but there were many lords with whom, now, he could take service. He could even go back to Bacalar or Chetumal. The Maya would not rebuild them, for they did not rebuild cities which had been desecrated, but they would certainly build another nearby. With his elder son, he began the long journey, across the peninsula, in search of his wife and daughter.

There was no hurry. Everything would be good now.

And so he did not hurry.

The provinces were now free, but it took a while for that flood of bellicosity to sink back into peace. With so many men in arms, there were small raiding parties everywhere, to stock the altars. One cacique was not above taking advantage of another. But Guerrero and his son now had the friendship, for a little while, of everyone. It was three weeks before they approached that hidden village where his family was.

Guerrero felt shy. It was two years since he had seen his wife and daughter. His daughter of course would be unrecognizably older, but his wife as always would be the same. He was sure of that. But he was not the same. He was forty-seven and he had aged. He was still a handsome man, still muscular, he thought he could still please her. But simply because he wanted so much to please, he could not help but feel shy. It is the little boy locked up inside us who always wants to be welcomed home, and little boys in that state are almost always shy.

Sometimes we are allowed to visit the human race. One is

grateful for the favour, but doubly careful, therefore, not to overstay one's welcome. Hospitality is so agreeable a thing that one does not want to see either its reasons or its other face. He had seen both, but did not care. One is always a stranger, but he had been allowed to stay on for life. He had had to change worlds to find his own, but he had found his own, and now for a while he might keep it. That made him very happy.

He had sent ahead a messenger to warn Ix Chan, and had had no answer, but that did not worry him. The last two days he had moved so rapidly, that the messenger had probably not been able to find him, and besides, to see her again would be answer enough.

The country was sparsely populated. He made rapid progress, slept, and early the next morning found himself on a hill behind the little bay. It had rained in the night. All the colours were crisp, the green, the white, the blues and zircons of the sea. The village was hidden from him, but there was a single fishing canoe, far out, towards the passage to the Caribbean at the head of the bay. The tide was coming in. He could see the darker colour pushing there, against the lighter shades within. The bottom was sand, so that the surface sparkled with a mottled, jewelled light. It was very still that morning. Even the tall dry forest was still.

He started down the hillside trail. It was not until he reached the bottom, that both he and his son began to feel that something was wrong.

There was no one about. There were none of the early sounds of a village. There was something definitely wrong.

They came to the village itself. It was made of thatch, with one stone building. The building was where his wife would have been lodged. They went inside.

It was empty and deserted. The fire was out. They looked at each other and hastily ransacked the other huts. In those fires still burned, though very low on their coals. It was quite clear what had happened, if not why. Everyone had fled.

They went down to the beach. The sand was loose and

dry. They could see the canoe approaching, borne back to shore on the tide. They could not see who was in it. They began to shout.

The effortless waves lapped two inches high on the shingle. The canoe came closer. There was no one in it but an old woman.

They seized the prow of the canoe, and helped her out, while she shrank away from them. She had been headed for the open sea, though she had a catch beside her, but the tide had turned her back, for she was too weak to paddle against it. She was very frightened. Clearly she knew who they were.

At last they made her understand she would not be hurt. Then they got the story out of her.

It was Lerma, with his need for slaves. His ship had appeared outside the reefs a month ago, and the villagers had watched its long boat come in. The place was obscure. They had not known what was happening. They had had only a moment to flee.

The headman had not been able to flee. The Spaniards had caught him in his hut, into which he had moved, leaving the stone house to Guerrero's wife.

Every man has an enemy, no matter what he does, for some men are born for enmity. It is their only means of self-expression. The headman had been well paid. He had also had to move out of his house to make room for Ix Chan. He was a great man in his own village, but that did not please him. It only left him with a hatred of anyone bigger.

Besides, it was a matter of sell others, or be sold himself. He knew what slavery meant. Lerma's men had at last heard of that renegade and turncoat Christian, Guerrero. Besides, Guerrero was far away. A lot of things could happen, and the headman had his own villagers to think about. So he made a bargain. If they would go away, he would give them the renegade's wife and daughter. The Spaniards accepted.

The headman sighed with relief and moved back into his

own house. And now, said the old woman, as soon as the messenger came, they had all fled.

Guerrero let her go. She was not to blame. There was nothing to do. He could only look at the empty water. They had rowed Ix Chan out that way, with his daughter. They would not put her in the mines. There would be no point in that. But there are other things men can do to women. Where had they sold her, and to whom?

Had they branded her, as the Spanish branded a thousand Maya, while the friars stood by to see the thing was done, never mind about the violated flesh, or their feelings, their pride, their integrity, with a proper respect for their souls?

Or had she killed herself? A woman like that would not want to live in that condition. That was what she would have done, and to her daughter too.

He stood there, and stood there, his eyes bulging, staring out at the water, which he could not even see.

Her name had been Ix Chan. His daughter's name was Ix Ceh, the deer who looks over its shoulder. When you see such a deer, it is an omen of parting and loss. And the little deer of Yucatan, who step so fastidiously through the underbrush, have soft muzzles and warm liquid eyes. When they look at you they are so confiding, so skittish, and so serious.

He could not even cry.

FOUR

XXVIII

It turned him into a madman. But then madness in a man of that calibre is not true madness, that bad inheritance which makes the defective so easy to tip over. It was instead a defence mechanism, a piece of self-indulgence, to protect him from the truth that life is not kind, that we are other men's means, that we cannot act for ourselves, that we are the sum of what we do. For though there is no punishment in this world, and no original sin, still what happens to us is worse than any punishment, deserved or undeserved. If we are lucky, we are bored, and that is horrible, but if we are unlucky, we can no longer enjoy ourselves, and that is far worse.

And yet there is a pleasure in pain. When we have lost the vigour to get rid of ourselves, in some seminal gush, then pain gives us that escape back again, as an implosion, muffled, but still exquisite. One cannot admire him much during those years. And yet one can understand him. Madness gave him strength, and he needed strength, for he was forty-nine.

It also made him a little vain. He now believed that he had seen through everything, as though any man had that much ability. That meant that life was no longer possible. He accepted that, for it was easier to accept it than to reject it. But there remained the imitation of life, and that was far, far better than nothing. Indeed it was all that stood between you and nothing.

In short, like most of us, even in madness, he held on. It is an insight into our fundamental belief in the finality of death, that almost biochemical and involuntary urge to hang on, no matter what fairy tales we tell ourselves about the afterlife.

We are quite willing to believe there is one. There is a heaven and a hell, we say. We shall meet in the afterlife.

But we know perfectly well there is not one. Once the loved are gone, they are gone for good. So are the unloved. And so we hang on.

We remember. Even when it is impossible, that makes life possible.

He was alone now. His son had gone out to hunt down the headman. But there was no point in hunting down the headman, for he had lost everything. When you lose everything, you do not want revenge. You want the dark to hide in.

He could not even have that. He was a hero. He was the only one remaining of an extinct, but once secure state. He had become Chetumal. He had also been their saviour. Everywhere he went he saw a new faint hope, which he found pathetic, but still, it was there.

They did no building. They had lost both the impulse and the art. But they were busy putting life back where it had been before, dusting it off, seeing what it had really been worth, seeing it again as always, for the first time.

He found it heart-breaking, because he could see the underlying timidity in it. History had lost them their assurance.

Yet it did not break his heart. He understood it, he sympathized, but it no longer moved him, for there comes a time when we have felt too much and can feel no more. In self defence we outgrow the passions. We determine never to feel them again, and then discover, once that decision has been reached and then outgrown, that we are trapped by it. Simply because we did decide so, it is true, we cannot feel passion any more, even though once more we want to. For something has gone wrong. Our bottom has turned shallow. Our feelings no longer break over us in waves, they are instead a constant undertow, which, though nothing appears on the surface, waits there, to drag us down, should we ever break that surface again and try to breast our old emotions.

For two years he wandered, from cacique to cacique. He had no purpose, no plan, except to fight the Spaniards, but there were no Spaniards to fight. It was all too much for him. He did not understand what life had become for him. Now when he sat eating or talking, he could see himself eating or talking, with a sort of detached horror, that made him wonder who he or anybody was.

He drank too much. He tried not to see. But he could not help but see. Everywhere he went, he was accompanied by that imitation of himself, who ate, and drank, and talked, and advised, and seemed alive, but had nothing to do with himself, for he was not alive. Sometimes, these days, merely to go through the motions of living maddened him, as the irrational always maddens us. Simply to watch himself alive was like a taunt.

For the first year he had no news of his sons. He did not even ask.

And then one long afternoon, in what was perhaps 1535, he found himself on the bay, close to the ruins of Chetumal. The Maya had not rebuilt them. Only a few fishermen lived there now. He looked at them almost fearfully, and then went on.

But something turned him back.

Timidly, a little rheumatically, with a sense of wonder for what he had once been and was not now, he wandered into the city. That which the Spanish had not torn down still stood. That which they had built, was a heap of confused ruins.

Here was the palace of Nachancan. It was already going back to the jungle. A tree had rooted behind the dais on which his father-in-law had sat, and already the sapling had pried apart the stones.

In his own wing, the tattered curtains still hung at the doorways. He ripped them down. Ix Chan had lived here. His sons and his daughters had been born here. Their coming of age had been celebrated with music in this court. Now it was dusty. There was no music.

He fled outside.

It was the same everywhere in the city. And yet he could not leave.

He was determined to sleep in the room he had always slept in that night. After all, there are such things as ghosts. Perhaps the dead do come back.

But he could not bring himself to sleep. He wandered until dusk fell. It became dark. And if only he had seen somewhere in all those weed-choked streets, even a silly fat plump hairless dog, sitting in the midst of nothing, waiting, it would have helped a little, for they were all here, even though they were not here. It would take the presence of something living to abolish them.

Then he saw a light. It was pale, and indistinct, and wavering, but it was there, high up, on the platform of the main temple, facing the sea.

He stared at it for a long time. Then, hesitantly, he put his foot on the first riser and began to climb. They were cunning, those stairs. He had forgotten. They were designed to straighten the spine, and they did. For a moment he felt like a younger man, in an earlier year. He began to climb more rapidly. The bay sparkled in the moonlight as it always had, but in all that city he saw no other light.

He went on up, and reached the platform.

Though the temple had been too well built to tear down, the Spanish had smashed the idols and scrawled crosses on the walls. They had even rolled the sacrificial stone out of place, and it rested, teetering, on the edge of the platform. He had no idea why they had not cast it down.

It wobbled there, on the edge of space, in the balance, and yet somehow it did not pitch over. Out of sheer despair he kicked it, and listened while it plunged below. As soon as he had done so he felt sorry, and looked fearfully towards the shrine. One should never harm any of the good. It is too much like throwing a scene in a sick room. Though ill, they were still powerful, and no matter what happened to them, they would have heirs. They always have heirs.

He could hear the crackle of burning incense, and, as the wind shifted, caught its acrid smell. He went into the shrine and found it empty. A low lamp was burning, and the incense ball glowed in its brazier. Not all the statues had been smashed. The stone image of Ah Puch was still in place. The Spanish had stolen his golden bells, but had not been able to move him. Crouched, his figure rose up, palms outward, above the smashed fragments of terra cotta and stone, still the master of Mitnal the ninth and lowest underworld. He was the god not of ritual sacrifice, but of inevitable death. Who could be worshipping him now?

The coals in the brazier subsided and collapsed and then flared up again. They gave only a little warmth, but they had not been deserted long. Guerrero walked round the platform.

On its sea side, in shadow, huddled against the wall, he saw a tattered priest, dressed as though to perform a sacrifice, and painted. He would not answer but drew away. Guerrero hauled him to his feet, and saw that it was his own younger son. He let go of him at once.

But the boy did not seem to recognize him, and would not leave the shrine. He seemed dazed. There was nothing Guerrero could do. He could not even make him speak.

It was a shock. The Maya did not go mad. That was not one of their diseases. Neither could they bear any physical uncleanliness, and the boy was filthy, his ears ragged and bloody with daily sacrifice. He even smelled of stale blood. European priests went mad that way, ascetic and filthy. But the boy had never heard of Europeans.

What did he want? What was he praying for?

There was nothing to do but leave him there. Guerrero went down the temple stairs, and wandered back across the deserted plaza to the palace. His skin prickled and he was worn out. Loneliness had become such a familiar ache that nowadays he only noticed it when he was in company. He did not notice it when he was alone any more.

He went into Ix Chan's quarters, and at least, when he was

asleep, he could lie there with a memory. He would never see her again. Most of the time he did not even think of her any more. But he would never not see her, either.

Outside the slippery magenta-thighed tree frogs began invisibly to chirp. The night was so empty and so wide.

The sunlight woke him, and though he had moved about mechanically now for over a year, it was damp here. He could not rise. He was hungry, and yet he did not want to eat. He wished he had brought a servant. Even the mechanical giving of an order made it possible to keep face. He lay staring at the sunlight, the weeds on the terrace outside, a spider web hanging in a corner. It took so long these days to make the body move. One could no longer move oneself. One was reduced to telling the body to move for one.

He went to the doorway, and looked out, one arm against the jamb. And then, there was no reason to stay. He went down to the court, remembered his son was out there, somewhere, and sat heavily down on a stone. Even the sunlight was not yet warm.

He did not know how long he sat there. The court had been whitewashed just before they had had to abandon the city. The whitewash was powdery, but thick, and still reflected a hard glare. The sun struck full against it.

The surface of the wall was irregular. As he watched, part of it rocked, and began to move. A very small part, no bigger than a knuckle-bone, edged out and began to climb slowly down. He stared, not quite understanding. Where it had been was a dirty spot on the whitewashed glare. The little knob moved painfully down, and something behind it glistened.

He jerked awake, got up, and went over. The blob was a foot from the ground. He reached out and picked it up, turning it over in his hand. He must have looked at it for a long time, while something clicked into place inside him.

It was a large snail. It had been whitewashed over almost a year ago. The thing was impossible. But here it was, alive. God knows how it had survived, but it was beginning to move again. It felt damp against his hand, and its head moved to and fro, its antennae were like two drops of quivering dew.

He put it down in a clump of weeds and laughed. It made all the difference. He had a reason for going on. He would wait and watch and survive, and when the Spanish came back, he would fight them. He would fight them until he died, wherever he could find them. All he needed was the chance. He had something to live for again. He had death.

He strode out of the courtyard, and on the edge of the plaza, stopped. Across it his son was wavering out of the ruins of the priests' quarters. The figure dodged back, and then came into view again, hesitated, and then beckoned.

Guerrero stood stock still. He did not want to be recognized by anything that had come to that. That would be too much. He tightened his lips. He had not had any use for that younger son for years, but what had happened to him was another reason for fighting back. He strode erect across the plaza.

He need not have feared. He was not recognized. He had forgotten. He was still dressed as a noble and a warrior. His son remembered nothing. He saw only someone in authority, and that was what he wanted, someone in authority. It was the absence of anyone to tell him what to do which had driven him to this state. He was one of those people who cannot survive the destruction of what they believe in, not because they believe in it so much, but simply because they have no spine of their own.

Guerrero let himself be led inside the building. He had never been there before. It was a rabbit warren of little rooms with high corbel vaulting and almost no light, narrow courts, and a shambles everywhere. The Spanish had obviously used it as a stable.

They came to a small room, smelly and occupied. On a stone bench was a pile of books, folded out every way, like little screens. Guerrero did not know what they were, but his son began to babble.

They were the katun books and histories. Across the sized

sheets the bright little gods and symbols confronted each other, each panel what had happened and what would happen again. They proved everything. His son said so. Life was not around them. Life meant nothing. Life was in the books. They told you what would happen. They told you what to do. They made the world safe and predictable. So long as they existed, the world would exist, unchanged.

His son looked up for a gloating moment of shy and stubborn pleasure. It said here they would all come back. The city would live again. Nothing was wrong. The high priest, now dead, had miscalculated, that was all. He had rectified all that, by collating copies. One had only to look here, to see that. The world was safe wasn't it? He pleaded to know. For an instant there was a dim echo of recognition in those eyes, but to Guerrero's relief it went away. He felt sick.

It said, it said, it said, the poor crazy voice rambled on and on, eager and cajoling, pointing a grimy finger now at this little ideogram and now at that. It was true wasn't it? It had to be.

Guerrero said yes. He had to get out of there. He was beginning to lose his temper with the world. Why couldn't this poor creature die?

It was worse than Aguilar. It was a punishment, but for whom and to what? Some people are born faulty. We cannot blame ourselves for that.

He did not get out of there, without having to take one of the books with him. He saw in his son's eyes the awful cunning of paranoia. The book was the future. He was to hide it somewhere, so the future would be safe. So the priests and the gods would come back again, and everything would be the way it was supposed to be. He wanted nothing for himself.

Guerrero took it and fled. He went on to Bacalar, where Nachancan's nephew now ruled. He wanted very much now to see Nachancan's nephew. But that afternoon he held the codex across his knees, in a clearing, glad that he could neither read nor interpret it. For madness is one thing, but suppose it told the truth? The future is something no one but a madman would *want* to know, for only the future can give us hope.

At Bacalar he learned that his elder son was safe at Sotuta. The headman was dead, and he had taken service there, under the cacique.

He sent for him at once, for he had learned something else. The Spanish were back, though not yet in Yucatan, and so was Montejo, though now he was younger and had a different name. He was called Alvarado.

He knew what to do now. That glimpse of his younger son had given him back his self again. Now he had no doubts. For he had seen something. Life is a little exercise. When we are young we think it is a rehearsal, and everything we do badly now, we will do better later. But he had changed lives, from a childhood in Spain, to what he had always wanted and respect, here. He had taken up another self. So more than most, he could see that anything we selflessly love, even it be our persona, is a parallel activity, less elementary than the Exercises of St. Ignatius Loyala, by which we achieve selflessness, even through absorption in ourselves, if our own lives be our hobby.

But like the process by which a mystic attains insight, every life has both a progression and a shape, which, if we follow it, gives us insight on our death-bed, but which if we flinch from that inevitable terminal act, and try to find a way out, means nothing.

He would no longer flinch. Like the society he had been accepted into, he wanted to go away complete. And he so attained insight, and could not be beaten. Every life has its signal victory, and the victory over the self is the best o these, for it leaves us free to be ourselves. And to be ourselves, we must sometimes die.

But die in the right way.

Now he knew that way. It too was inevitable.

And as do all irreversible acts, decision gave him a magisterial freedom. It gave him back that second youth, which comes after decisions have been made, a second adolescence, if you wish, since adolescence is the age of choice.

He felt young again, but a little heavier about the gut and chest. And yet the gravity of a trim fifty is very like the gravity of youth: at least in a man.

XXIX

Events were to assist him.

For Montejo was also a man who could not be beaten, because he could only be killed. Perhaps he wanted Yucatan merely because he could not have it, perhaps because there was nothing else he could have. He wrangled a grant from the Crown which made him Governor of all the disputed land between Tabasco and Honduras, not because he was greedy, but because he believed that every piece of land on which he or his lieutenants set foot belonged to him, just because there might be some profit in it, and because he had your true banker's innate respect for real estate.

But Honduras was far away and inaccessible over mountains to the south. It was closer to Guatemala than to Mexico. Therefore Alvarado, the conqueror of Guatemala, appeared in Higueras, the capital, and took it for himself.

That was what Alvarado was, a conqueror. He was one of the men who had helped Cortés sack Mexico, but he was also a man who would be young on his death-bed, and who was incapable of an interest in cautious investments, long-term gains, or real estate. He did not see the world in those terms, for his passion was for power, pomp, and war. Like a feral creature, say a jaguar of these jungles, he suffered from boredom. It was boredom that drove him to kill more than he could eat. He killed for sport.

Of all that Guerrero knew nothing, but refugees from Honduras brought the news soon enough, that the Spaniards were back, marching from the mountains of the interior, towards Higueras and the coast. The battle was on again. And the only way to keep these devils out of Yucatan, was to fight them where they were.

Even the Maya were willing for once to co-operate, for the uplands of Guatemala and Honduras were their heart land. It was from there they had first come, and to there, a hundred years ago, that the Itza had gone, back to their origins, on an island in Lake Tayasal.

The Spanish were driven out of Yucatan, and yet you heard a little about Lake Tayasal everywhere now. It was the palladium, the redoubt, the refuge of their world, the last stronghold, a place no Spaniard could touch. Their world was in ashes. But there, it was said, it still burnt and flickered on, as in the days before the Spanish arrival.

A good many priests, in particular, had gone there, to keep themselves and the old religion alive, to be able to go on bribing the gods for the good things of life, and for the survival of the Maya. It was said that the Christian friars were coming back to Champoton, and a priest knows a fellow fanatic when he sees one. It was better to take the gods off to some place of security. It was better to take the old life off somewhere where it was still understood, and where there would be no one to touch it.

Honduras was holy. But that did not prevent Cerezeda, the Spanish governor at Higueras, from beginning a campaign against the cacique of Coçumba, in the valley of the Rio de Ulua. That was too close to Tayasal to be countenanced. So far he had had no success, but now Alvarado was coming, and everyone knew what that would mean.

Guerrero agreed to lead a force of Maya warriors across the Bay of Honduras to Coçumba. But he refused to leave without his son. Yet time went on, it was the summer of 1536, and still his son did not come. Guerrero could not delay much longer. He set out for Sotuta to fetch him.

Yucatan had already become unreal to him, as a place does once we have decided to leave it. Since we never expect to see it again, already, even though we are still there, we do not see it. He knew what he was doing. He knew he could not win. His journey had the unendurable pathos of a prolonged good-bye.

Yucatan was still like a garden, in which he had played for years, it was still recognizable, but it was like a garden after the heat of summer, when the flowers, though still gorgeous, wilt, and the last buds, even though the sun has sprung them open, we know will never bloom. There was a tendency to move on tiptoe, where formerly they had moved with assurance. There was a desperation now in what had once seemed a matter of course, the doing of the same old daily things.

And again and again he heard that word, Tayasal.

Never mind. He had his own plans for Tayasal.

Everyone knew he was raising an expedition. A few of those who saw what had happened to their world, looking at that mask which his face had become, may even have known, and agreed with, his real purpose. There were many who were willing to go with him. He had his pick, and a pick was what he needed. He would take only those men who had had experience in fighting the Spaniards, and, as he crossed the peninsula and found them, he sent them back to the rallying point at Bacalar, where canoes were being prepared for the crossing of the gulf. One never knew. Because one has decided to die, does not mean that one will not fight for one's life. Indeed, honourably, such a decision makes one fight all the harder. One must meet the conditions.

And all those who had something more than themselves to lose, the caciques, the priests, those who were less individual men than embodiments of the sacred nature of the race, chose to go with him, for the same reason that he himself was going: because it was better to take their world away with them, than to survive it.

He travelled swiftly, through partially dismantled, partly damaged towns. Nothing had been repaired. It was as though even the common people knew, or were at least waiting, to see if perhaps, against all hope, their worst fears might not be unjustified.

He soon reached Sotuta, found neither his son nor the

caciques were there, learned they were south, at the smaller capital of Otzmal, on the borders of Mani, and hoping that did not mean another suicidal internecine petty war, hurried on.

He was now travelling in some state, suitable to a man of his age and position, or the pomp with which Cleopatra was conducted the first time to her pyramid, with the difference, that being a man, he knew that hope, though a good companion, is a poor adviser, and therefore meant to go to that pyramid only once.

As for pomp, he could not be bothered about such things himself, but it was the habit of the country, and made travelling much easier.

No matter what we do, even if, as he had done, we have changed worlds to free the self, eventually we become trapped in our own character. Even though we think differently than we have conditioned ourselves to do, believe otherwise, feel in another way, as soon as life begins to turn down, we cannot resist or hold back, even though we want to, our lives flow down the same groves of habit, willy nilly, in response to the gravity of that character we inhabit, which is not the shell of the hermit crab, but the creature inside it, who too late to change shells finds the one he has chosen leaves him no more room to grow.

So every man of public eminence, as he was now, every person of decided character, as he had always been, is, if you look, only an impersonal mask, a work of art, a jointed doll, out of whose eye-holes stare the eyes of a trapped child, who moves the arms and legs, speaks through the mouth, articulates the facial muscles, but absent-mindedly, expertly, wanting very much some less constricting persona to play with, but doomed all the same always to be shut up in the same inexpressive, mortal, and decaying automaton, saying, I am young, let me out.

A group of such people, talking, is not very reassuring. For they all share the same trade secret, they all want to get out and play with each other, say what they really mean, confess at last to someone like themselves, that they are only seven, but they have so perfected the performance with those jointed dolls, themselves, that they cannot even say so.They have to go through the same motions. Only the expression in the eyes allows them sometimes to show what they really are. For to be locked up in the self is so lonely, and quite inevitable. It is only before the character is formed that we can get out for a while, with someone else, and be ourselves.

So Guerrero thought, I am killing this body, because I do not want to live in this world any more. I would prefer to die myself, rather than see what they will do to this body, to this world. And yet, since the performance was about to be over, he rather liked to watch it, as an actor, finally giving in to curiosity, on the 1,000th night of the play, lets his understudy go on, only however, if the understudy is not apt to make a sensation, and slipping into the back of the house, watches himself in the play.

For really, he had never got over the sense of wonder that here was he, Gonzalo Guerrero of Nieto, who might have seemed a peasant to the world, fitting the role of Ah Ceh so well, that never again would he be allowed to play, or even want to play, any other part. For do not character actors become, for all but a small either delighted or discomfited segment of themselves, the part which has so well served them in the world? Your actor with a genius for disguise, who never plays the same part twice, is a rarity, an anomaly, and personally, a distress. For an actor like that has never become aware of himself. He seeks the self in a diversity of appearance, becomes a plural schizophrenic who changes so often, that he had never been caught out in one role long enough for the disease to be identified, or to catch up with him. No, the actor is not himself. So he is the person he has become. It is a form of protective mimicry. One becomes oneself, in order to escape detection. But under what a thing is lies what it really *is*. It is a great collaboration, a secret *entente*, which in turn has secret treaty clauses, which we call mental reservations, and which give the play its true though not its apparent meaning.

Indeed, we are so lonely, in this busy emptiness of life, that it is only so, wandering in our persona on the stage, that we can meet other people at all. For we can never meet other people at all. We can only meet personas like ourselves, with whom we act out an intimate drama, to the applause of the cosmic opera house. Drawing-room comedy is only Greek tragedy for those who cannot feel any more; the morality play, the miracle play, and Everyman, only the best part for those whose abilities are limited.

The analogy was endless.

Before the cathedral, on that two-storied cart the world, the tinker acts out the drunkenness of Noah, the privations of Job, and the madness of Nebuchadnezzar. Before the altars and the palaces of Otzmal, he danced, as years ago the priest of Tulum had in dancing inside the skin of Valdivia given Valdivia a meaning, the life of Ah Ceh. But the play was over. The repertory company had split up. His wife, his daughter were dead, his younger son was mad, and had always been despicable. The theatre was condemned.

And now, he was here for one last theatre party, on the familiar stage, but with the houselights out.

Of course Guerrero did not think of it in those terms.

But he did think of it in that way.

He looked at his son. He was no Job, nor was there much dignity in the Lamentations of Jeremiah. He preferred this Maya world. It was the highest honour and the best place, it meant something, he hated to see the old traditions torn down, or what was worse, made meaningless. He knew they would be. The old order passes and no one seems to care, in particular, the greater number of those who will pass with it do not seem to care. Only long afterwards, when the time has come to dig the old order up again, do those who won out over it see how much they thereby lost.

The Maya were a processional people. They looked neither to left nor right. In a stately manner they moved off gravely into eternity, and he had joined the procession. That was as it should be. It was what he had wished. It even filled him with a certain awe. But he was almost fifty. His son must go on. The name must survive.

For even more than what we are, we want what we love always to be there, untouchable, after us.

But in his day they were not so far from reality as that. The Spaniards, though ignorant of India, still played circular chess. The prime minister was called a queen. Time had elapsed so much as that. But a bishop was still a bishop, a rook a rook, a knight a knight, and a pawn was a pawn. All of them, in the co-operation of that enormous two-sided parable the board, which in circular chess, such is the refinement of the oriental mind, had no sides at all, knew their movements and their places.

But the Maya were an oriental people. It was the Wheel of the Sun they followed, not the triune verity. They were a subtler people than the Occidental. They could see that we know where we are only because the same constantly revolving pattern reaches over and over again the same position, only to pass on to the next, and that nothing, like a pyramid of smoke, goes up to heaven and that's the end of it. Even the gods die and are replaced and come back again. Brahma breathes the world in and out, and is himself breathed in and out. It and he are the same in all respects each time, and yet they are not the same example of themselves. He does it by the katun, the aeon, and momently. Just because it is, nothing is. And simply because it is not, it is eternal. Everything is passing, because it does not pass.

And yet it makes one a little weary, to realize all that.

And one must make one's exit, before the carpenters come to tear the theatre down.

So one gives this last, perhaps a little hurried, performance.

So Guerrero travelled in pomp, with a small guard of warriors, and ten slaves to carry his litter, though unless he were leaving or approaching a town, he preferred to get out and walk, which was faster. But he kept up the proper forms, out of piety, to his wife, his daughter, this world, Chetumal, and Nachancan. Out of piety to what he was.

He could not be sure of his reception in Sotuta. Nobody ever could. The more panoply he travelled with the better. For like most men, the Cocom of Sotuta had a respect for such things. Indeed, now he was capable of them, he respected them himself. Now they had no meaning left, he knew what they meant. Since we are to be destroyed anyway, we may as well keep up the proper forms, until such time as we are to be. There is a protocol to be followed, on that last tramp towards the pyramid. Otherwise we offend both our survivors and ourselves.

He found Sotuta festive, with the intangible pathos of flowers, that are so triumphantly there, and yet they must die. The day before they were not. The day after they will not be either. That makes living in today a little strange. The Maya were a people in love with flowers, and who could blame them for that? But their flowers were not the sedate ornaments of Europe, but a parable which leapt savage from the pod and hung there, on their stalks, as though quivering at the leash, scorched in an hour, and therefore, while they blossomed, doubly terrible.

His bearers swerved on to the sacbe leading to Otzmal. Running straight and well kept into the city, it was as deserted as that to Tulum, twenty-five years ago.

He soon found out why.

The Lords of Xiu were coming.

So, for that matter, was he. He had sent messengers ahead, as the form required, and now had himself announced by conches. That meant nothing, all this pomp was terminal, though sometimes he thought only he, and some of the priests perhaps, realized that. But it was also necessary. One did not, if one wished to survive, approach the Sotuta as an underling.

It was also something he owed to Nachancan, that benign warm ghost who sat smiling in his heart, and to Chetumal, which was now a ruin.

And to his wife, of whom it was better not to think.

He wondered what had brought the Lords of Xiu here. It was unbelievable that they should come here. They were too unscrupulous ever to humble themselves, too proud, except among equals, and they recognized none, ever to humble themselves.

It must mean that at last they too suffered from some doubt. At last doubt had touched them, after a thousand years. They were on their way to ask the gods to do something about their appointed and anointed sons.

He entered the city, and there were those who came out to see him. For in a way he had become their last magic person, their ultimate sacrifice, the thing they would give to save themselves, even though that meant going with him to the sacrifice.

The Cocoms received him well. He was a great man, as they reckoned such things. But in twenty years he had come a long way. He now knew certain things it is not right for a peasant to think of, such as that greatness is only a disease, that pulls us down in time. We have not the stamina to withstand it. It destroys us.

It destroys everyone.

It had destroyed him. But then, so would have squalor. It was better to end this way. It at least had dignity.

The bearers carried him into the square of Sotuta. He could tell at once that his arrival was not welcome, by the degree of politeness it evoked. It was not his place to ask questions. His son was among the first to receive him. Everything was as it should be. And yet it was not. His son, too, who had always been so honest, seemed evasive here. Yet it was good to see him.

He did his best to shrug it off. Whatever it was, it had nothing to do with him.

The cacique and his nobles he did not trust. They seemed on edge. He had the feeling he had interrupted something. There was something a little too deliberate about their cordiality, a little too evasive about his son. Hun Imix was grown up now. He had become a handsome stranger. Guerrero would rather have had him for a friend.

He had begun to think of these people as strangers again, no longer as a group he wanted to belong to, but as a group he had outgrown.

If life was a walk through a suite of rooms, he had opened one door too many, by accident, and found himself outside. There was nothing outside. All the same he did not want to go back in, and he certainly did not want to retrace his steps to the beginning of the stroll. Nothing was something not entirely unenjoyable, like physical exhaustion, which means you will sleep well. But unlike fatigue, it makes you sharp-eyed about what is under your nose.

Why were the Xiu coming?

Because they had asked to come.

Why had they been given permission to come?

It wasn't exactly permission. It was a safe conduct they had wanted, through Sotuta territory, to Chichen Itza. They were on a pilgrimage.

The cacique smiled. No doubt Guerrero was surprised. It was what he had always advised, that they should forget their feuds and unite against the possible return of the Spanish. It was the only way they could keep their country, to unite. Was that not so?

Guerrero said nothing. He was not exactly a pessimist, but he had once been an optimist, he was older now, and experience had made him cautious. He was given now only to deliberate risk. Besides, if you believed the worst of people, rather than the best, you were seldom disappointed and sometimes delightedly surprised. With his son he awaited the arrival of the Xiu, in the plaza before the palace. Otzmal was not a capital, but even so, it was grander than Chetumal, for the Cocoms were a richer and older people. He looked around the company.

Bernal Diaz, the *conquistador*, had once bribed his way back to Cortés in comfort with a handful of quetzel feathers. There were enough quetzel feathers here to feed a city. Both priests and nobles were top-heavy with wickerwork headdresses from which sprouted ciliated plumes, and were gorgeous in jade, in gold, in ceremonial armour and embroidered, jewel infested breechclouts. Nachi Cocom himself sat cross-legged in the midst of all that, elevated on a carved wooden platform, under a canopy. He was talking amiably. It could have been any state company, receiving a deputation of an equally powerful state, but Guerrero did not like the way his son avoided his glance. He could not help but try to ask a question.

The Xiu arrived in the afternoon, preceded by musicians playing drums, the armadillo ocarina, owl and frog and bird whistles, bone scrapers, and maracas. It was not a visit but a progress, and though they travelled only with their high priests and assistants, slaves, and a bodyguard, the Xiu were more gorgeous, more full of pomp, and more stately even than their hosts. It was haughty, not tactful, but it was certainly magnificent.

It was almost ten years since anyone had made a state pilgrimage to Chichen Itza. This progress was a holy and almost divine event, and besides, pilgrims were sacred. They were going to offer human sacrifice at the Sacred Well, to appease the gods who had for so long behaved so badly, and now, it seemed, had had a change of heart. It was not merely a procession for the Xiu, but for the nation, which is perhaps why the Xiu had undertaken it. They were not stupid to the uses of propaganda. It was something the Sotuta had not thought of, to embody the nation in such a way.

Guerrero found it sad, simply because it was so assured, the magnificence so touching. He was moved perhaps to join the thanksgiving himself.

The company swayed down the sacbe and into the town. The sacrificial victims walked in a hollow square of priests, some girls, and two pretty boys brought up for that purpose, and trained toward no other. The high priest was in a closed litter high above them. A Xiu himself, he could not be seen, and would stay at the temple quarters.

Behind the priests came the guard, and among the guard, on the shoulders of the slaves, Ah Dzun Xiu, and Ah Ziyah Xiu, his heir, together with forty of the chief men of the nation, all cousins and cognates, some of them walking, but some in litters almost as rich as Dzun's.

The litters were set down in the plaza, which had been purified. Now the high priest of the Xiu, together with those of Sotuta, purified it again, and the Xiu stepped out on to the flags.

If they were nervous, nothing of that showed in their manner. The father was a little wrinkled, but one had only to look at the son, to know that he was also proud and wiry. The nobles had the same look. It was easy to see how closely related they were.

Guerrero tried to press forward. The Xiu had been so self-centred and so foolish, that he wanted to speak with them and see what manner of men they were. He could not contrive the meeting. Somehow something always happened. He did not think it happened by chance. The deference with which his hosts treated him was too firm.

Yet for four days nothing happened. He began to relax. He was introduced to his son's wife, who pleased him. It pleased him even more that she was gravid. But though he was treated with respect, he knew very well that his son had been given orders not to talk to him, except in front of witnesses.

He wondered why not. He could not get over a certain uneasiness. The Cocom hated the Xiu. A diplomatic agreement was one thing, but all this affability did not ring true.

Unless it were meant as an irony.

Late in the afternoon of the fourth day Nachi Cocom gave a farewell banquet, for the pilgrims were to advance the next day. Guerrero had decided to go with them. It could do no harm, and might do much good. For his coming expedition he could use the best omens and auspices. His son would also go, as would the Cocom leaders. They, too, had had the time to think about the uses of propaganda. They had to go.

Guerrero was seated well down the room, drowsy with wine, tired, and even bored. There had been too much liquor, too much food, too much music, and far too many dancers and acrobats. Even the Xiu seemed relaxed. They were not, of course, drunk. Drunkenness was a serious criminal offence, as well as a lapse from dignity. But they were not sober either. The caciques of Xiu and of Cocom sat on a dais at the end of the room. The music stopped for a moment, and the acrobats filed out two of the four doors. There was a longish pause.

Outside somewhere somebody sounded a conch.

Nachi Cocom had been leaning over, talking to Ah Dzun Xiu. Ah Dzun Xiu abruptly screamed, and Nachi Cocom drew back, holding the sacrificial knife he had had hidden about him somewhere.

Guerrero tried to get up, and found his arms held at his sides by the men to his left and right. There was nothing he could do but watch.

Warriors came in through the doors. The Cocom guests, too, had hidden weapons. So did the Xiu, but they had been taken by surprise. Guerrero saw his son pull out a knife.

He had forgotten. This son, like the other one, was half an Indian, and so more Indian than the others. He enjoyed revenge, even when it was not practical. The Spanish only when it was practical. It made Guerrero feel hopeless. All men want revenge. One cannot blame them for that. Our emotions are as irrelevant to politics as the weather. But battles are sometimes lost because of the weather, and with battles, causes, and that they should want revenge even at the price of their destruction was inopportune.

He had wanted revenge himself. This sight sickened him, and he realized that for some time he had not wanted it any more. He had only wanted to save a world, not for himself, but just because it was one, and because men should not be able to destroy everything, simply out of greed.

But there was a stronger force even than greed. It did no

good even to hide behind poverty. There was that hate that springs from a worse than Castilian pride. And hate is a hydra with a hundred different heads. It belongs to the best causes, and fights in the most justified wars. When it purrs we call it love, but even when it is well fed, it is still there, a mechanism that allows us to survive the little crises to go to a worse death.

He knew he must not think that way. He would not think that way. But he felt so futilely tired. For the world is beautiful after all. There should be somebody there to see it, after we have gone.

He was an old man. He realized it suddenly. Not middle-aged, though he had a youthful body, but an old man. It was because he did not want to be young any more.

He watched his son killing, and not altogether because he was paid to kill. Perhaps it was because he had been trained properly to do so, that he enjoyed it so much.

Then it was over. The high priest they had slain at the temple, separately. But hatred is less efficient than love. There were forty Xiu dead in that room. They lay about on the floor, gorgeous as crumpled pheasants. Even Nachi Cocom seemed taken aback at the sudden quiet.

But there was another Xiu, at Mani. The Spanish need only to get to him, to be able to win the war, when they were ready. Guerrero would not see Chichen Itza now. Nor would any vast procession ever again wind through that city.

His guards had let go of him. Nachi Cocom smiled at him. It was supposed to be a lesson in how to fight a war. Nachi was pleased with himself, or would be, once his priests had absolved him, and he had apologized to the gods.

Guerrero could not smile back. It was too much like congratulating an incipient corpse on the skill with which it had arranged for its own death.

He could only curse. Why do men, even more than their involuntary skill to destroy each other, make such an effort, and succeed so well, to destroy themselves?

And what can you do when it is over, except go with it, and never say a word?

For all the beauty, all the love, all the glory, all the splendour, and everything personal and touching in this world, is purchased out of the bigotry, the hysteria, the self interest, and the desperation of those whom we call, since, in transferring their squalid little desires into something outside themselves, they seem to have an interest beyond themselves, disinterested and selfless people.

And why not? Why complain about that? That is the way animals and plants, at enormous cost to their own numbers, still save their own generic being. They mutate, and then persecute the mutation that will survive them, almost unconsciously to try it out, to see if it will hold up. The concentrated hatreds of this world, by which the race perpetuates itself in order to have a moment to spare to devote to love, are only the laboratory conditions which reproduce the conditions of survival. And those who condemn us, do so (though they do not know it, for if they did know it, they would not co-operate in the survival of the species even that much) only in order that through us the race may be conditioned to survive.

But it was very saddening. For those who live to love, must regret the passing of that moment when love is possible, and must with a sigh settle down to assure the return of that moment which will be nice for others, but which they themselves, even while, and because, they fight for it, will never see.

XXIX

It was time to get to Honduras, before his warriors learned what had happened and could turn on each other instead of the common enemy.

He had to move at once. He knew now the Cocom did not trust him, and knowing he had been there, neither would the Xiu. And if he was not trusted, neither would his son be. Nor was it wise to leave his son's wife behind, to be mistreated as a hostage, against who knows what civil war? His son could understand that.

They slipped out of the city before dawn, and got back to Bacalar in a week, travelling mostly at night. His son's wife was in her eighth month, but sturdy. She scarcely retarded them.

There was no time to worry about the child.

News of the massacre had got to Bacalar before them, and demoralized everyone, for they knew what it meant. It was the one thing too much. The only thing to do was to embark at once.

Guerrero took both his son and his son's wife in his own canoe. The flotilla headed out into the lake, Bacalar fell behind, they went down the river, reached the Bay of Chetumal, passed the ruins of the city, and fanned out into loose formation as they paddled down towards the open sea. There were drummers to keep up the stroke. The weather could not have been better. Fishing boats put out from shore, to cheer them on their way.

It could not have gone better, yet Guerrero refused to look back. His son's wife had been doing so. She swallowed, gave him a wistful smile, settled herself as well as she could, and stared forward towards the currents of the open sea. Behind her the rowers bent their backs.

He knew he would never see Chetumal again. He did not know why.

At the entrance to the bay the water was almost purple, and quite abruptly cold. The current caught them, and the rowers relaxed. In a curving arc the canoes swung one after another into that wing of the returning Gulf Stream which had brought him to Yucatan in the first place. The drums were still, but to pass the time someone was playing a flute.

The coastline shimmered in that sparkling air. It was only a line of white, of ochre, and the 150-foot continuous towers of the rain forest, the blue-green tufted pile of the peninsula. It should not have been so moving. And yet he was moved.

They were not a sea people, but they knew their own shores, and how to manage both the currents and their canoes. At no time was that trip ever an easy one, but they had a better passage than Davila had had. There were no storms. The weather held, but still it took them weeks to navigate the irritable boredom of that sea.

Each night, if they could, for sometimes the current kept them offshore, they ate and slept on the beaches. There were no habitations, and very few natives. The region was poor, swampy, and impassable.

Slowly the shore on their right began to rise, until at last they saw the faint blue of hills above the line of the forest. They were exhausted, and had not even come half-way. Their passage was now more difficult, floating among islands, a few feet above vast submerged sand bars. They had to move swiftly, or the tide would strand them on one of them.

Off the mouth of what is now the Belize river, his son's wife began to have labour pains. There was a settlement at Belize. He signalled to the others to follow, and then urging on his own rowers, peeled off from the flotilla, and headed for the shore.

It would be a good place to rest and get provisions, and the child could be born there.

To his surprise he was expected. The natives came out to meet them, bearing gifts of fruit and food. They had no news of Yucatan, but much of Honduras. Alvarado had arrived and founded two towns. Everyone knew what that meant.

The natives called a midwife and settled Guerrero and his relatives in the stone building of their chief. Where was their chief? He had gone to Tayasal. When would he be back? They did not know.

There was a reason for that welcome after all. Their leaders had all gone to Tayasal, for good. Their river led up country, to the uplands, and was the chief local means of getting there. Many travellers came through, and they hired themselves out as guides. There was a party here now, on the way. Things were disturbed in Honduras. The caciques there had not been able to hold Alvarado. He was now in the valley of the Rio de Ulua, trying to defeat the cacique Coçumba. The Spaniards could not be held. Neither could they be borne. They pulled down the temples.

At Tayasal the temples could not be torn down. They stood in the middle of the lake. Even Cortés had had to turn back there.

Guerrero went to talk to the party on its way, small nobles from Honduras. They did not have much to say. They had had more of the Spaniards than they had yet had in Yucatan. Refugees are much the same everywhere, but the rich are exiles, and exiles are different. It is not so much that they have more to lose than the poor, but they have power to lose, and that makes them haughty. They wander over the face of the earth, trying to find someone who remembers who they were. They are much given to waiting, like birds ruffled in an unexpected storm. Unlike refugees, they have no now. That made them shiver in their pomps. It made Guerrero shiver. One does not have to die to become a ghost.

His son's wife was in labour for eighteen hours. It gave him a long time to find out about Tayasal. At least the old life went on there, or something very like it. And something very like it is better than nothing, when we have been pushed too far.

But how long could they hold out there?

Longer perhaps than any other where, unless the Spanish could be defeated.

He went down to see his men. It was now twilight. There had not been room enough for them in the village, so they were bivouacked on the beach. Out there, somewhere, across the dark gulf, lay Honduras and the Spanish army, perhaps a week away.

When he got back to the chief's house, the child had been born. A slave brought it out to show it to him. It was purple, wrinkled, and male. It made him feel angry. He knew now what must be done, for it contained a little bit of Ix Chan,

Nachancan, his son, and even of himself. The child, its mother, and his son must go to Tayasal.

For he knew now why they loved children and hated death so much. It was because they loved the world so much that they wanted someone else always to be there to see it too, even though they were dead and could no longer see it themselves. And indeed their world was beautiful. It must be allowed to go on. It was well worth the seeing. It would be some victory over the Spaniards if even this little of it could survive to be seen.

And what did men like Montejo and Alvarado see? The better of them marvelled at what they saw, but all the same they destroyed it.

This was something they should not have.

It took him a while to talk his son around. His son was eager to fight. But his wife and child could not make the journey alone, and someone would have to treat with the rulers of Tayasal. Guerrero was still a rich man. His wealth had shrunk to a bag of jades, but jade, for which the Spanish had no use, was to the Maya the most valuable of all substances. And a warrior of the prestige of his son would not be unwanted in Tayasal, for the city was, among other things, a heavily armed camp.

Guerrero went with them up the river, saying he would be back in a week. His men could use a week's rest. They did not grumble. Something about his manner must have told them he would be back.

He did not go with Hun Imix all the way. There was not the time, and besides something inside him did not want to see Tayasal. The men of the village were excellent guides, and there were slaves along for portage, when the river turned into rapids and became impassable.

They passed out of the foothills, and came into the rolling mountain savannah country. The going here was easier. And here he left them. From the edge of the forest he watched them out of sight. They disappeared round a bend. Then he was alone, as he had been at the beginning, when first he had come to this world. He had said he would send word to his son in a month or two, but he knew that no word would be sent. Instead he sent them on, into that future which to the Maya was always the past of their race come round again.

Perhaps, one day, he would come round again, but somehow he did not think so.

What does one say to a son? It is someone one sends into the future, to get things ready for the family worship of the gens. The gens is even more important than the lares and penates, which by and large are only superstitious vanities, of whom we ask the same profitless questions, generation after generation.

But though we think we are thinking creatures, thought is just one of the hard-bought little luxuries of the nature of the beast. Since usually our grandfather's bought it we think it both our nature and our right. But if we buy it for ourselves, in our own lifetime, we see it differently, and understand it is nothing, beside the perpetuation and the unconscious worship of the gens.

Yet it is just that worship which alienates our children. We can never know them. They resent us too much, first for loving them, and second for refusing to let them be themselves. For we love in them not themselves, but the perpetuation of the gens and the repetition of ourselves. And since it is not until forty that they realize they do repeat us, or take any pleasure from the fact even if they do realize it before, since it will not be until then that they will feel about their own children and the gens as we do, then alas, there is always the barrier between. He might adore Ix Hun's physical perfection, the muscular certainty of his calves, the open, innocent honesty of his chest, but these things he adored only as an idealized summary of his own lost youth.

So parents and children can never get along, except uneasily. And yet we love our children. We miss them. We always want to see them again. We never give up hope, that at least they will survive, and that one day, though the day never comes, we and they may be at ease because equivalent.

He had sent Ix Hun not to Tayasal, but to the future. It was what Ix Chan would have wished. Now he was left with the present. It seemed a little empty.

The guides and bearers left him alone. He was glad of that. He felt empty and torn to shreds. He had so much to remember, and so little, now, to do. But still, it is better to feel, even though it hurts, than not to feel. It was good to be alive, even though some men would say contrariwise. It was good to know that one would be continued, up there, at Tayasal.

But good or not, it did hurt. He had loved them all. He had even loved this son, who was half Ix Chan.

He had even loved the other one. For fool or not, the other one was also his.

So he did not go back at once. He had one last thing to do. The bundle of jade he had given to his son. But there was another bundle.

That night he spent in the ruins of Tikal, which was not far away. It was, though he did not know it, the oldest of the Maya cities, the one they had come from. The bearers did not like to be there very much. It was two thousand years old, and like all such places, was not exactly reassuring.

He had spent much time in their ruins, and always times like this, in between, just after or just before something. He sat up very late, beside a campfire, in the rustling clearing that had once been the main plaza. The tall narrow temples climbed up to the sky, confused with shrubbery and trees. The foliage seemed full of their gods, but they did not frighten him. Like himself, like forest animals, they were going away. There was only the sound, now and then, of a twig incautiously stepped on and so broken.

They had gentler gods in their pantheon as well as fierce. But those were always the first to leave. Those had already gone: the goddess of maize, the goddess of childbirth, the goddess of marriage, and even, sometimes, the god of death.

He fell asleep.

In the morning, some distance outside the ruins, he found

what he was looking for, a shallow cave in the limestone, half hidden by ferns, but dry. Caves were sacred places. The others would not go in. He went in alone. There was a rude stone shelf, packed with little clay idols, old and dusty and brittle to the touch. He placed his bundle there, without bothering to unwrap it.

It contained that katun bundle codex his second son had given him, without recognizing him. Alone in the cave, wrapped in hemp, the little coloured gods would march after each other year after year. Perhaps someone would be able to read them someday. He stood there for a moment and then left.

Outside the cave he interrupted the intently meaningless ruminations of a female deer. It stared at him and then loped away, but its eyes had been soft and large.

It would have been an omen, had he believed in omens. As it was he was merely touched. He went back downstream to the village, and set out across the Gulf.

Yet his name was Ah Ceh, which meant "the deer", so he must have thought about that deer a little. He must not forget his name.

For the deer is the symbol of loss. They come down to the water, they watch us from the edge of the meadow, those creatures. Slim, spotted, young, by their nature aristocratic, tentative, uncertain, wide-eyed, innocent, naked, they yet know what the world means. Their sides quiver. Their slim, brittle, dangerous legs scarcely seem to support them. They stare and stare. They reach that kind of decision which is no decision, but only an experience older than they are. They watch, they examine, they whirl and gallop, as though strangulated, away.

In a stream, deliberately, they drop their green excrement.

And with a slightly painful, heart-twisting elegance of their necks, they droop to browse, and even so, they watch, their big lustrous eyes full of the pain of beauty.

Together, as at a signal, no matter how harmless our intent, how surprised our wonder, they turn and stare at us, with the awful gravity of the condemned, who condemn us, just by being, for hunting them.

And their little pleasures, their little sexual delights in a moonstruck meadow powdered with flowers, have such a stolen transience, and such a pathos. They are aware, and yet have not the brains to know they are. It is because they see everything always for the first time.

And their vulnerable streaked and spotted foals, wet, and hiding in the grasses, have such a slightly bothered, wet-muzzled, reserved way of finding themselves alive.

And then they stand up, rickety, their glass legs wobble, their bob tail going up has the effect of the midwife's smack into life, and utterly astonished to find themselves where they are, they have to go on living.

They grow a little thick. They grow a little sedate. Though always aware of danger, they are always willing to play.

And then, sometimes, they come down to the stream, and if we are there, they watch us, watch us, watch us. Their big eyes are mirrors, in which we may see what we know of ourselves, which is not what they know of us.

And when, having made up their minds, they dart away, it is as though we too had vanished. As though we had been ripped away, out of the now where we think we are.

And so they are the animal of leave-taking, of loss, of parting.

And while we watch them, our hearts are torn out.

XXX

He was right. The Spaniards could not be beaten. And behind him, somewhere, Sotuta and Mani were at war. The Xiu, it was said, had sent for some friars who had arrived at Champoton. The Xiu meant to win. What could they win?

Honduras was not Yucatan. The people were more fierce, and the landscape gave better cover. But Alvarado was not Montejo, either. The cacique of Coçumba was locked up in a strongly fortified town on a plateau above the Rio de Ulua, and Alvarado was outside it, and had been outside it for two weeks. He had cut off supplies, and water was running short. Guerrero had glimpsed him once or twice, in the distance, riding along his lines, a tall, black clad figure who knew exactly what to do. Among other things he knew how to keep himself and his men out of arrow shot, and safe from marauders.

He had harquebuses, archers, and small cannon. He had settled down to wait.

It seemed to Guerrero that he had seen him once before, somewhere, he could not remember where, but only that wherever it was, it had been raining. He crouched to watch, but he knew it was only a matter, now, of days. How much of his life had he spent crouched in the weeds, watching? How much of his life does any man spend in those weeds, watching?

Inside the fortification they could wait no longer. They knew very well the battle could not be won, for Alvarado was not the man to be taken by surprise, but they also knew they did not mean to be starved into submission either.

To die in battle is not exactly suicide, but if his world was going down, Guerrero wanted to go down with it. So, apparently, did the cacique of Coçumba. Neither man said anything, but each dressed with care. The men could desert. They could not.

Coçumba was only a strongly fortified hill fort. It was austere. Yet it had within it all the elements of their own world, which were precious to them, and which they must leave, because they were not precious to this new world outside.

They knew that. It did not make them solemn. It made them a little too gay.

Self-immolation, unlike suicide, or the terminal taunts of self-contemptuous saints, is not such an easy, and yet is a more amiable matter. Iphigenia, at least, though at the behest of the inexorable, had the justification of personal, reasons for her sacrifice, was translated, and ascended, even out there, at the end of the Black Sea. But this was a final situation. Hers was a personal world, but theirs an impersonal situation. The decision had made it so.

And yet, even when we are glad to leave, we are never glad to say good-bye. They took a last look round, and a little after dawn, on 14th August 1536, they left their fortifications and attacked. The men did not desert. There is some contagion in a good example, after all. They streamed, screaming and yelling, the last exemplars of an exemplary race, uphill towards the slight rise where Alvarado's men were mustered.

Alvarado was a good commander. He was not taken by surprise. He was only surprised, and a little suspicious, that it should be so easy. He fired his cannon.

The Indians wavered, but came on. It took time to reload a cannon in those days. Therefore he brought up the harquebuses.

Guerrero had hoped for a last personal duel. He and the cacique were out in front of the charge. The splay of shot hit them both in the face, and that was the end of it.

It was what in the despatches is called an instantaneous death. Merciful, they say. Yet no death is instantaneous. They must have had the time to think of everything before they fell. The world must have looked so agonizingly crisp and worth living for, just because it was there. They must have found so much to say good-bye to in so little time.

Then they lay still.

The Spaniards went on fighting. It was easy for them. There were so many on the other side who wished to die. So of course they won. They had the cannon.

Then the smoke cleared and the battlefield came up into focus, with its abandoned dolls, lying here and there.

The Spaniards went out to loot the dead, found Guerrero, and reported his death to Alvarado. A little uncomfortable, despite himself, Alvarado went out to look.

He had no idea why he felt uncomfortable. Yet as he stared down at that body, he had a feeling of lost identity, a sort of panic went through him about who he was, about what life was.

Yet he saw, since the Spaniards, like most people, recognized no excellence but their own, only the body of a common sailor, a renegade, and no Christian, disgracefully got up like one of the heathen, but for that reason, a dangerous enemy, and now at last dead.

He was not a man ever to ask difficult questions. He spat and walked back to camp.

And yet he felt uneasy. Something, he felt, had got away from him.

XXXI

It was the end. The Maya would fight on, they fought until 1917, they will always fight, but still it was the end. They were left, but their world had gone away.

At a few of their altars, even now, deep in the jungle, you may find a candle burning, as they left copal burning, in their day, in empty Chichen or Coba. But that means nothing. That is only piety that has forgotten what it worships.

But in 1536, even the Spanish, surrounded by that suddenly hushed world, sitting in their canteen, who had no use for the world, felt awkward all the same. Perhaps they felt all around them the presence of something they did not even know the name of, the inexorability of lost time.

That night the moon rose as usual, over all the ruined cities and the cities soon to be ruined of that empire. It was a solemn sight, it was like a sigh, but there was no Spaniard out to see it. They were an indoor people, like all those who feel safer when the landscape is bleak. They were not haunted by the beauty of the now, except to know what it was worth to them, and if it was worth nothing to them, to tear it down.

It was worth nothing to them.

Guerrero's body still lay on the battlefield. It had been stripped of everything of value, but the wind ruffled its panache slightly, as it lay there, in the midst of a landscape haunted by itself.

Yet who is not haunted by himself? We take the *doppelgänger* and we go. If we are lucky, when the time comes, we go away complete.

For him it was complete. He had had his victory. He had helped it to go on.

For in Tayasal there was still somebody left to see that moon. The joys there may have been visible, but false, the chagrins hidden, but real, yet they too intended to go away complete. The last coming of Katun 8 Ahau would not occur until 1697. They were a people to whom coherence and tradition meant everything, and if we have respect for such things, it does not matter that life is meaningless. There is still order. We must still put things back where we found them. And so up there they managed to hold out until then.

The Spanish, who thought it a poor place, could never understand why.

And yet the victory of honour, though never admitted to, is sometimes felt, by those who conquered it, since, to go, with honour, is the signal victory over a world which has none, and the conqueror, who has none, feels that.

As for Tayasal: now it is an island, with a few huts, a stone wall, and some palm trees. It has not been dug up again. We prefer to restore Chichen, which means less.

For the world is full of Mexicos, of Yucatans, and the emblem of Mexico disturbs us. There is the eagle, seated on the cactus, holding the snake. It was by that sign that they founded Tecnoctitlán, 600 years ago.

Eagle succeeds eagle, but each holds the same snake, the worm *Ouroboros*, the snake of the world, the snake of Eden, the snake of Lilith, whatever snake you call it, we are all held in the same claws.

As for those Spaniards, whoever our Spaniards may be, they may take away from us our lives, as they have taken away our reasons for living, but they shall not take back those things given at birth, which are inalienable, dignity, honour, the ability to bend but not break; a little insight; and the ability to admire that which will not love us: the world of nature; a sense of order, and the ability to be kind, out of a sense of duty; the cruelty to punish those who offend the idea of grace, by taking away their ability to besmirch anything, even at the cost of suiciding what they would besmirch; the willingness to die, for it takes self-restraint not to bolt at the last moment; and a vast tenderness to oblige those who are themselves tender.

Where have all those virtues gone?—those virtues which, willynilly, whatever our choice might be, make us virtuous despite ourselves, those things innate to the self, bred to the bone, and affirmative, unlike those vulgar little nervous Christian virtues, by which we have lived too long, only to find ourselves, out of honesty, pagans again?

They are still there, waiting to receive us. They have gone ahead of us. We shall join them soon. We cannot join them yet.

And walking round those ruins of Yucatan, one takes thought. We look up at that indelible sky. The hawk in the air, we have seen his course, and like the rabbit in the field, dodge as we may, we know we are the object of his hunger. For we, too, have been that hawk. That is why we have this interregnal leisure to observe his passage.

The watching is unendurable.

In the meantime we wander round these ruins, with a curiously tentative movement. The truth is so horrible that there is nothing for us to do but face it. Yet who, not a Medusa, could stare the Medusae down? Who could outface those snakes?

And in the Ball Court at Chichen, since we avoid it, perhaps we remember the eternal judges of the secret court, whose horror is to pass no judgment. It is we, before them, who stand self-condemned.

And so we search for someone, anyone, to teach us how

to die. It is the only way, any longer, that we have to live. Is there no one, anywhere, to teach us even that?
  Not even Guerrero?

Saddlebag
November 1958–April 1959